BRUTE OF ALL EVIL

ORDINARY MAGIC - BOOK 9

DEVON MONK

ODD
HOUSE
PRESS

Brute of All Evil

Copyright © 2022 by Devon Monk

ISBN: 9781939853295

Publisher: Odd House Press

Cover Art: Lou Harper

Interior Design: Odd House Press

Print Design: Odd House Press

BRUTE OF ALL EVIL

In two weeks, Delaney Reed will marry the man of her dreams. Everything's perfect. So why are the gods following her around like she suddenly needs a bodyguard?

It might be because her fiancé is forced to serve an outsider god who hates Delaney and the town she protects. It might be because the local Valkyrie hired a social media star who is determined to expose Ordinary's secrets. Or maybe it's because the king of hell wants to take over the world and Ordinary is standing in his way.

Whichever disaster has the gods on edge, Delaney isn't going to let anything get in the way of walking down that aisle. But when an attempted murder and kidnapping hit with a one-two punch, Delaney must take on the pain-in-the-neck gods, the nosy streamer, and all the demons in the Underworld, before her chance to say "I do" is lost forever.

For my family, and all the dreamers and magic makers in the world

CHAPTER ONE

If I, Delaney Reed, ever found a genie in a lamp, I knew exactly how I'd spend my three wishes.

Wish one: for the jerk god who'd tricked my fiancé, Ryder, into worshiping him to drop dead. Wish two: for my wedding to finally, finally be over. Wish three: for a nice, quiet evening on the beach with Ryder, sharing a blanket, the sunset, and a beer.

But instead of three wishes, what did I get this fine Tuesday morning? Two knuckle-headed gods fighting in the middle of the road.

"Go over it again." I pushed at Crow, who was the god Raven. His long black hair was pulled back in a single braid, and he wore a T-shirt advertising his glass blowing studio THE NEST. He stood his ground and glared daggers—no make that swords—at Odin, who was the god Odin.

"He's an ass." Crow tried to side-step past me. I moved into his space, body checking him and shoving a hand on his chest again. He took a quick backward step.

"He started it," Crow said, stabbing his finger

toward Odin. "But I am more than fucking happy to fucking end it."

Behind me, Ryder warned Odin to stand there or get ready to explain things while cuffed and cooling his heels in jail.

The seagulls called out overhead, hoping someone had brought french fries to the fight.

We hadn't gathered a crowd yet, mostly because it was Tuesday, and the two gods had decided to duke it out on a side street.

Also, now that summer had faded into early autumn, the crowds of nosy tourists had drifted away from Ordinary, back to their work-a-day lives. We'd still have tourists—the ocean and our local Valkyrie, Bertie's, constant community events, festivals, and contests would make sure of that. But I, for one, was looking forward to a little quiet around here.

"Settle down, Crow." I gave him another push just to make sure he was listening.

His brown gaze flicked to mine, and there was amber fire there. "Stay out of this, Delaney."

"No," I said mildly, "I don't think I will. Do you want to tell me why you two are going at it like kids in a schoolyard?"

"No."

Odin was telling Ryder much the same. Just a short, blunt denial.

"Are you going to start fighting as soon as you're out of my sight?"

That stubborn set of his jaw told me all I needed to know.

"Ground rules, then." I stepped back. "Keep the conflict resolution reasonable. That means words, not fists. And if you absolutely must fight, no property destruction, no hospital stays for you or others. Got it?"

Crow's smile was hard and flat. "Sure, Delaney. No property damage." He shifted his glare over my shoulder to Odin.

Odin's gray hair was wild around his head, his beard cut shorter than usual, his plaid shirt dusty and smelling of cedar.

The eye patch he wore today was forest green and set off the light in his one clear blue eye. He looked scruffy, temperamental, and every inch the chainsaw artist he was.

"I have better things to do than come back here and drag you to jail, Crow," I warned. "For cripes sake, can't you just drop whatever this is?"

He looked away from Odin and focused on me, really focused on me as my almost-uncle instead of as an angry god. His smile this time was kinder, less mocking. "I won't guarantee I won't hit him again."

"Crow."

"But I can promise he won't end up in the hospital." He shrugged. "For long."

He was still annoyed: the clench of his jaw, the sharper line of cheekbone, the square of his shoulders. There was war in him, but it was, at the moment, tempered.

"You want my advice?" I asked.

"No."

"Let it go. Whatever is between you, set it down. You're supposed to be living a quiet, relaxing life here, remember? You can fight with the other gods when you leave. Kiss and make up."

"He can kiss my ass, that's what he can kiss," Odin grumbled.

Crow rolled his eyes.

Ryder's phone rang. "Just stand there, all right?" he told Odin. "I'm not going to change my mind."

Well, that was interesting. "Does this have something to do with Ryder?" I asked Crow.

"What? No. Why would you think that?"

"Because I know what a lie looks like on your face."

He stuck his tongue out at me.

"I swear, if this is somehow about the wedding—"

"He picked Crow over me!" Odin bellowed.

"Because I'm the best man!" Crow shouted.

I stared at the sky. "Is there a god I can pray to that will make you two shut up?"

"No," they both said.

I shook my head. "I blame you for this, Ryder. I told you to leave the gods out of the wedding ceremony."

Ryder was gorgeous. His sun-lightened hair was threaded with copper and gold, and he'd been keeping a sexy five o'clock shadow that carved his jawline. He had on a light blue flannel over a black Henley—which made his shoulders look even wider—jeans, and heavy work boots.

He waggled his eyebrows, then stuck his finger in his ear and answered his phone, turning his back.

"You're not the best anything," Odin growled. "You're a trickster and a thief, and Ryder should have chosen me as his best man."

"You're a groomsman," Crow argued. "That's second best."

"Odin," Odin said, "is *not* second best."

"I dunno," Crow cooed. "Have you seen that

chainsaw artist in Boring? Now, he's good. Really good. Way better than you."

"Delaney," Odin said coolly, his one-eyed gaze flicking to me. "I'd like to report a murder I'm about to commit." He curled his fingers into a fist, knuckles cracking.

"No," I said.

"No," Ryder said to whoever was on the phone. "No, it is not a good time, and it is not in our agreement. It can wait."

His shoulders were stiff, his spine straight. There was only one person who could make him that angry, that quickly.

Mithra, the god who'd tricked Ryder into a contract pledging his life to him. The god who had always hated us Reeds, hated that we enforced the rules and laws of Ordinary, Oregon, the little vacation town for gods, and home for supernaturals.

"He's a dick," Crow said, watching Ryder. "Mithra, not your boo."

"I know," I said. "But we haven't found a way to break the contract yet."

"Mithra is a dick," Odin agreed, "but he knows how to make a contract stick. Is he still dragging Ryder around by the ear to do his petty bidding?"

I nodded. It hadn't been too bad to start with, but in the last year, and especially since Ryder and I had been engaged, Mithra called on him every day, sometimes several times a day and sent him out to uphold and enforce outdated, and frankly ridiculous, laws for the god.

"Between Mithra and the wedding, he's exhausted,"

I said. "But the only ways to break the contract come with even higher prices."

"Such as?" Crow asked.

"Giving Ordinary over to Mithra and letting his law become the only law in the town."

"Fucker," Odin said, which was followed by a couple other short words in a language I didn't know.

"It's not gonna happen," I said. "He can't have Ordinary. This place will always follow the agreement of the gods who made it. The way gods put down their powers, how those powers are kept safe, will always be handled under a Reed."

"We know that, Boo-boo," Crow said. "Is Ryder taking your name?"

"What?"

"The wedding. Is Ryder taking your name? Because if he becomes a Reed..."

I nodded. I'd been thinking about that. "He said he wanted to, but yeah, I know. If he's a Reed, Mithra will use it as a loophole to try and take over Ordinary."

"Traditionally..." Odin started, "...well, current tradition is that the bride takes the groom's name."

"I'm keeping my name," I said.

"Because of Mithra?" he asked.

"No, because I want to keep it."

"And what does Ryder want?"

"He said...well, he told me he'd like to take my name. We haven't really had time to talk about it. There are still a lot of loose ends and decisions that have to be made."

"Cutting it pretty close, aren't you?" Crow asked. "Wedding's in a week, right?"

"Two weeks," I scowled. "And it's going to be fine."

"No, it is not," Ryder said to the phone. "I *am* working and you do *not* need me there to shut down a garage sale."

A police cruiser rolled down the street.

I sighed. That would be Myra. If she was here, it meant she'd take over for Ryder while he left to do Mithra's chores.

Her family gift meant she was always in the right place at the right time.

"Fuck," Ryder growled as he jabbed at his phone. He squeezed it so hard his knuckles went white. "As if I don't have a million other things to deal with."

"Delaney." Myra stood out of the car and strolled to us. "Need a hand?"

"You leaving?" I asked Ryder.

He turned to me, stilted movements, like he wanted to have his own little boxing match with a god right about now.

"I know," I said before he could say anything, before he could apologize.

"I'm sorry," he said anyway.

"Don't. Just be careful, okay?"

He nodded.

"Garage sale?" I prodded with a grin.

He nodded again, the movement finally unlocking some of the stiffness in him. He rubbed the back of his neck. "Coos Bay. Someone is putting on their third garage sale of the year. The horror."

"How many are they legally allowed to have?"

"Two." He inhaled, exhaled, accepting his fate. "I should be back in a few hours. By tonight, latest."

"If you need backup in Coos Bay, I know a few people," I said.

"As if Mithra would let someone else handle it. No, I'm good. It's...I'm good." He turned to leave, then strode back to me, closing the distance fast.

And then he was there, in my space, in my world, breathing the same ocean breeze, shining under this same sun. "I love you," he said softly, all his heart reaching, wanting me to know he would try to fix this, too: his connection to Mithra. That he would try to make our life better.

"I love you," I told him, because this wasn't just his problem to solve. I wanted a lifetime of quiet, uninterrupted moments with him on the beach, watching the sun set, sharing the warmth of a blanket, or just walking hand in hand. I would find a way to break his contract to that god if it was the last thing I did.

He bent, and I met him halfway for the kiss which was brief, but heated, Ryder's anger a warmth of its own.

"I'll be home soon," he promised.

"Good," I said. "You're cooking dinner."

"Damn right I am." His fingers brushed my hip, lingering and reluctant to leave. Then he walked over to his truck, nodding to Myra as he passed. "Good luck with them."

"Drive safe," she said. She put her hands on her hips and looked between the two gods. "You two done fighting?"

"It was just a tiff," Crow said airily.

"So you're done fighting?" I asked.

Crow grinned. "Let's just say if I want to punch him, I'll do it where no one can see me."

"The fuck you will," Odin said mildly.

"Not the message I was delivering, but I know when

to count my winnings. Just in case," I said, "Crow, you're with me."

"What?"

"Odin," Myra said, "How about I escort you to wherever you should be right now, which is nowhere near Crow."

There was a moment, a tension in the air, when I thought both gods would decide they really, really wanted to get kicked out of Ordinary, but then Odin inhaled and gave Myra a little smile.

"I was going to deliver a few orders," he said. "I don't need you to escort me back to my property."

"Pretty sure I'm going to anyway," she said.

That got a low, fond chuckle out of him. "All right. I wouldn't mind a lift."

He turned and walked to the cruiser without once looking back at Crow, ignoring the other god completely.

"Three o'clock, right?" Myra asked me.

"What's happening at three?"

She blinked. "Really? I reminded you yesterday."

"Oh."

"And the day before, and four times last week. A month ago, you told me you wrote it in your calendar."

"I... Right. It slipped my mind?"

She squinted at me. "Dress shopping."

"Right. That."

"Your wedding. Shopping for your wedding dress. We have an appointment." She pointed at her chest then at me. "Me, you, Jean. Sister time. We are looking for your dress. Today. Because we cannot put it off any longer. We shouldn't have put it off this long. You need a dress."

"At three," I said. "Got it. I'll see you at the shop at three."

She studied me for a minute, looking for how I was going to try to weasel out of it this time.

It wasn't that I didn't want a dress, it was just that I hated clothes shopping on general principle.

"Super excited about it," I told her with a thumbs up. "I'll meet you and Jean there."

"At three," she repeated.

"Yup."

"You won't forget."

"I won't forget."

"Don't make me have to find you and drag you there by your ankles, because you know I will."

I grinned because she was being funny, but from the frown she threw me, she very much was not being funny.

I gave her another thumbs up, and she finally turned toward the cruiser.

I waited until both Myra and Odin got in the car before stepping a little closer to Crow.

I slapped his arm. "What was that all about?"

"Ouch," he laughed. He rubbed the spot where I'd smacked him. "I don't know. Why don't you want to shop for a wedding dress?"

"That's not what I was talking about. Why were you really fighting with Odin? Honestly, if there's something more going on between the two of you, I need to know."

"And yet, my personal life is none of your business. What? Don't give me that look. This may come as a shock, but even vacationing gods can get on each other's nerves."

"Uh-huh." I waited.

"This is where I change the subject so masterfully,

you drop the whole thing and never ask me again. I hear there's gonna be a wedding, and we haven't settled on a dress yet. Are we thinking pantsuit? Jorts?"

"We're thinking the dress thing isn't your problem."

He tipped his head back and stared at the sun, which peeked in and out of the high, crystalline clouds that draped fine lace across the silken summer blue.

"Would you look at that? Almost lunch time. You hungry, Delaney? Maybe want a burger and a little time to chat with Uncle Crow?"

I narrowed my eyes. "Is this a trap?"

He scoffed. "This is *lunch*. Wow, you are really wound up."

"I wasn't the one in the middle of the street punching people."

"Person. And he deserved it. Tell you what. Lunch is my treat. Come with me, and you can make sure I don't track him down while he's doing his deliveries to punch him in the schnoz."

My stomach growled loud enough, Crow grinned.

"Is that a yes?" he asked.

"Is this part of you all taking turns stalking me?" I asked.

He scrunched up his face. "What? Who?"

"All of you. The gods. One of you is always hanging around me lately, ever since..." I paused, thinking back. It had happened so slowly, I wasn't even sure when it had begun. Definitely after the demon queen Xtelle had come to town. After the demon king's right-hand man, Avnas, had come to town too.

After the monster hunter had come to town and almost discovered the ghoul in our midst.

But that had been months ago, and the god tag-team

had come on slowly. It had taken me most of the summer to realize it was happening, that there was always, unexplainably, a god in eyeshot of me now.

"Has your paranoia set in just since the wedding planning started?" he asked. "Or have I just not noticed it all this time?"

"You can't tell me one of you hasn't been showing up at everything I do, everywhere I am."

"I *can* tell you that." He nodded toward my Jeep. "Give me a lift?"

My stomach rumbled again. Since I'd skipped breakfast and gone on a run instead, I knew I'd better eat while I had the chance.

With Ryder out of town, we were officially down an officer, though things had been slow with the dwindling tourist visits, and he was part-time anyway.

"Come on," I said. "I'm ordering the most expensive thing on the menu."

"Ooooo, scary. I can take it. We're eating in town, I'm guessing?"

"How does the Blue Owl sound?"

"Cheap and greasy. I mean, good. Extravagant. Why the diner?"

I shrugged. "I want pie." I swung into the driver's seat while he got in on the passenger side.

He glanced in the back. "No dragon-pig?"

"At home, with Spud. I don't bring the dragon to work, Crow."

"You could."

I put the Jeep in gear and drove past coastal pines whose extended limbs spilled pools of shade onto the road.

Crow was silent, looking out the side window like he didn't have a care in the world.

I let the quiet between us stretch as we exited the neighborhood and took the main drag—Highway 101—north to the diner.

I wasn't used to my mouthy uncle being this quiet and almost asked what was wrong with him, but decided to come at it from a different angle.

"Is the thing with Odin old or new?" I asked quietly. I caught his slight wince, before he sort of loosened, slouching in the seat and propping his elbow so he could pick at the weatherstripping around the window.

"We haven't always gotten along, he and I," Crow said. It was one of his standard non-answers, but my gut told me this wasn't something I should let pass.

"The last couple months, things have been going good in town," I said, "now that the monster hunter is gone, and the demons and ghouls have settled in a bit. But if there is something that has you on edge, something that's bothering Odin, I would rather know than be caught unaware."

The corners of his eyes tightened, and his breathing changed. I thought he was going to say something, was going to share whatever had the gods on edge enough to follow me around, but he turned a smile my way and shrugged.

"Like you said, things have been going good in town. Maybe that's what has some of us on edge. *Some*," he repeated. "Others of us are just loudmouth jerks. Like Odin."

I eased the Jeep into the diner parking lot, which was pretty full. I found a spot near the garbage dumpsters and parked.

"You are not being helpful."

He wagged a finger at me. "Now, now. I thought you wanted pie."

"I do."

"Look at how helpful I am. This place has pie!" He winked and pushed out of the Jeep, then strolled to the front of the diner.

I watched him for a minute, trying to figure out what he wasn't telling me. But since Crow was a trickster as a god and also as a god on vacation, I had a bad feeling there were plenty of things he wasn't telling me.

CHAPTER TWO

THE DINER SMELLED like grilled meat, french fries, salt, and rich, buttery caramel.

The place was packed, and the rise and fall of voices overtook Hall and Oats singing about how they can't go for that.

I stood just inside the doorway and scanned tables and booths, noting faces I recognized and a few I didn't. The mix of truckers, tourists, and families made the place feel cozy.

Four people sat at the curved corner booth: Two women, two men, one man with gray hair, the rest younger, maybe in their thirties, a mix of light and darker skin. They didn't look related. Friends? Tourists?

They drew my attention. Not because they were doing anything to draw notice, but because they were doing the exact opposite.

While the rest of the place was laughing, making noise, they were all silent, quietly drinking coffee, eating desserts, and very carefully not looking my way.

The silence, the almost robotic movements, pinged my radar and made me want to keep an eye on them.

"Delaney?" Ahead of me, Crow spun on his heel, momentarily pausing in following the waitress to an open booth by the window. "You coming?"

I nodded and sat across from him, taking the side of the table that gave me a clear line of sight to the corner booth.

The waitress, short, plump, with the most gorgeous brown eyes I'd ever seen, was a new hire I hadn't met before. Her name tag said Maria, and there was a winky-face drawn beside her name.

She put two menus down for Crow and me, then got busy filling water glasses.

"I'll give you a minute unless you know what you want?" She paused, her pen poised over a small order book.

"Yeah," Crow said, "I want—"

"Give us a minute to check the menu, Maria? Thank you," I said over the top of Crow.

"Sure, sure. I'll be back in a shake."

She bopped over to the other tables, water pitcher in her hand.

"They've never changed this menu," Crow said. "Do you really think there's something on the menu you haven't seen?" He picked one up and flicked something off the laminated surface, then put it down, already bored.

"All the same pies. All the same eggs and bacon and burgers. All the same everythings." He folded his fingers together, propped elbows on the table, and rested his chin. "You look tense. Why are you tense? I said I'd buy. Lunch *and* dessert, since I am your favorite uncle."

"Do you notice anything weird about those people in the corner booth?"

"They're quiet?"

I hummed, which made him look a little closer.

"Does that seem out of place to you?" I asked.

He settled back in his seat. "Not really. Humans behave in a lot of different ways. There are reasons for groups to be quiet. This is more of your paranoia isn't it?"

"I am the chief of police, you know."

"So...is that a yes?"

I raised one eyebrow.

"It's okay," he said, "I gotcha, Boo. Tell Uncle Crow everything that he totally won't use to rat you out in a memoir which will make him rich and famous."

I shook my head. "Lunch better be fan-fuckin'-tastic," I grumbled.

Maria showed up, pad and pen ready. "Did I give you long enough to look over the menu?"

"Yep," I said. "I'll take the fish tacos with a side salad, please, and some coffee. Oh, and I'm going to want dessert. Which whole pies do you have to go?"

"Sure, sure. We have apple, blackberry, cherry, and I think we might have a strawberry rhubarb left."

"Oh, she wants the rhubarb," Crow said.

"No, I do not want the rhubarb," I said, spearing him with a glare. "But that blackberry sounds delicious."

"Sure, sure," she said again. "I'll put your name on it just to make sure we don't cut into it...uh?" She glanced at my uniform jacket on the seat beside me.

"Delaney," I said. "Delaney Reed." I gave her a smile. "Welcome to Ordinary, by the way."

She smiled. "Thank you. And what would you like?" she asked Crow.

He gave her a panty-melting smile. "What do you recommend, darling? You look like a woman with excellent taste." He followed that by leaning back to show off his chest and cupping the back of his head in his palms, flexing his arms. He gave her a big wink.

"You look like oatmeal," she said.

I sputtered a laugh.

"I look like...what?"

She shrugged. "You wanted my recommendation, and you look like oatmeal would do the trick."

"The trick?" he asked suspiciously.

"Man of your age? It's good for the heart."

"My age." Crow tipped his chin up.

She waited with a pleasant smile.

I still couldn't get a read on her. Was she insulting him for the whole "darling" and posturing thing, or was she teasing him to see what he'd do?

Crow gave her a very judgy look.

"Red meat, please. I'll take a burger," he said. "With bacon and avocado, if you have it."

"Cali burger coming up. You want fries with that?"

"Yes."

"Sure, sure." She pursed her lips then made a big production of mouthing *"oatmeal,"* as she wrote on the pad.

"Anything else?" she peeped, fluttering long lashes at him.

He deflated in the booth and gave her a new look. One that said he liked her spunk. "Delaney?" he asked.

"I'm good. Thank you, Maria."

She gave me a grin then bopped off to the kitchen.

"She's fun," Crow said. "Wanna bet I'm getting a bowl of mush?"

"Oh, yeah, no. You are totally getting a bowl of mush."

"So," he said, "this dress thing. You and Myra later today?"

"Apparently it's traditional for the bride to wear a dress to one of these things." I glanced over at the silent booth again. They were slowly making their way through their desserts, as if they had all the time in the world. They were also throwing quick glances our way.

"Good," Crow said. "I happen to have a clear schedule this afternoon."

"What?"

"To help pick out the dress," he said. "I'm free all afternoon."

"No."

"But I'm family." At my look he tapped his finger tip on the table a couple of times. "Close enough, right? And as your uncle, I want to be a part of this special time in your life."

"No. You'll be lucky if I invite you to the ceremony."

"What do you mean? I'm officiating."

I laughed at him. "Weren't you just fighting over being the best man?"

"Maybe that hasn't been decided yet. Maybe I'm going to be the officiant."

"No, you very much are not."

He looked shocked. "Who? Who is going to marry you, Delaney Reed? My one and only niece—"

"I have two sisters."

"—one and *only* niece who is getting *married* in two

weeks. Who else would you possibly consider giving you your official vows?"

"There are dozens of gods in town, several religious leaders, judges at the courthouse, an entire dory fleet of ship captains, not to mention I'm pretty sure Jean took one of those online quizzes to make it legal for her to notarize stuff and marry people."

"Other than those people?" he demanded.

I took the napkin off the table and dropped it in my lap. "We haven't decided. No, don't get your hopes up. From how much Ryder keeps being called out of town, I don't even know how we're going to pull everything together on time."

"I have plenty of time," he said. "Let me help. You can start by letting me be there while you're picking out the dress. Consider it an audition. A chance for me to show you how supportive I can be. Way more supportive than your sisters, especially Jean with her fake certificates."

I opened my mouth to tell him the whole point of dress shopping was so we three sisters could spend a little time together outside of work and all the other busy things that filled our lives. Then I noticed he was still tapping his finger on the table.

Like a nervous tick.

What was he nervous about?

"It's a girls-only thing," I said, watching his reaction.

"Absolutely. Girls and their favorite uncle."

"Why are you trying to elbow your way into my dress shopping, Crow?"

"There you go again, Delaney. So suspicious. You know I love you, right?"

"That was so not an answer."

"No, no. I understand. You don't want me there. I heard you, loud and clear. I won't push."

I waited, expecting him to push.

"What?" he asked.

"I was waiting for the push."

He pressed wide-spread fingertips against his chest. "Offended. You clearly have a boundary you don't want me to cross."

"Clearly," I slowly agreed.

"So I won't cross it."

"Just like that?"

"I've always respected your boundaries, Boo-boo."

"Is that so?"

He smiled. "Dress shopping is important. A...tradition, a ritual. It's for women only. I heard you. I hope *you* heard that I am more than willing to help with the wedding. With anything you might need to make it easier. Especially officiating."

He might be angling for only helping with the fun stuff, but at least he was offering his help.

"Thanks," I said, actually touched to know he was there if I needed him.

Maria popped over to our table, balancing plates on her arms.

"Here you go, Delaney." She placed the fish tacos, which smelled delicious, in front of me, then set down a small side salad and tartar sauce.

"Looks amazing," I said.

She nodded. "And for you."

I half expected it to be oatmeal, but instead it was a burger, with generous portions of avocado and bacon peeking out from under the bun.

"Well, look at that," Crow said. "Thank you, Maria. This looks great."

She added ketchup and other condiments to the table. "Anything else?"

"No, but thank you." I lifted one of the tacos and took a big bite. It was delicious.

Crow's phone rang, and Maria took that as her cue, working her way toward a table that was asking for more coffee.

Crow frowned at it his phone, then slid out of the booth.

"Problem?"

"I don't think so. But I need to take this."

"That better not be Odin challenging you to a duel," I said.

He pointed at his fries. "Stay out of those. I counted. I'll know if you steal them."

I snorted, but had a mouth full, which I decided was more important than a snappy comeback.

He walked past me and out the door where, even with mid-day traffic going by, it was probably quieter than inside the diner.

The music had rolled through several feel-good love songs, but now Taylor Swift was getting her chance to shake things off.

I tapped my boot along with the song while I looked around the diner again.

Just people having lunch.

Then why were my nerves on edge? I'd thought it was just Crow being annoying and the lingering anxiety and, okay, I could admit it, fear over the wedding planning. But now that Crow was out of the place, the slight feeling of wrongness remained.

I stole three of his fries, rearranged the stack to hide it, then ate them one by one. Nothing seemed out of place, except that group of four quiet diners.

But the longer they remained there, quietly finishing their meal, the more they seemed to fit in. As Crow said, humans behaved differently, and silence wasn't that unusual.

I didn't have my sister Jean's ability to know when something really bad was going to happen, nor did I have Myra's family gift for being in the right place at the right time.

But that didn't mean I should ignore my instincts.

The gods had been acting strange, well, stranger, around me.

And there was something up with those people in the corner booth.

Maria swung by the corner booth folks. She smiled and laughed.

Like someone had flipped a switch, they smiled and laughed, too, suddenly breaking their silence, breaking their spell.

My gut still said something was up, but now they just looked like regular people out for lunch. Maybe people on their way to or from something that had them contemplative and silent. Like a funeral. Or a training conference.

That seemed to fit. They didn't look like friends, more like work associates.

I dug into another taco while the group settled their bill, worked out who was pitching in for the tip, and gathered jackets and purses.

They strolled out the door, and I watched them through the window. They split into male-female pairs, got into two cars, and pulled out of the lot, heading south.

South toward Ordinary. South toward a lot of towns, really, including Coos Bay. Maybe they were headed to an illicit garage sale.

"You stole my fries," Crow slid into the seat opposite. He picked up his burger and took a huge bite.

"Quality control test," I said. "Did you see those people drive off?"

"I did." He took another huge bite.

"Did you get any weird feelings off them?"

He shook his head and started in on the fries. "Looked like regular humans to me. Why? Did you?"

"Nothing I could put my finger on."

He chewed thoughtfully. "They're just human."

"Yeah, but humans cause trouble too."

"Don't I know it?" He popped his fingertips one by one into his mouth to clear them of ketchup and salt, then dragged the same fingers over his napkin. "You're worried."

I shrugged. "That's part of my job." *Part of my life.*

"You don't need to worry. You've got a wedding coming up. A dress to choose. Let some of the rest of us worry instead."

I frowned. "Is that why all you gods are acting so strange? You're worried?"

"We've always been strange. And I'm not worried about a bunch of humans who like to eat without a lot of chit chat." He pointed at his mouth, my plate, and made some exaggerated chewing motions before demolishing his meal.

I finished mine, too, and just as he'd promised, he picked up the tab.

Not too much later, we walked out of the diner. I was full, in a much better mood, and an entire blackberry pie the richer.

"Want me to drop you off somewhere?" I asked.

"That'd be great. What are you doing the rest of the day until the dress thing?" He ducked into my Jeep, and I sat behind the wheel.

"First, I'm going to get rid of you so I can do my job. And then, none of your business." I put the Jeep in gear. "You know what you're *not* doing the rest of the day?" I asked.

He raised his eyebrows.

"Getting into a fight with Odin."

"Well, not where you can see it anyway," he said with a grin.

I shook my head and took us both back to town.

CHAPTER THREE

I STRODE INTO THE STATION. Death was waiting for me.

"Reed Daughter, you are late," Than, the god of death, intoned.

He was looking particularly dapper today, from the brown trilby to the brightly flowered Hawaiian shirt, which was covered in smaller brightly flowered Hawaiian shirts, to the crisp black slacks.

He stood partially behind the counter that separated the waiting area from our desks. I couldn't see his shoes, but I would win money if I bet they were polished within an inch of their lives.

"Late for what?" I asked. "And since when are you in charge of my schedule?"

His eyebrows lifted slightly as he gave me a look that indicated this was not the subject on the table.

"I do not follow your schedule," he said. "However, there are three people who have indicated you were to meet them here. The half of an hour ago."

I mouthed: "*the half of an hour*" and glanced past him to my desk.

Yep. Three people waiting for me. Three people I very much did not have on my calendar.

"Bertie," I said, pushing past the front counter and surly god to face the Valkyrie who looked annoyed at my cheerful tone. "I don't recall us having a meeting today."

At first glance, Bertie seemed like a petite elderly woman with short silver hair and an office chic taste in fashion. Today she wore a plum and gold jacket and slacks, the silk blouse a vivid pink that really pulled the whole suit together. But her power-suit and pearls exterior hid the ferocious heart of an ancient creature born for the battlefield.

"We did have a meeting," she informed me. "I called an hour ago. Than explained you did not have anything on your schedule this morning. I've been waiting."

I threw a dirty look at Than. He slowly lifted his mug of tea, and took a sip, watching me the entire time.

Unrepentant, that god.

"I didn't know he'd promised I'd be here, or I would have cut lunch short. Hi, Tish."

Tish lifted their fingers in a wiggly little wave. They were a ghoul and one of the newest members of Ordinary.

Bathin, the demon who was dating my sister, Myra, had granted Tish a bodily form of their own so they didn't have to keep eating things or people and turning into them. They were a good looking, dark-haired, copper-skinned person who was wearing a white T-shirt, leather belt and designer blue jeans.

I'd never met a ghoul before Tish, but they seemed to be settling into our town and their job as Bertie's assistant surprisingly quickly.

I'd made sure Bertie understood Tish had basically

27

been forced by the demon Goap, who was Bathin's younger brother, to invade the god realms and steal god weapons, strangely delivering some of them here to our town. Goap had made a couple plays to try and get Bathin to fight their father, the King of the Underworld, for the throne, but Bathin said he didn't want the throne.

He wanted to stay here in Ordinary, dating my sister and volunteering at the animal shelter.

Bertie had brushed off my concern of demon influence over Tish, and had spent the last couple months training Tish to help in the various festivals Bertie was constantly coordinating and throwing, teaching them how to be organized and professional.

If Tish ever got tired of being Bertie's right hand person, they'd have no problem finding a job in any business of their choice.

The other person sitting on the edge of my desk was a man I didn't recognize. "And you are?" I asked, offering my hand.

He was blond, fit, and had that everything-always-goes-my way attitude. Handsome enough he could land a commercial strolling a tropical beach with a lime balanced on top of his beer bottle. His smile, when he switched it on, was bad-boy rock star in a boy-next-door package.

Dangerous.

His handshake was warm and somehow carried the intent that, if he wasn't my friend yet, he intended to be so by the end of our meeting.

"Patrick," he said. "Patrick Baum."

"Nice to meet you, Mr. Baum."

"No," he said, holding my hand for an extra beat. "So nice to meet you. And it's just Patrick, please." His voice was easy, the burr of it a finger across the back of my neck. A shiver rippled down my spine.

He was not human, but I didn't know what he was, exactly.

"Welcome to Ordinary," I said, drawing my hand back. If he didn't want to tell me what type of supernatural he was, that was fine. But if he wanted to stay in Ordinary in any permanent way, I'd need to tell him the rules. "Are you here for the weekend?"

"Oh," he leaned back on one foot, but managed not to move out of my personal space at all. "I'm leaving my options open. Been moving around the country. Looking for a vacation home. Stopped by Boring, as a matter of fact. And what a lucky break that was."

Bertie, who had been waiting for us to be done with our pleasantries with as much patience as she ever managed, went ramrod straight.

Tish eased away from Bertie. Patrick didn't appear to notice her discomfort at the mention of the town where Bertie's sister and rival Valkyrie, Robyn, had set up her nest.

His attention was on me, unwavering, his gaze intent. That smile was just so friendly, like we were both in on a private joke against the world.

I hated it.

I lifted my left hand and gestured at Bertie, but made sure my engagement ring was in full view. If that didn't make him turn that smile down to battery saver level, I'd tell him I was engaged, and wouldn't have been interested in him if I weren't.

"How do you know Bertie?" I asked.

"I invited him here," she said stiffly. "To…assist my efforts."

Uh-oh. I didn't like the sound of that. "Which efforts?"

"Marketing and outreach. Social media."

"You probably recognize me now don't you?" he asked, doing the gosh-ma'am humble act that I was pretty sure was just that—an act. "Everyone does when they hear 'social media.'"

Bertie glared at me like I was the slowest bus at the station. Tish's eyes went wide.

Okay, I was missing something.

"I don't recognize you," I said. "Should I?"

Than, still watching from the counter behind us, snorted softly.

"Well, I'm embarrassed," Patrick said, working the boy-next-door angle.

"He is *very* well known. On the social medias," Bertie said, and I couldn't tell if she was complimenting him or insulting him. "He is an influencer."

"Bauming Down the Road," he said. "You know, I pick little places full of big fun. Find all the sweet road bombs for road lovers who're looking for places to visit that still have a little of that old-fashioned magic in them."

Magic. Did he mean that literally or figuratively? "I haven't seen your stuff, sorry. Are you telling me Ordinary is a place with old-fashioned magic in it?"

Bertie cleared her throat. "That is what I invited him here to find out."

"Well, *invited*," he dragged out the word with a smile.

"More like the events coordinator in Boring...what was her name?" He snapped his fingers. "Robyn. She spilled the beans that I was coming by."

"Yes," Bertie said tightly. "And then I invited you."

There was something more to all this, something that didn't sit right. There were rules in Ordinary, and one of them was that supernaturals, except for gods and demons, were free to come and go. But if any of them decided to stay for an extended time, or live here, the rules changed.

So as long as Road Bomb didn't break the law, he was free to tourist the town.

"Like I said: Welcome," I said. "I'm sure Bertie has someone in mind to show you around town. Unless there was something I could do to be of help?"

"There is," Bertie said. "I already extended my offer to be his personal tour guide, but Mr. Baum has certain needs. One of his terms is that he is allowed to move through town without much supervision."

"Any," he corrected with that billboard smile. "Any supervision. Too many cooks ruin the video spontaneity. I don't like things scripted."

"Uh-huh." I put a little more authority in my tone. "My job is to look after and protect all the people in this town, Mr. Baum. You are, of course, free to move about town just like anyone else. But if I find you've broken a law—any law—I will arrest you just as quickly as I would any non-influencer."

"I didn't say I was going to break the law," he said.

"And yet, you're here, in my station, asking for an all-access pass. Property damage is breaking the law, trespassing is breaking the law, drunk and disorderly is breaking the law, and if those are the sorts of things you want to do—if those are the sort of things that make for good "video spontaneity"—then I need you to know I won't allow it."

"I have money," he said. "And sway in a lot of circles. Social circles. Political circles."

"Good for you," I said. "Bribes are a crime too."

"All right." He dropped the smile and gave me what I thought might be the first honest expression of the day. It was thoughtful, maybe even impressed. "That was pressing my luck, wasn't it? I'm used to people getting excited when I show up, kind of going along with me."

"We're excited," Bertie assured him. "Delaney is not a woman easily swayed by glamour cast over her eyes."

Nice. I liked how she opened up the opportunity for him to tell us what sort of supernatural he was.

His head jerked up. "Glamour? Like…fairytales? I mean, I'm a good storyteller, but there's nothing but a bit of the bullshit to me."

Was it possible he didn't know he was supernatural? Maybe. Some people grew up sheltered and never found out they were more than human. It wasn't our place to tell them.

"Bullshit your audience, but don't bullshit law enforcement," I said. "If you do, you're on the hook for the consequences, though we can provide a lawyer for you if needed."

"Nice of you," he said.

"We treat everyone here, residents and bullshitters, the same." I smiled.

"All right," he said. "All right. That's good enough. I won't break any laws. But I'm an old pro at this, and I know it's best if I introduce myself to the local law and let them know I'll be nosing around, talking to people, asking questions. On my own."

Bertie opened her mouth to argue, and then *closed it.* Okay, there was something really wrong with this whole deal if Bertie wasn't arguing him into doing things the way she wanted them done.

"I'd prefer that you'd have someone local with you," I said. "But since this is your show, and you know what your viewers want, I won't insist."

"Beautiful," he said, "That's just what I was hoping for. You've been a big help to me, Chief Reed. I do need a contact though. Someone I can call if I have questions."

"Bertie can set you up with a contact."

"I offered my number," Bertie said. "He refused."

I crossed my arms over my chest. "You should take Bertie's number. There is no one who knows Ordinary better than her."

"Well, I heard you were born here."

"Lots of people are born here," I said.

"But lots of people didn't become the youngest chief of police, are also female, and have a record of the fewest civil complaints per capita as you. You are *interesting*, Delaney Reed."

There was the shark beneath the waves I was waiting for. Maybe he wasn't fairy folk. Maybe he was some kind of were-shark come ashore to cash in on an easy lunch.

"You have my number," I said. "It's 911. If you have an emergency, a real emergency, call it. Myself or one of my officers will reach you as quickly as possible."

He dragged his fingers back through his hair once

and shook his head. His hair fell perfectly back into place, making him more handsome.

It had to be fairy magic. No one lucked out on looks that flawless.

"I don't want to strain your emergency line," he said, "but I would love your number. For emergencies of a less dangerous sort."

"I'm sorry. I can't take time out of my duties to show you around. If you need help from law enforcement, call our non-emergency line, or 911. If you just want to know which of our restaurants has been in business the longest, I'm not the person you need to talk to."

"All right," he said. "I can take a hint." His expression changed into something calculating. "Would you have coffee with me? Any time that works for you would work for me. I'd love to ask you a few questions about what the town was like when you were growing up here, and what it's like now. That sort of life-in-a-small-town thing. People love that shit."

"Are you going to video it?"

"Just a couple clips. I won't have the camera running the whole time. It can be as professional or personal as you'd like."

Bertie was giving me a look that said there would be consequences if I refused.

"Sure. I'll let you know when I have time. Good luck with your project, Mr. Baum."

He gave me a little quirk of the lips, like I'd just told a great joke. "Thank you."

"And there you have it, Patrick," Bertie said. "I'm sure Chief Reed will find a moment to speak with you later. Would you like to begin on your solo adventure now, or is there something I could provide you with?"

Bertie had the perfect blend of being friendly, but also being done with the whole thing, down pat.

"No, I'm good, I'm good. I'll just see myself out."

"Mr. Baum?" I called out.

He paused with his hand on the door.

"It's not one of our most historic businesses, but we have the best bakery on the Oregon coast. Puffin Muffin. Just drive south and you can't miss the line of people waiting for pastries. Hogan's the owner. Tell him I sent you, and he'll give you a donut on the house."

"They also have an excellent tea selection," Than noted.

Patrick grinned. "Why am I not surprised the cops know the best donut joint in town?"

I faked a laugh and waved like it was the first time I'd ever heard a joke about cops and donuts. "Drive safe."

He gave me one last look, then finally walked out of the station.

The door shut on a wash of cooler air that mixed with the over-cooked coffee smell of the station. None of us said anything. Not until we heard an engine start and saw his car pull away.

"Interesting," Than said, breaking the silence. "I assume you sent him there so Hogan will tell you what supernatural he might be?"

"Yep. It pays to have a Jinn with the ability to see true forms dating my sister."

Bertie gave her head a choppy shake. "Patrick is much less tolerable than I'd prefer."

"I'm curious why you're tolerating him at all. That's not like you, Bertie."

"I tolerate people all the time, Delaney. But yes. He

35

may have his uses. There is a contest, a contest certain small towns in Oregon have entered."

"Small towns like Boring?"

"I believe it was mentioned."

"And what is this contest?"

What was good enough that Bertie would let a schmoozer like Patrick work his own angle on our town without her keeping him under her thumb? "Did you really invite him here?"

"Yes. And it's not because Robyn had him for three weeks. Three weeks, Delaney. I have no idea what he could have possibly found to do in Boring for three weeks. I checked the medical records to see if he may have slipped into a coma for two and a half of those weeks, but if he did, he didn't report it."

"Rude of him," I said.

"Yes. His interest in our town enters us into a contest for a prize Ordinary desperately needs. It's not money," she said, even though I wasn't thinking it would be. "It's having our town registered as a Road Bomb. His social media has the ability to bring a lot of people to a town. Some who will want to sit at the same bench he sat at, or eat the same meal he ate."

"And those tourists will bring money to the town without it having to be part of a community event," I said. "Passive advertising. Are you wanting to slow down a little? You know we appreciate everything you do, but if you wanted to ease off on the events, we'd be okay with that."

"Of course I don't want to slow down. Do I look like the retiring type? Really," she grouched.

"This will give Ordinary a wider reach into the world. More people will see us and know our town is filled with more festivals and artistic events and natural beauty than any other small town in Oregon."

Such as Boring. I hated to admit it, but for the first time I wondered if Bertie's drive to prove she was better than her sister, Robyn, might mean she wasn't making the best decisions for Ordinary.

"Do we really want to draw that much attention?" I asked. "This is supposed to be a small town, a vacation town for gods, a place where humans and supernaturals can live quiet lives. Bringing so much more attention could be a problem."

"Are you questioning me, Delaney?"

"I'm questioning why you want to put Ordinary on the map in this way. What you do for us is above and beyond. You keep the heart of this place pumping, keep it fun and make wonderful memories for all of us."

She colored just slightly. "It's my job," she said, "to keep Ordinary vital and up-to-date with the world. Having a larger social presence is keeping Ordinary up-to-date."

"Sure," I said. "I understand that. If we get too far behind, we'll draw attention we don't want. But having an influencer trumpet all our secrets to the world?"

She lifted her chin and dropped her shoulders. If she'd had a sword at her hip, I'd probably have the tip of it at my throat right about now.

"He won't trumpet our secrets. Do you think I haven't assessed the dangers of inviting someone with his number of followers into our town?"

"He said he's looking for places with real old-fashioned magic. And when you accused him of using glamour, that act he pulled to convince me he was non-supernatural was bull."

"Yes, I know," she said, "and no, I am not certain what kind of supernatural he is, but I do know he's not a demon who would need to sign a contract to be here."

"Social influencers like to discover things other people haven't," I said. "He's smarter than that boy-next-door routine he's selling. I don't like the idea of him walking around town without oversight."

Bertie gave me a look that I was going to interpret as tolerance. "I'm not going to set him loose on the town and expect him not to get into trouble. Someone from my office will follow him at all times."

"Your office."

Bertie didn't have permanent staff. She was too hands-on. Oh, who was I kidding? She was too controlling to let other people handle important things.

"Who?" Then it hit me.

Tish.

"Tish will follow him." Bertie nodded toward her ghoul protégé with a sparkle of pride in her eyes. "They can be very inconspicuous when they want to be. They will follow Mr. Baum at a discreet distance and report to me in regular intervals. We'll make sure we have measures in place to lead him away from anything of a sensitive nature we don't want him to stumble upon."

"You've already planned for this, and I shouldn't have doubted you, right?"

"Of course. I've gathered a team of volunteers who are willing to be distractions or interference, if needed. Non-violent, of course. We will keep a close eye on Mr. Baum for the remainder of his time here."

"How long is he planning to be here?"

"Three weeks in Boring, Delaney. *Three*."

I raised my eyebrows. "But we don't really want him

here for three weeks do we, Bertie? We have…um… some things coming up that we don't really want splashed across social media."

"You're talking about your wedding," she clarified. "I would expect a grown woman such as yourself to be able to at least say the word."

"Yes, Bertie. I'm talking about my wedding. I don't want a social influencer filming it to share with a bunch of random people worldwide. I want it to be a private event."

"Nonsense. You understand that at least half of the entire town will be attending."

"We're whittling down the guest list."

"You aren't. I've spoken with Ryder who is actually coordinating and planning the event. He's recently decided on an outdoor setting, so more people can attend."

He had? He hadn't told me any of that, though with him being constantly called away by Mithra, and me being…how had he put it…psychotically weird about wedding planning…I wasn't surprised I was out of the loop.

Still, there was a pang of regret, of sorrow, I guess, that I hadn't even known how my own wedding planning was going.

"Nice," I said with what I hoped was a convincing smile. "Outdoor setting."

Bertie could read a person, well, me certainly, like a large print menu. "He's still working out the details, Delaney. There are two weeks left until the wedding. I am sure there will be changes up until the last minute. That is just how it goes. You should know that."

I should know that? Because of how many weddings I'd actually put together, which was exactly zero.

"Sure," I said. "I know all events have last-minute changes."

"Good," she said. "Which only gives us two weeks with Mr. Baum since I expect he will be out of our town before the nuptials. I assume that is your preference?"

"That is very much my preference."

"Consider it done. Tish will take on the form and appearance they need to follow Mr. Baum and report back to me if they see anything of concern."

"Please keep a very low profile," I said to Tish. "Can you do that?"

They gave me a smile I never would have thought they had in them just a couple months ago when they'd first come to town.

Bertie had not only employed Tish, she had also given them a sense of confidence and self-worth they'd been sorely lacking when they'd been used by Goap.

"Yes?" Tish said, and then to my surprise, they corrected themselves and didn't couch it in a question. "Yes, I can."

"Listen to you," I said. "Good. I think you'll be excellent at it. If anything feels dangerous, or if you are uncomfortable, contact me or Bertie immediately. You are not to put yourself in harm's way, okay?"

They nodded.

"We've already gone over this," Bertie said. "They know I am instantly available for any situation that may arise."

"Sounds like we have a plan. Baum gets to look around town, Tish keeps an eye on him, and you check in to make sure nothing goes sideways. If something goes wrong in any way, I expect one of you to tell me."

"I remember when you didn't even know how to tie your shoes," Bertie said. It was either an uncharacteristically nostalgic moment, or she was reminding me that she had been alive for several dozens of my lifetimes and didn't need my permission to do her job.

Probably that second thing.

"Look at how far I've come!" I said. "Keeping the peace. Telling demons if they get to live here. Dragging gods out of fistfights. Go, me."

She studied me for a moment. "In any case, I am behind schedule now, since you left me waiting for over half an hour."

"I didn't even know you were here."

"Details. I assume I'll see you tonight?"

Uh-oh. "Tonight?"

She exhaled, every second of that breath informing me of just how irritating I was.

"After your dress shopping," she said, "you are coming by my office to look over my expectations for the murder mystery this weekend."

"Right." I'd forgotten all about that since I'd signed off on it at the beginning of the year.

"Don't disappoint me," she said. "And don't keep me waiting. Tish, let's get back to work." She strode past me in a swish of silk and perfume, her low heels clacking on the hard floor.

Tish gave me a wave and smile before falling in step with their boss and exiting out the door.

Than just made a considering sound and went back to sipping tea and staring at our phone line which was not doing anything worth staring at.

"Why did you tell them I was going to meet them here?" I asked.

"Did you not?" he asked.

"No, I did. But you gave them a time limit."

"Would you have preferred I didn't?"

"No, yes. You could have called and asked my ETA."

"Ah."

He sipped tea, watching me over the top of a cup that was much too delicate to be held in fingers that long and boney. I had the impression he was laughing at me.

"Did you know I was at lunch with Crow?"

He hesitated a little too long before saying, "No."

I narrowed my eyes. "What has gotten into you gods? That was you calling him at the diner, wasn't it?

Than took the time to carefully place the cup down on a delicate saucer. It was a set I hadn't seen before. I thought he and Myra had been trawling the online sites to one-up each other's cup collection. They were a bad influence on each other.

"Perhaps," he said, giving me his full attention. It should have been uncomfortable, bearing the weight of Death's gaze, but Than had a glint of humor behind that blasé expression.

He couldn't fool me. He liked me.

"I'm never out from under the watch of a god lately," I said.

His eyebrows ticked upward ever so slightly. "Do you think? Even while you slumber?"

I rolled my eyes. "You can deny it. All of you can deny it. But I know when I'm being watched. I'm being watched."

He made that considering sound again.

When he didn't say anything else, I scowled. "One of you is going to crack. One of you will tell me what you're worried about."

"I see."

"You are the worst," I grumbled. I pulled my phone out of my pocket and dialed our local baker.

"Puffin Muffin, this is Hogan," he answered.

"Hey, Hogan. Delaney. I sent a guy your way. He's a social media influencer looking into small towns. Bertie's brought him in to give Ordinary a review."

"Who is it?"

"Some guy named Patrick Baum."

There was a pause on the other end of the phone. I could just make out the soft, tropical music playing in the background and the burble of customer voices.

"Road Bomb is in Ordinary? Here? Patrick Baum is coming to my shop? Mine?" His voice went up with each question. Not panic, but not just excitement either. "Holy shits."

"You've heard of him?"

"Who hasn't heard of him?"

I didn't acknowledge that with an answer.

"I told him to try your bakery. I have no idea if he will or not. We have Tish following him in a subtle sort of way, just to make sure he isn't getting into any trouble."

"Holy shits."

Hyperventilating. Was he hyperventilating?

"Hogan? Hoges? You still with me?"

"I didn't have any idea. I would have…I would have made something better, something special."

"Okay, first of all, everything you make is amazing

and special. Everything you make is better than the best out there."

"I'm not ready."

"You are. You're going to be fine, going to be perfect. You have four out-of-town businesses begging you to keep delivering to them…"

"Six," he breathed.

"Six. Hey, congrats. You're a fantastic baker. All I need you to do is give him a free pastry when he stops in. I'll cover it."

"No, it's good. It's on the house. No worries. I got it."

"Maybe give him a cup of coffee or tea?"

"Sure, yes, whatever he wants." He sounded a little more like himself, the shock having worn off quickly.

"So other than being your normal spectacular self, and letting him enjoy one of your normal spectacular treats, I need you to do one more thing."

"I'll try."

"Take a good look at him, and tell me what kind of supernatural he is."

"Oh," he said. "He's not a normal, huh? Okay, yeah. Yeah, I can do that."

"Thanks, Hogan. You are going to impress the hell out of him."

"Thanks, yeah, I gotta go. See ya."

"Bye."

I disconnected and called Jean.

"Wedding dress shopping at three," she said.

"Myra already chewed me out about it. Hogan has a social media influencer who might be visiting his bakery today. He sounds a little star struck. Can you stop by and help him stay calm?"

"Which social media influencer?"

"Patrick Baum."

"Road Bomb! Oh, man, that's sweet! Why is he in town?"

"Bertie invited him. There's a small town contest he's doing. Also she wants the marketing that comes along with one of his visits."

"Yeah, of course she does. I heard he was in Boring for three weeks or something."

"Bertie heard that too."

"Oof."

"Yeah, but Jean?"

"Yeah?"

"Is Baum really that big of a deal? Should we brace for outside impact?"

She paused and I heard her truck door clack shut.

"Yeah, I'd say yes. He's a big deal. He draws attention everywhere he goes. He's been popular for over a year now. There's a chance his fame will fade and we won't be swamped, but he has a lot of fans out there. A lot. People like to follow the places he's been to, to recreate his experiences."

"How often does he put out videos?" I asked.

"Four times a week. He's on his Boring series right now. So I'd say we have at least a week before he posts about us."

"Or more, right? He was in Boring for three weeks."

"Yeah, but he started posting a week or so after he got there."

"Okay."

"He's not going to mess up your wedding," she said.

"That's not what I'm worried about."

"Delaney."

"That's not the *only* thing I'm worried about."

"What else?"

"The gods following me around. Mithra being an ass to Ryder. Goap sending weapons into our town. You know, all the regular things."

"Goap?" she asked. "Has there been some other contact with him, or with the king of hell?"

"No. I keep waiting for some kind of blowback from us taking Tish in, and sheltering Xtelle, Bathin, and Avnas. Everyone says a war is coming, though."

She was quiet. I wondered if she was using her family gift to work her way through what I was really asking her: Could she tell if something big and bad was about to blow our collective house down.

And if so, was it connected to Patrick? Was it connected to the demon Vychoro, who was the King of the Underworld?

"I don't feel anything bad," she said. "Really bad. Nothing soon, anyway, you know I sometimes can only tell minutes before it happens. But if I feel anything, I'll tell you."

"I know. I'm just tired of waiting for the hit I know is coming. Whenever it lands, we'll be ready for it."

"Yes, we will."

"Good luck with Hogan," I said.

"See you at three. For wedding shopping."

"I'll be there. There better be wine."

"Already got you covered," she laughed. "This is fun, you know, you getting married. This is exciting. Be a little excited. You are picking out your first wedding dress."

"First? Only. Only wedding dress."

"Right. That's what I said. Your only wedding dress,

because Ryder is your one true love, your knight in shining armor, the king of your hill, your smoochy-smoo—"

"Good-bye, Jean. Go be a supportive girlfriend to your boyfriend."

I disconnected to cut off her cackle.

CHAPTER FOUR

HATTER AND SHOE showed up at the station around two-thirty to take over. I usually worked later, but everyone insisted I get out of there.

"Perhaps," Than said as we both walked out of the building into a September late afternoon that was still clinging to summer, "you would provide me a ride?"

I glanced around the parking lot, then pointed at his gold pimp-mobile. "What's wrong with your car?"

"Nothing that I am aware of, Reed Daughter."

"Delaney," I corrected absently. "You aren't avoiding anyone are you? Leaving the car here so they think you're not at home?"

"I didn't ask you to take me home," he said primly.

"That wasn't a no. Who are you hiding from?"

"May I remind you I am the god of death?" One long, boney hand rested on the passenger door handle of my Jeep. "There isn't anyone from which I hide."

"Is it Talli? I haven't seen her around lately. Did you break up with your girlfriend?"

"Perhaps we could continue this discussion never."

He delivered that so dry and flat, it took me a second before I realized it was a joke.

"Oh, no. If I have to deal with gods paying too much attention to me and my love life, then turn about is about time. If you want a ride, you're gonna talk."

I opened the door. He opened his and folded gracefully into his seat. "You will be late for your dress event," he noted, before buckling the seatbelt.

"Trust me, if I don't show up, they'll find me and throw dresses at me. It won't matter if I'm a couple minutes late. Spill. What's going on between you and the vacationing goddess of morning and the evening star?"

He folded his hands in his lap and gazed out the window. "Do you know one of the things that convinced me to sample the experience of setting my power down and vacationing here?"

"Other gods were bragging about it? Plus, that ancient vampire Lavius was here, and you had vowed to extinguish his non-life?"

He hummed. "The gods don't, as a matter of fact, brag about vacationing in Ordinary. Quite the contrary. In the larger world, in the larger universe, Ordinary is very rarely mentioned. Not, I think to hide it, but instead because to understand it, for a god to understand it," he clarified, "it takes some very human thinking."

"Gods vacation," I argued. "There are plenty of stories of gods lounging around doing whatever they want."

"There are very few stories of gods willingly putting their powers down to take time off from being a god."

"Well, Odin," I said, "Frigg."

"In those tales they appear as human. That does not mean they gave up their god powers."

"Okay," I said, taking the Jeep out of the parking lot and heading north on the main drag—Highway 101. "So giving up your power isn't a thing most gods think about."

"No," he said, "it is not. It does, rather, fly in the face of being a god."

"The power is pretty much the thing," I said, "right?"

"Yes. The power is 'the thing,' as you put it. We gods like to keep our power. It is the most important thing to us. Wars may wage and planets may fall, but gods will hold their powers above all."

"This is going somewhere?"

Than blinked, then turned to stare at me.

I tried to keep the smile off my face.

"Because if this is going to take a while, I'm going to be late dropping you off at your house and getting to my appointment."

"I did not ask to be taken to my home."

"Where then?"

"The antique store will suffice."

I frowned. "The one right next to the second-hand clothes shop?"

"Does Ordinary have another antique store?"

No, it did not.

"You're into antique shopping now?"

"It is a mildly pleasant way to pass the time."

"Tea cups, right?"

"I believe I was explaining what convinced me to come to Ordinary. Would you rather I explain my requirement for tea vessels? The thickness of china I prefer? The pattern and age?"

"No, I would very much not like to listen to you talk about china. Please. Go on. What was one thing that convinced you to come to Ordinary?"

"Whipped cream."

I let that sit between us. "Whipped cream? That was…that was nowhere close to what I thought you'd say. When did you have whipped cream?"

"When you ordered that ridiculous drink you then assured me was coffee."

"At the casino? But you had already called and told us you wanted to vacation in Ordinary. You'd already made up your mind."

"No, Reed Daughter, I had not."

"Okay, back up. So you heard about Ordinary and decided to look into it, so you called us?"

"Yes."

"And when I brought you the contract to sign, you didn't listen to the rules, or that you'd have to put your power down, or any of that, you just saw that pile of whipped cream and chocolate and coffee and thought, 'Yeah, I need a vacation'?"

"No. I listened to the rules. I listened to *you*, Reed Daughter, and then I watched. You bought for yourself plain coffee. You bought for me a…confection. Something you thought I would not understand was not coffee. You were testing me."

"Hey, it was coffee. For the price I paid, it better have had coffee in it. And it wasn't only a test. I was…I don't know…teasing you I guess. It was such a frilly drink, and you looked so serious. I thought it would cheer you up."

He was silent for a few moments longer than I expected.

"Than?"

He cleared his throat, and I was certain it could not have been emotion that gave his voice that roughened edge. Still, it sounded an awful lot like emotion.

"What you should know, Reed Daughter, is that whipped cream, a frilly drink, and the woman who ventured to buy that particular beverage for the god of death because he looked serious, is the reason I entertained the actuality of setting my power down and vacationing in this very small town, on this very small world, in this very small universe."

"Oh." I nodded, not quite sure how to take that all in. "It wasn't just you wanting to kill Lavius?"

"It was you, Reed Daughter. You who shine bright. I would not have you underestimate the regard in which we gods hold you."

I suddenly couldn't speak. All I could do was swallow and, strangely, try not to cry.

"It was also wanting to kill Lavius," he added.

I choked a laugh, the moment broken. It was a lot. It was more than I thought I'd ever hear him say.

"Why bring that up now?" I parked in front of the dress shop. The antique store was just a few shops down. Myra's cruiser was here. So was Jean's truck.

I turned to the deity in my passenger seat.

"You asked why the gods are not acting as we usually do, which apparently, is to largely ignore you.

"We are satisfied with you doing the job you were born to: Bridging the supernatural world and the human world, Bridging our powers to then be safely contained and at rest.

"We are satisfied with your carrying out of the laws built into the roots and marrow of this place. God laws, mortal laws, magical laws.

"We are not willing to have you be nothing but a pawn on the great chessboard of the worlds. To that end, we are watching you more closely so that there is no harm to you."

"Okay," I said, a little breathily. "Harm. From who? From what?"

"From many things. From those who would oppose us, of course. Now. Enjoy the dress tradition of shopping. Good night, Delaney Reed."

"Wait—"

But it was too late. He swung out of the Jeep and briskly strode down to the antique store without a single backward glance.

Dang it.

Gods. Always right to the point, but so vague it was impossible to know what they said.

I sat there a minute and tried to come up with an excuse for not going into the dress shop.

I checked the parking lot, checked my rearview mirror, but unfortunately there were no crimes going down.

I sighed and trudged up to the shop. The door opened with a jingle, then a joyous, "Here comes the bride!" chorus, sung more or less on key, filled the air.

The shop wasn't very big, but the goddess Tyche, who went by Cheryl and was the owner, had rearranged it to open up more floor space. A raised, carpeted circular platform off to one side was centered in front of full-length mirrors angled along the curve.

The racks of everyday clothing had been pushed

against walls, and roses and sunflowers in vases were scattered everywhere. There was a wine station with delicate glasses, sparkling lights, and bottles chilling and bottles airing.

But it wasn't the shop that made me catch my breath, it was the women in the room.

Cheryl, Myra, and Jean, my defacto aunt and town witch, Jules, and two other gods: Hera, who ran Mom's Bar and Grill, and Frigg, who owned the towing company, Frigg's Riggs.

They each held a glass of something in their hands and were absolutely beaming at me.

"Wow," I said. "Thank you? For coming?"

"And miss our chance to see you try to talk us all out of you wearing a dress for your wedding?" Cheryl asked.

She'd pulled her bouncy black hair back with a coral and green headband, gold earrings dangling. Her dress was a short-sleeved sundress of oranges and bronze that complemented the deep brown of her skin. Olive-green tights and natural-fiber sandals finished the look. "Wouldn't skip this for all the monsters in the sea."

"You knew we'd be here." Myra strolled over to me, Jean next to her. Myra was dressed in a soft blue blouse with tiny yellow butterflies on it, pedal pushers, and bobby socks in black Mary Janes. Her makeup was perfect: pale pink lipstick, smokey eyeliner in a wing. She did rockabilly better than anyone I knew.

Jean wore a wrap skirt with a huge starfish tumbling across the blue and green waves printed on it. She had on a tie-dye tank top, her lavender hair pulled back in a single high pony. It made the light dusting of freckles on her cheeks pop. For a moment, I saw her as the girl she had been, and found myself caught by memories of a much younger pair of sisters. My childhood confidants, my blanket fort co-conspirators.

Myra pressed a glass of white wine into my hand, and Jean grinned as the echo of who we had all been spread out into the song of who we all still were.

"I lost a bet," Jean said. "I thought you'd be an hour late."

"Hey, I'm not that bad."

She leaned forward and gave me a hug. "I love you. You really are that bad. Worse even."

She pulled back. My sisters were radiant with shared joy, both of them looking like they were ready to spend the night poking fun at me. I was suddenly very, very happy with my life.

"Just trust your gut," Myra said. "Or better yet, trust ours. We've both agreed to double team you until you pick the dress we like best. Or pick a dress at all. Or let us pick one for you."

"No way," I said. "I am the bride. What I say, goes. Got it?"

"Since that isn't different than any other day you're bossing us around?" Jean said. "Uh, I mean, yes, sure, boss, I mean Delaney, Sister, Sir, Bride. Whatever you say."

I pointed. "Fired and fired. But I still love you, so let's get the dress shopping over with!"

Myra lifted her glass, Jean lifted hers, we clinked, and everyone else gave a short cheer, then Jules started to chant: "Dress! Dress! Dress! Dress!" Everyone else joined in.

I was shoved to the front of the room as my audience settled into seats, except for Cheryl who rolled out a rack with dresses in fifty shades of white.

"This might look overwhelming," she said, "but I wanted enough of a selection to follow whichever way your tastes might fall. I have an idea of what you'll like, but you might surprise me. We talked, and you said white, right?"

"I think so?"

"We're going with white." She pushed the dresses apart with one clean movement, like a good blade cleaving through bone.

"Have another sip of wine," she suggested, "and sit down. I'm going to pull out the kinds of dresses I have, and you can give me a love, like, or hate. Okay?"

"Hang on." I gulped wine, letting the burn fortify me. Then I took the seat that Myra and Jean emptied between them. "Bring it."

"Spoken like a true warrior," Hera leaned forward and gave me a wink.

"White is a good choice," Frigg said. "It shows the blood of your enemies much better. Warns those who think they can make you bow to their whims."

"We are talking wedding dress, right?" I grinned. "Holy matrimony, not holy war?"

"Sure, we are." Hera dragged out the words. "Bliss. We're talking about wedded bliss. All the bliss."

Frigg snorted and drained her glass. "Refills! Who wants one?"

Everyone raised their glasses except Cheryl, who was wrangling lace and wrestling fluff like a pro.

"Delaney?" Frigg offered.

"No, I'm good with one. I don't want to regret this anymore than is necessary."

"Boo," Jules called out. "I thought I raised you to enjoy life, young lady."

"You did. I'm going to enjoy watching you all have your wine, then when you fall asleep, I'll slip out the back and get to wear sweats and a T-shirt to my wedding."

"No sweats!" Myra said.

"Drink more wine," I suggested.

"The dress will be as comfortable as sweats," Cheryl insisted. "We still have time to tailor. Once that is done, you won't even want to wear sweats anymore."

I shook my head, because, yeah, there was no way any dress could be as comfortable as sweats.

She wagged her finger at me. "Just you wait." She pulled the first dress off the rack with a swirl of lace and a flash of some kind of jewels. Pearls, maybe?

The collective "Ooooo," was impressive.

"All right," I said, eyeing the fabric that didn't give me any idea of what the dress would look like on a person—on me—I self-corrected. "Talk me through this baby."

Cheryl grinned. "This little model is a classic. The lines are engineered to really show you off, bumper to bumper, if you know what I mean." She bumped her hips out, side to side, with each word.

"All right. I like what I'm seeing so far, and your sales approach is spot-on. Close the deal."

"Generous leg room," she fluffed the wide skirt, "easy on the straightaways, and perfect for that long, relaxing ride down the aisle."

I applauded, so did everyone else.

"So, like, love, or hate?" Cheryl asked.

"Can I try it on before I answer?"

"Yes, you absolutely may. You can also tell me on first blush what you don't like about it. No, it's fine. I can see it in your face. Something about this isn't what you're looking for."

"She doesn't even know what she's looking for," Jean said.

"I think it's too…spangly."

Cheryl blinked. "Spangly? The jewels?"

"Yeah, aren't they a little…flashy?"

"It's your wedding," Myra said, bumping her shoulder into mine. "Live a little."

"Hear, hear!" Jules crowed. "Spangle that bitch!"

"We can do a little less flashy if you want," Cheryl said.

"Let's try this one. This little beauty is for the gal who likes feeling the wind in her hair. The detachable skirt allows for tight turns and easy handling. Once Ryder sees you in this convertible number, he's never going to remember to keep his hands at ten and two."

I grinned. "I'm willing to try that one too. No sparkles and smooth, uh, is that satin?"

"Yes."

"I like that the long skirt comes off, and there's a shorter one under it. But that…um…convertible bit on the top?"

"It's sleeveless, yes?"

"I don't want that much chestage out in the open."

"Oh, my gods," Jules moaned. "Delaney. Dearest. You will wear a turtleneck at your wedding over my damn dead body. Even then I'd rise from the grave with a pair of scissors and make emergency alterations."

"Wow," I said. "That is…something."

"That is love." She toasted me with her glass and took a sip. "You're welcome."

"Is this a yes for trying on?" Cheryl asked.

"Yes."

"Fabulous. This is going much smoother than I expected. Okay, I'm going to pull out one more kind of dress. Ready?"

"Lay it on me."

"This is something that might catch the eye of a collector. Modern, clean lines, while still carrying the fine heritage of the designs that have come before it. You will note the luxury exterior is made all the more remarkable with fine attention to the details: Lace. Only white lace.

"No spangles. No fluff. Nothing that detaches or removes. The discerning eye will note a smooth under-carriage—nothing too over done—understated elegance, easy elegance. Timeless."

She held up the dress: a long sheath with lace covering it, and what looked like fitted sleeves made of that same white lace.

"Okay," I said. "I can see the appeal of this one. It's simple."

Cheryl grinned. "Well, no wedding dress is simple. Elegant, maybe. But yes, this one is understated. Refined."

Jean made a rude noise. "Understated is dumb. You are the first Reed sister to get married. You should go for all the sparkle they can glue on the thing."

"I'll try it," I told Cheryl.

"Fantastic. I'll set these up in the changing room for you in the order that we've seen them. Go ahead and undress, and I'll help you with any tricky buttons, laces, or zips."

She scooped up the dresses like they were made of

nothing but bubbles and wishes, then got to work setting up the changing room.

"Put on the sparkly one first," Jean said. "It's my favorite."

"No," Myra insisted, leaning around me to scowl at Jean. "We agreed the one with the detachable skirt is the best."

"We didn't agree on anything," Jean said.

"Yes, we agreed that I am older than you, so therefore I am always right."

Jean widened her eyes at me. "Delaney, she's being mean to me."

"Sure, she is," I said. "Poor little Jean couldn't be trying to manipulate me into taking her side on the sparkly dress at all."

Jean chortled. "Yeah, I figured you were going to hate the sparkly dress."

"Reverse psychology won't work either."

She gave me a big thumbs up and sipped.

"Delaney?" Cheryl asked. "Ready?"

I heaved to my feet, and my audience offered very polite golf claps before giggling their heads off.

I shut the curtain and just stood there in the changing room a moment. They might think I hated shopping for dresses—and they'd be right—but this experience was different. It was more about having my sisters there, blood family and chosen family. It was about being held up by their joy for me, their happiness.

I didn't care which dress I wore down the aisle. This, hanging out with my sisters and aunties and friends, was something I'd never forget.

I put on the first dress and tromped out to the platform.

It fit nicely, and the skirt was so puffy, I felt like a storybook princess.

"But the spangles are blinding," I said, as I did another spin at Jean's request.

"It's so pretty, though," Jean said. "Don't you all think it looks amazing on her?"

"No," Myra said.

"Yes!" Jules piped up.

"I agree," Hera said.

"I'm not ready to take sides on this yet," Frigg said with a grin. "But you do look amazing in it. Very….floofy and bright."

"Three for, one against, one abstained," I said. "Pretty much where I thought the chips were going to fall. Care to give an opinion, Cheryl?"

"Nope. Not until I see you in all three of them. Let's give that sporty little convertible a spin."

Another trip to the changing room. This time I came out with a little more dramatic sass to my step.

"What is she doing?" Jean asked in an overly loud whisper to Jules. Apparently while I'd been in the changing room, they'd all played musical chairs. Jules was now next to Jean and had absconded with a bottle of Riesling, which was on the seat of the empty chair next to her.

Myra and Hera had claimed two other chairs and moved them just that extra bit away from Jean and Jules, declaring war.

Frigg was slouched in a chair behind the row of four, arms crossed over her chest and a small smile on her face.

"Is she possessed? Did a zombie bite her?" Jean whisper-shouted again.

"I'm strutting."

"Are you craving brains? Should we start doing the Thriller dance?" Jean asked.

I flipped her off with both fingers, which sent her into a gale of giggles.

Cheryl ushered me up onto the platform so I could get a good look at myself from every angle. Not bad.

"Now that," Myra announced, "is gorgeous. And practical. It looks so easy to walk in."

"Bor-ring!" Jean announced.

Myra scowled but didn't look at Jean. In a perfect hostage negotiator voice, she said, "Delaney, isn't this much easier to move in? You don't have to deal with all the layers and fluff of the first dress."

"True," I said, doing another runway strut.

"No!" Jean said. "It doesn't even sparkle. It doesn't have lace!"

"Let me just undo the ties and take off the long skirt." Cheryl came up behind me to do exactly that.

"And now it doesn't even have a long skirt!" Jean complained.

"Oh, Delaney," Myra said, her voice utterly rapt. "You look fantastic. Why are you always hiding your legs in pants? I can't believe you don't live in short skirts."

"And think of what Ryder would say if he saw you coming down the aisle in that," Hera said.

"No," Jean said, "don't think about Ryder. Who cares what he says? Think about all the sparkles you don't have. Think of all of the plain sadness you're wearing."

"It's more the parts I'm not wearing that I'm thinking about." I didn't own anything sleeveless, and Myra was right, I never showed this much leg.

"Frigg?" I asked.

"Again," she said, "you look amazing in it. I want to see the third one, though, before I declare the winner."

"All right. Let's get the third one over with."

Cheryl raised her eyebrows at me.

"I mean, yay!" I said. "Third dress!"

She pushed me into the changing room and told me to behave. I told her she should go ride roughshod over my sisters, which made her laugh, and leave me alone.

The last dress was the easiest to get into. Long, without a poofy under layer and no tricky absence of sleeves, it was soft against my skin. The lace seemed a little over the top since it covered every inch of the dress. It cut square just beneath my collarbones, covering my shoulders and all the way down to my wrists.

But it was easy to move in.

I didn't know how I felt about it.

"This one is giving me mixed feelings," I called out to the crew.

"Let's see it," Jules ordered.

I walked out, and just like with the other two dresses, Cheryl got me up on the little platform.

The dress fit much better than I'd thought it would. It wasn't skin tight, which I liked, and it skimmed the right places and pulled away from the others. The lace, which I'd thought would be too much, really did look... what had Cheryl said? Elegant?

I was surprised how much I liked it.

"Okay," I said, not looking at any of the women. "You are all being awfully quiet. Is it that bad?"

"Turn around and give us a walk," Cheryl said.

I turned to a sea of faces that held the same expression.

I couldn't tell if that expression was surprise or something else, so I did my walk, just my normal walk this time, turned, and then stopped in front of them.

I planted my hands on my hips. "Somebody better say something or I'm going to decide dresses were a bad idea and go back to the sweat pants plan."

"No," Jules said. "We covered that. Death scissors. No sweats."

"It's your dress," Frigg said.

Hera nodded. "She's right. It's lovely. You're lovely. This suits you, Delaney."

"Plot twist," I said. "Do I sense changing alliances here?"

"I wasn't allied with anyone," Frigg said.

"What do you think, Jules?"

"It's perfect. Damn it," she said. "I always imagined you in a princess dress. But this. This is the one."

"There's still a chance you two could team up with Cheryl and vote for your favorite," I said to my sisters. "I promise to take everyone's opinion into account before I decide the winner."

"How about I weigh in?" Cheryl stood by the platform, and finally took a sip of wine.

I nodded.

"I love you in this dress. I love you in all of them," she said, "but this is you. It fits you in every way. You glow."

"Myra? Jean? Would you like to submit your complaints?"

"Just, why?" Jean said. "Why do you have to look so beautiful and elegant in that dress? It doesn't even have any sparkles."

"It has a lot of lace, though," I said.

"True," she said with a sigh. "I like lace. I love it. It's perfect."

"Myra?" I didn't think I'd change my mind if Myra's vote was lukewarm. But if she absolutely hated it, I would ask her for ideas that would make her hate it less.

"I could probably stick a ribbon on it somewhere, or have someone take up the hem a little," I said to her. "People do that with wedding dresses, don't they?"

Myra stood and stepped over to stand right in front of me. "I hate to admit I was wrong. You know that. But I was wrong. This is everything. This is your dress. And oh, my gods, Delaney, you're getting married!"

She laughed but it was also part sob and I felt my throat tighten with emotion.

I grabbed her and hugged her and tried not to cry while all the girls let out little comforting sounds. Then Myra pulled away and made noises about not wanting to mess up my dress with her makeup, and Jules was there to wrap her in her big soft embrace and, somehow my wine glass was in my hand again.

There was a quick toast to the wedding dress, then Cheryl took a couple minutes asking me if I wanted it tightened or loosened anywhere. I realized I loved this dress in ways I couldn't put into words.

Some of it was because it was chosen for a singular purpose. The dress would mark an event I would hold in my heart for the rest of my life.

But some of what made me love this dress was that it had brought my sisters, friends, and family together, to share this one-of-a-kind joy.

Eventually, I was ushered off to the changing room.

I slipped out of the dress and into my regular

clothes, my regular life. It was nice to be back in normal clothes, but a part of me was still thrumming with excitement. That dress was mine, and I was going to marry the man of my dreams while wearing it.

I couldn't stop smiling.

I pulled my hair back with a band and exhaled slowly. Like it or not, tonight had changed something in me. Changed something between me and my sisters too.

It had made, for a moment, my wedding seem like a real thing. A wonderful thing, yes, but also a solid, unstoppable change barreling my way.

My life, my relationships with those I loved would shift in small ways. New ways. It would never be the same. The weight of that, the importance of it, had taken root somewhere deep inside me.

It was new, thinking of myself as a married woman, but I was beginning to think I was going to like it.

When I finally stepped out to join them, they were finishing off glasses of water. Hera who had drunk one glass of wine and tea the rest of the evening, was ready to drive everyone home.

"I'll make those adjustments," Cheryl said. "Ryder can pick it up by the end of the week."

"Or I could," I said. "I could pick it up."

"Sure," she agreed like I was a child who promised to put their shoes away and never did. "I'll send him a message and let him know when it's ready."

"And me. I'd like you to send me a message too."

"Oh," she said, hearing me that time. "You really want to pick it up? Ryder told me not to worry you, that he was handling the details."

"Well, it's my dress. He has enough on his hands. I can pick it up. At the end of the week." I pulled out my phone and made myself a note to check in if I hadn't heard from her.

"Good," she said. "I was afraid he might want to take a peek, and you know the groom seeing the dress before the wedding is bad luck."

I had a feeling we were going to need all the luck we could get.

"Do you need a ride home?" she asked.

"I got her." Frigg wandered over to us. "I had half a glass of wine and water after that. Let me drive you home, Chief."

"I only had one glass of wine too," I said.

"I know." She didn't add anything to that, but her gaze was warm and steady and seemed to see into the deeper parts of me, the shaken parts that hadn't quite settled into place yet.

"This is supposed to be a celebration," Cheryl said. "Let her drive you home, so you can just sit back and relax. I know trying on three dresses must have exhausted you."

That? Sarcasm. Which was exactly what I expected out of her.

"It did. I can't believe I only had to try on three to find the one I didn't hate."

"Never doubt my ability to know what will look amazing on you, *and* what you will hate the least."

"Love," I said. "I love it."

She blinked and took a moment to study my face. "Well, good," she finally said with a soft smile. "Love is what it's all about."

"Thank you for doing this." I gestured to take in the whole of the shop. "I really appreciate it."

She waved me off and started gathering up glasses

and buckets of ice. "My pleasure. I relish the challenge of trying to talk you into things that look fabulous on you.

"Go home, relax, think about the dress…or don't think about it. You'll be the star of the day, I promise."

"That reminds me," I said, as I started to the door. "Patrick Baum is in town to socially influence Ordinary. He's some kind of online star…"

"Road Bomb," Frigg said. Cheryl nodded like she'd heard of him too.

"Is he here for the murder mystery?" Cheryl asked.

"No, he's doing a contest Bertie wants to win."

"Of course she does." Cheryl chuckled.

"My car or yours?" Frigg asked.

"Mine, if that's okay with you."

"It is." She pushed the door open, and I walked out into more cheers and hugs from my sisters, my family.

CHAPTER FIVE

Frigg parked my Jeep in the driveway of Ryder's and my house. "Everything okay?" she asked quietly.

We'd been sitting for a couple minutes in silence with only the muted hush of wind and the cooling click of the engine breaking that quiet.

"It is," I said.

She leaned an elbow against the door. "You and I haven't spent a lot of time hanging out together lately. Understandably," she added. "We both have busy jobs, busy lives, and then there's summer."

"So many tourists," I agreed.

She nodded. "But sometimes it's nice to be able to talk to someone who isn't your family, who will just listen to the things on your mind with no judgement."

"Who said things are on my mind?"

She shrugged. "Maybe there aren't."

She waited, and there was comfort in her presence, a feeling of being on familiar, safe ground.

"I'm worried about the wedding. Not that it will happen, not that there will be last- minute loose ends.

It's more…what it stands for. It's a big change. A change I want, but it's still a change. We've had a lot of that lately," I said. "Things changing."

She hummed and waited, and I stared at the house that Ryder and his dad had built. A house that was mine now, too, more home to me than my family home had been.

"I don't want things to be the way they were," I said. "Or at least not all the time. I wish… I wish my dad were still here. Mom too. I miss them.

"But I like my life now, who I am. I love this ridiculous town." I shook my head. "So ridiculous."

"It's a good place," she said quietly. "You're a part of what makes it good."

"Thank you. I know the gods are worried about me."

"Oh?"

"Than told me. Not directly, but in his way. He said you all think I might be the target of some trouble."

"We gods aren't of one mind on, well, anything, really," she said. "Our kind, godkind, isn't well known for being all on the same side."

"Crow took me to lunch, Than escorted me to my dress event, and you brought me home."

"We've talked about keeping a closer eye on you. The weapons coming into town reminded us that, even though we're vacationing, there are still events we should remain aware of. Especially if they involve the demon king."

"Goap was behind Tish bringing in the weapons," I said, "not the King of the Underworld."

"The demon prince's reasons are his own. But it is Vychoro, the demon king, who is the most dangerous."

"You think he's going to attack Ordinary?"

She shrugged. "We would be stupid not to assume so. The Queen, well, former Queen, of the Underworld is in Ordinary. The prince who should inherit the throne is in Ordinary. The king's brother is in Ordinary. All of them within the last year or so. And now, several god weapons and two stolen demon weapons have been deposited into Ordinary. If the Brute of All Evil decides to attack the human world, we will all stand to stop him. I think he's realized the power we represent."

"Do you think the spell book of the gods is involved?"

She stared out the window for a moment even though the sky was darkening, shadows thickening, so there wasn't much to see.

"That is a very old thing. Very old. I know the page torn from it fell into the hands of demons, but the rest?" She shook her head. "We'd know."

"So if the spell book isn't involved, how do you think Vychoro will attack?"

She hummed, then turned to me. "You know when we vacation it limits our access to our god powers. Finding out what Vychoro is doing would require we pick up our powers.

"We want to keep you safe. We want to keep Ordinary safe. But picking up our powers comes with consequences."

"You'd have to go do your god business for a year before you could come back."

"And we recently did that. The consensus is that we'll keep an eye on things and pick up our powers only if there seems to be no other choice."

"Okay," I said. "Do you all think I'm the demon king's target?"

"No. But you are the Bridge. You are the crossing, the entrance to the town for powers and magic. If I were wanting to attack Ordinary, or trying to hurt the people or demons or gods within it, I would disable you first."

"Aw, you said disable, not kill. It's nice to know I'm loved."

She flashed me a smile. "I do love you, but you are, by definition, a target. A demon target."

"I'm not stepping down as the Bridge."

"I wouldn't ask you to. I'm not sure you could just decide you don't want the job anymore. I think you'd have to train your replacement first."

"Yeah, but I'm not giving it up, so…"

"So that means we'll keep an eye on you."

"For how long?"

"What do you mean?"

"How long are you all going to watch my every move?"

"We're not watching your every move. We're just keeping a general knowledge of where you are and what you're doing."

"Stalking."

"Friendly oversight."

I shook my head. "Can I talk you out of it?"

"No. This is one of the first times in many, many years that we all agree on something. It's a novel experience."

"What about Ryder?"

"What about Ryder?"

"If the Brute… You know that is such an arrogant

name. If the demon king, if *Vychoro* is attacking, how safe is Ryder? If I were a demon, I wouldn't hit me. I'd hit someone I loved. Ryder or Jean or Myra to start with. Why aren't you gods keeping a close eye on them?"

"Ryder is tied to a god who is an ass, but Mithra wouldn't allow demons to take away his favorite Ordinary plaything."

"Yuck."

"Jean would know if something dangerous was headed toward her."

"The family gift," I said.

"The family gift. And Myra has Bathin. That demon would know if his father was launching an attack or trying to harm her."

"So that leaves me."

"That leaves you and every single god in this town. We'll keep you safe, Delaney. You don't have to worry."

"I can handle myself. You know that, right?"

"Yes."

She said it so simply, so easily, the annoyance drained out of me.

"Do you want company?" she asked. "Until Ryder comes home?"

"No, I'm good. Really. No need to babysit. Do you want me to call you a ride?"

"I think I'll walk. It's a nice evening. And I need to stretch my legs."

"Thanks, Frigg."

"Anytime. And by the way, that dress? You made the right choice. You are going to knock Ryder off his feet."

I chuckled, pleased. "We'll see."

She handed over my keys and got out. I gathered my jacket and gun belt, then locked the vehicle.

Frigg meandered toward the shore of the lake. That wasn't the fastest way back to town—around the lake and through the neighborhoods—but she was a god. She had all the time in the world on her hands.

I jogged up to the front door. Before I opened it, I noticed a shadow retreating down the side of the house in the narrow space between the rose bushes and siding.

Someone was in my yard. We weren't close enough to the lake for someone to mistake this as public property.

Someone was in my yard.

And the demon king might be targeting me.

Someone was in my yard.

My head cleared as training kicked in. My heart thumped steadily and hard, the adrenalin pumping. I filled my lungs and exhaled.

I dropped my jacket, strapped on my gun belt, and checked it was securely holstered. For all I knew it was just a couple kids messing around out there. But I didn't want to leave my weapon unattended on my porch either.

I moved down the stairs, out onto the yard, then back along the edge of the house into the space between the side of the house and the rose bush hedge, moving as quietly as I could. Even in the falling light, I could make out footprints pressed into the sandy dirt. At least three different shoe sizes. None of them child size.

Branches rustled in the rhodie bushes along the back. A blue jay squawked and darted into the churning sky.

Whoever was back there was around the corner, out of my line of sight.

"I know you're there," I called. "You are trespassing

on private property. Come on out. We don't need any trouble."

The rustling got a little louder, and the sweet scent of something like pastries drifted by. I wondered if Xtelle was back there, hiding out and eating her way through a sheet cake again.

"Xtelle? Is that you?"

Footsteps crunched through sand and brittle leaves. Someone was approaching.

"Sorry," a woman's voice said. "I got turned around."

She came into view. Medium build, dark hair, dark eyes, jeans and a T-shirt. I had seen her somewhere before but couldn't quite place her face.

"I was down at the lake." Her smile was fake. "I didn't mean to trespass."

"Okay, that's fine," I said, not getting any closer to her because my gut said something was wrong here. Something wasn't as it seemed.

"Just follow me this way. I'll point out the easiest way back down to the lake."

"Thank you."

I didn't turn, didn't take my eyes off her as I took a step backward.

That was the only reason I saw her gaze flick away from my face. That was the only reason I saw her expression go hard. That was the only reason I knew, in the pit of my gut, that I had walked right into a trap like a damn rookie.

There was someone behind me. In the split instant I realized it, I dropped to my knees.

The fist meant to connect with my head whiffed above me, fast, and hard enough I could feel the wind generated from the blow. I spun while still crouched and punched at the knee of the attacker.

He swore, overcorrected, and slammed shoulder first into the side of the house.

There were more feet, more legs, more people behind the man, but before I could twist and scramble to my feet, the woman jumped on my back and started punching.

She wasn't a skilled brawler, but with the slippery ground and limited space, I took a couple shots to my ribs and one to the back of my head before I bucked her off.

Being on the ground was bad. Being on the ground with my weapon in someone else's reach was terrifying.

I heaved away from the house, through the rose bushes, then rolled up onto my feet, pulling my gun at the same time. "Freeze! Police. Stay right where you are."

My pulse roared in my ears. Sweat dripped down my neck, slick between my shoulder blades. I knew I was injured, but the lightning spike of adrenalin sharpened my sight, my hearing, my sense of smell.

My mind burned through possibilities, sorting and throwing out options.

The man had regained his footing and taken a couple steps toward me, the roses still between us. The woman was on her ass.

The other legs—two people—had taken off at a run, and were already out of my sight. Not worth pursuing.

A second, two had passed. The pair in front kept their eyes locked on my gun.

"I said freeze! Turn toward the house. Both of you."

I moved to better cover them. "You," I ordered the woman, "stand up slowly. Palms on the house."

Her eyes were wide. She nodded and swallowed, then rose, slowly, her hands in front of her. She turned and placed both palms on the house.

"You too," I told the man. "Palms on the house."

He narrowed his eyes, and there was a moment where I saw him consider rushing me, but his gaze fell to the gun, and then rose to my face. Whatever he saw there made him do as I asked.

"You picked the wrong house to try and rob," I said, grabbing for the zip ties in my pocket. This was the tricky part where I'd have to manage the gun and secure the attackers.

I approached the man first. "Hands behind your back."

He complied and I secured his hands, keeping an eye on the woman.

"You next." I zipped her wrists, then took several steps back putting the rose bushes between us again.

The adrenalin sloshed through me like an ocean with a heavy undertow and my stomach soured and churned. I knew the shakes were going to follow soon. I needed backup.

I pulled out my phone to dial Myra or Jean, but they weren't on duty.

I put the call into Hatter and Shoe instead.

"Hey boss," Hatter said in his ever-shifting southern accent that was leaning pretty darn Kentuckian lately.

"Got a situation," I said. "My house. Two people cuffed. Two on the run. I need you and Shoe."

"On our way," he said in a hard clear tone. "Are you injured?"

"No."

"Are you alone?"

"Delaney?" Frigg called out.

"Not any more. Frigg's here."

"We'll be there in two minutes."

I disconnected and glanced at Frigg. She had a crowbar in her hand, though I had no idea where she'd gotten it. "Couple of people were running from your house."

"Did you get a good look at them?"

"Yep."

"Can you give a description?"

"Sure, but you can take a look at them yourself. They're taking a little nap in your driveway."

I nodded, but kept my gun pointed at the two by the house. "Thank you."

"I said we'd be close."

"I don't like you putting yourself in danger like that. You are not a part of the police force."

"I didn't even get a scratch, and I only hit them hard enough to knock them out."

"You saw someone running and decided to club them?"

She blinked, then narrowed her eyes. "They attacked you."

"Yes." There was no denying that. "But you didn't know that."

"Yes, I did."

From how she said it, I knew she wasn't lying.

"I'll need a statement."

"You'll get it."

"Okay, stay here for a bit. There's about to be a lot of paperwork in our future."

Hatter and Shoe pulled up a minute later. I'd secured my weapon and told both attackers they could turn around.

After that, everything fell into the familiar procedure drilled into me from when I'd become a law officer.

The adrenalin spike made me shaky, but even that passed, leaving me stiff and tired.

The man and woman Frigg knocked out came around eventually, and Hatter and Shoe took all four of the people into the station to process them.

Frigg said she was driving me to the hospital to make sure I didn't have any cracked ribs or a concussion. I very calmly refused, in a loud voice, until I got my way.

Somewhere in the endless hours that both crawled by and seemed not to move one iota, Myra and Jean showed up, both of them mad as hell.

"Inside," I said. "I want to get out of the wind."

We moved the conversation into the house, and Spud, who had been barking his head off for hours whined and wiggle-rubbed beside my legs, happy to finally see me.

Dragon-pig looked like it wanted to eat a small building, spit it out, then eat it again.

"Give me a minute, they need to pee," I said. "Well, Spud does."

"No," Jean said. "You sit. I'll take them out. Come on, Spud. Good boy. You coming dragon-pig?"

Dragon-pig grumbled and growled, stomped its little pink hooves, then stopped in front of me and snorted spouts of fire.

"I am fine," I said. "Go out with Spud and Jean."

Dragon-pig gave one more spout of fire, then, to my

utter surprise, bumped the top of its head into my shin, in a little love tap.

It trotted off after Jean, who had hooked a leash on Spud and was holding the door open.

Myra sat on the couch next to me and pulled me into a hug. "I hate that I wasn't here," she said.

"You would have been there if you needed to be. Family gift, remember?" I hugged her back, trying not to wince as my ribs reminded me that, even though the woman couldn't brawl, she'd sure wanted to bring the hurt.

"I should have been here anyway."

"Frigg was here," I said. "That's probably why you didn't need to come. I had backup."

"I'm your backup," she said fiercely.

"Yes, you are."

She searched my face, assessing my mood, which was calm, then nodded. "Okay."

"Did you smell cinnamon, Delaney?" Frigg asked.

"Outside?"

"On the people."

I thought back. The scent of water and moss, the smell of dusty sand, the broken green of roses and rhododendron bushes. The man behind me, so close I could see the weave of his jeans, did he smell like cinnamon? Did the woman who jumped me smell like cinnamon?

Yes.

"I wasn't paying a lot of attention to it, but yes. There was a sweet spice smell. Why? What does it mean?"

"I think they were sent here by demons."

Neither Myra nor I said anything because that was not what either of us expected.

"Not the demons inside Ordinary," she clarified, looking between the two of us. "A demon outside of Ordinary."

"Well, fuck." I rubbed at my eyes. My head hurt. "I know where I've seen them before. They were in the diner this morning. Eating and being creepy."

"Creepy how?" Myra said.

"They were totally silent the whole time they were eating, and kept throwing little looks my way."

"That's not really creepy."

"The way they did it was."

"Is cinnamon a demon marker?" Myra asked Frigg.

"It's not cinnamon, but it's a claiming mark—a demon claiming a human mark," Frigg said. "I don't know if they sold their souls, or if they made a deal and signed a contract. But there is a demon mark on them."

"A demon who wanted to what? Clunk me on the head?"

"Kill you," Myra said, like I'd lost my marbles. "They wanted to kill you."

"No, if they'd wanted to kill me, they would have sent humans who knew how to kidnap someone, or shoot someone, or frickin' fight, without getting caught."

"They attacked you," she said.

"They didn't even have weapons. Or training."

"Maybe they thought you would be easy," Frigg said.

"Hello, I'm the chief of police."

"Sure." She shrugged. "Some demons are well-versed in humankind. But some don't pay attention to human details. Just like some gods don't pay attention to

81

human details. It's a form of arrogance grown from power.

"The demon king or a demon in a high enough position of power might not think a human would be difficult to kill. Especially if the odds were four to one."

"Yeah, that makes sense," I said. "We should be able to get information out of them. Who they made a deal with, why, exactly, they were hired. Find out which demon is behind this."

"Unless their memories have been tampered with," she said.

Jean and the beasts strolled back into the room. Spud ran off to his pile of toys by the fireplace and brought me his favorite shark.

I let him put it on my lap, then he rested his big fuzzy head on my knee. I rubbed behind his ears.

Dragon-pig jumped on the couch and pushed its way between me and Myra. It placed one hoof on my thigh and grunted.

I looked down at it. "I'm okay. I'm fine. Really."

Dragon-pig smooshed its way onto my lap behind the shark, resting its head on top of the toy. It grumbled, but settled, like a warm little rock.

"So we're dealing with people who made deals with demons." Myra pulled out her phone. "I'll call Bathin. He can come look at them. Maybe he'll recognize the mark."

"Is that what the king wants?" Jean asked, sitting on the couch arm beside me. "Will he expect us to take the attackers to the station, then expect us to send the next in line to the throne to go look at them? Could it be a trap?"

"You think the humans aren't really a trap for me," I said, "but for Bathin?"

"He's the one who can kill the king, right? A first born..."

"...spawned," Myra corrected.

"...first spawned. If I were the king, he would be my target not you, Delaney."

"Although taking you out," Frigg said, "could also work, if his final goal is taking over Ordinary."

"So we don't send Bathin, or any of the other demons, to the station," I said.

"Maybe not," Myra said.

"But we could go at it from the contract level," Jean said. "If it's a contract between the humans and demons, Ryder should be able to see that, right? Might be able to tell what demon is involved?"

"Probably," I said. "Because Mithra's the god of contracts."

"Is he still in Coos Bay?" Myra asked.

"I think so," I said around a yawn.

"Let's get you in the shower," Myra said. "I want to see how badly you're hurt."

"I'm fine," I repeated for the millionth time. "I'll call Ryder."

"Jean, call Ryder and see when he's going to be back," Myra said, ignoring me.

"On it." She pulled out her phone and dialed.

Frigg stood. "I'll make us all some tea. You do have tea, right?"

"Probably? We have coffee and cocoa for sure."

"I'll investigate."

"Come on." Myra stood and offered her hand.

"But I just got comfy. With a dog. And dragon-pig."

Dragon-pig growled, and Spud thumped his big fuzzy tail on the floor.

"Don't be a baby," she said. "We'll be back in a minute."

Dragon-pig stood and watched us walk up the stairs. Spud hopped up and curled on the seat where I'd just been sitting, but the dragon-pig didn't look away from Myra and me until we were out of sight.

That intense focus from dragon-pig was new. I wondered what was going through that dragon head.

I sat on the toilet lid, pulled off my shoes, then socks. Getting out of my jeans wasn't too bad, but pulling off my shirt and undershirt made my ribs twinge again.

"Okay," Myra said quietly, her eyes assessing my ribs, shoulders, arms and thighs. "You are going to be a variety of colors for the next couple days. I don't see any deep cuts that need stitches."

"I would have noticed deep cuts," I said dryly. "You know, there would have been blood."

Her blue eyes, lighter than mine, flicked up, unamused. "How about you stand in front of the mirror and take a look at yourself? I'm going to poke at the back of your head to check that hit you took."

I sighed and closed the door so I could get a look in the mirror hung on the back of it.

Okay. Maybe I was a little more banged up than I thought.

My arms were scratched and bloody—rose thorns—and a paint pail splash of blue and black bruised my ribs and down one hip. My chin and cheek were scraped from going face down in the sand and rocks, and one of my eyes was swelling just a little.

"Turn," she said.

I did and caught glimpses of the back of my thighs —bruised, like someone with really boney knees had body slammed me—and more bruises spread up my back.

"How bad is the headache?" she asked.

"Pounding."

"Your eyes are dilating correctly. I'll get you some painkiller."

I turned on the water, then unlatched my bra and stepped out of my underwear. I moved into the shower, closing the sliding door behind me.

When I ducked my head under the spray, grit from my hair washed to the tiles beneath me, creating a slight traction under my feet.

I closed my eyes and let water wash away the sweat, the fight, the dirt.

Myra tapped the door.

"Painkiller." She stuck her hand in the shower.

I took the two ibuprofens and swallowed them down with warm water.

"Thanks."

"Take your time. I'll be downstairs."

I heard her close the door, and then, finally alone for the first time, I thought back through what we knew about the attack so far.

Almost nothing.

I wanted to know what those people's orders were.

I wanted to know who was behind this.

On top of that, I wanted Ryder home.

"He will be fine," I said. "He will be home soon."

I lingered, but finally turned off the water, dried myself, and walked into the bedroom where I dressed in sweats.

I heard the front door open downstairs and wondered if Jean was taking Spud out again, but then I heard his low, soft voice.

I leaned against the dresser, hung my head and just listened to him: Ryder.

He was curious, happy, a little tired. But then there were other voices, my sisters explaining things to him. Frigg too.

Before they could finish giving him the rundown, his heavy work boots crossed the floor.

The whole of him was a storm stomping upward, thunder cracking two stairs at a time. His hand slapped and released the banister as he surged, wind-pushed, furious, to our room.

To me.

But he stopped there.

He didn't storm into the room.

No, not Ryder.

He waited on the other side of the door for a moment. His breathing settled. He cleared his throat. Small sounds of his arms shifting, his shoulders rolling.

The man was trying to shed his own fear and anger before he stepped into the room with me.

"I can hear you on the other side of the door," I said quietly.

"You can, can you?" he said just as quietly, not opening the door yet.

"I'd know you were there even if I couldn't hear you."

"How?"

"Your presence. You're becoming something familiar to me, Mr. Bailey. Something a little bit precious."

"A little bit?"

"Maybe more. You'd have to come closer for me to decide."

The door swung slowly inward, and the love of my life, the boy, the teen, the man who had always held my heart, walked into the room.

He was tired and windblown, like he'd been standing in the sun all day. There was a fine layer of dust on his face. Maybe Mithra had made him do road work: shovel gravel. Ryder didn't always tell me what the god made him do, just that it was usually menial tasks or enforcement of petty laws.

Anything to remind Ryder that Mithra owned him. That the contract Ryder had agreed to when he impulsively pledged himself to the god, was something no mortal could break.

But even tired, windblown, and covered in dust, Ryder was the most handsome man I'd ever laid eyes on.

"Hey," I said. "Long day?"

He nodded, frowning. His steps were soft now as his gaze swept over my body, searching for injuries.

I smiled. It softened the look on his face.

"What did that jerk deity have you doing today?" I asked. "Digging ditches?"

"Judging a dune buggy contest."

"I thought you were going to shut down a garage sale?"

"Did that too."

He stopped in front of me. The smell of dust and motor oil, sweat and the deodorant he kept in his truck, filled my nose.

Beneath all that was the warmth of his body I had grown so used to, the slight hint of his shampoo he hadn't changed for years.

I opened my arms, and he paused.

"I need a shower," he said.

"You do."

"I'm going to get you dirty, and you just got out of the shower."

"I did. I don't care."

He stepped into my arms and wrapped his around me, holding me like one of us might break. "How bad?" he asked.

"Which part of the day?"

"All of it."

"It doesn't get five stars, that's for sure," I said. "Some of it was pretty good, though."

"Which part?"

"This."

He settled, holding me. Then, when I loosened my arms, he leaned back just a bit, his eyes such a dark green they were almost black.

"Tell me all of it. Jean, Myra, and Frigg went over some of what happened, but when they said attackers, everything else went blank."

"Do you want a shower while I talk?"

"They're making hot cocoa," he said.

"It will wait."

He drew me with him into the bathroom, not ready to let me out of his sight, and I perched on the edge of the counter top.

He shucked out of his clothes and didn't bother testing the water before he got in.

I gave him the basics on how the fight between Crow and Odin had ended, told him about the people at the diner, Than admitting the gods were watching me, and that we had a social influencer in our mix.

I told him I'd had a good time picking out my dress.

"You actually picked one?" He turned off the taps and grabbed the towel I'd slung over the top of the door for him.

"Wasn't that what I was supposed to do?"

"Yes. But you are, as always, a woman of surprises."

"It was just a dress."

He opened the door, the towel wrapped around his head, and all the rest of him very nice and very naked.

He was muscular, but not carved like a body builder. His muscles were from working a physical job. An architect by trade, he still spent most of his time in construction, building and remodeling. That hands-on physical work kept him in shape.

"It was more than just a dress. I'm proud of you for choosing one."

"Like I want to dress shop more than once. I wasn't leaving that place without picking something to wear. My sweatpants plan was aggressively vetoed." I let my gaze trail over the tattoo of da Vinci's hand in sepia with Nature Never Breaks Her Own Laws on his shoulder, the drawing compass at his hip bone, and the star constellation low on his stomach.

I loved the ink on his body, loved that each tattoo reflected who he was—a builder, a dreamer, an artist.

"Your sisters said they'd make it a lot more fun than normal shopping. Was there wine?"

"Yes. And strippers. And puppies."

His smile was quick. "They told me they'd only let you bring one of those things home."

"I know. His name is Rex Flexible. I gave him the spare room."

"He better be a dog."

"Oh, he's a dirty, dirty dog."

"All he's getting to eat around here is the generic kibble Spud likes."

"Kinky. He might have an opinion on that."

He leaned toward me and gave me a quick kiss. "No strippers."

"Except you," I said.

"Except me." He did an impressive body roll, then strode out of the room to get dressed.

"Hey, just a kiss? And only one body roll? With all that nakedness? I have dollar bills around here somewhere. I am willing to stuff them anywhere you want them." I followed him into our room.

"We have a house full of guests, two of whom are your sisters. No Magic Mike when my soon-to-be sisters-in-law are in the house."

He pulled a Led Zeppelin T-shirt—that was almost worn out—over his head, and the image of Icarus settled into place on his chest.

"Can I see your injuries?" he asked quietly.

"It's just a couple bruises."

He reached out. It was automatic, as if he didn't want to be that close to me and not make a connection. As if he needed to know we were both here, alive, and a part of each other's *now*.

This was a part of living together, of sharing our lives. We'd become accustomed to the other person, and we sought each other out without hesitation.

When we'd been dating, we looked for each other in the crowd, and of course would draw together, happy to make that connection.

But here, now, in our home, we still reached for that

contact, that assurance, that joy of knowing the other person was there.

"You sure you don't want to get some rest?" He hooked his fingers into mine and tugged just a little. "We've got a very comfortable bed. Right over there. Just waiting for us."

"Tempting, but I want to take care of this situation while it's fresh. Let's go downstairs, drink cocoa, and figure out how to deal with this mess."

CHAPTER SIX

SPUD JUMPED off the couch and wiggled and wiggled to Ryder, begging for the attention of his favorite human on Earth.

Ryder knelt and made good-boy noises, giving him a thorough petting while Spud licked his face and whined happily.

The dragon-pig just sat on the couch and glared at me. Puffs of smoke curled up from its nostrils.

"Cocoa?" Frigg asked.

"Please," I said, eyeing the dragon-pig.

"Coming right up." She unfolded her long legs from the armchair and headed into the kitchen. "You too, Ryder?"

"Make mine a double."

"So you're a marshmallow and whipped cream man, are you?"

"Tonight I am." He dropped down onto the couch and draped his arm across the back. Spud was there already, the shark offering dropped instantly onto the altar of Ryder's lap. Then the dog rested as much of his body as he could over Ryder's thighs.

The dragon-pig was still glaring at me. It growled.

"Hey, buddy," I said to the little pink menace. "Are you purring?"

The sound it was making wasn't quite a purr, but I'd never heard it make that noise before. "Do you want a cup of cocoa too?"

"I think it's mad at you," Jean said.

"No, it's—"

The dragon-pig *oink*ed.

"Okay, you're mad? What did I do?"

The dragon-pig *oink*ed some more, adding in growls and grumbles and a weird bird-like whistle now and then.

"Wow," I said. "I do not speak dragon, but if I did, I'd think it was chewing me out."

"It is." Frigg brought in a serving platter loaded with cups of cocoa and all the extras. She offered the platter to Ryder, and he took a mug.

"You speak dragon?" I asked.

She tipped her head back and forth. "A little. This one has an accent I can't quite place, but yes, it is angry at you."

"Why? What did I do?"

She paused and listened to the grumbles.

"You got attacked."

"Well, yes. That goes with the job, though. Sometimes there will be a tussle."

The dragon-pig snorted, ending it with a foghorn hoot.

"It doesn't like that," Frigg interpreted.

"Buddy," I said to a creature that could swallow me

whole, "I'm the Bridge for gods. I'm the chief of police. I'm the one who stands up to people doing bad things."

It made little popping sounds.

"If I'm understanding it correctly," Frigg said. "It wants permission to eat them."

The dragon-pig *oink*ed.

"No," I said. "You may not eat humans. Ever."

More smoke curled out of its nostrils, and its eyes flashed red.

"Huh," Frigg said.

"What?"

"Something about an older law, a dragon law about a dragon guarding its hoard? Protecting what is valuable to it? I can't pick out the details, but it has something to do with stomping on houses."

The dragon-pig stared at me and stomped its feet one at a time, slowly and purposefully, dreams of crushing Tokyo becoming clearer and clearer with each movement.

"Nope. No destroying buildings either," I said. "Everything we agreed on when you first came to town remains in play. Now scoot over so I can drink my cocoa."

It moved over just enough I had room to sit. Then it climbed onto my lap and settled down heavily, as if determined to keep me there.

Frigg handed me a cup. "Need to fancy it up?" She tipped the platter, offering marshmallows, whipped cream, and hilariously, a tiny bottle of rum she'd dug out from somewhere.

"No, this is perfect."

"Are you sure you shouldn't be in bed?" Jean asked.

"Already tried that," Ryder said.

"To briefly recap," I said to Ryder. "Frigg drove me home from dress shopping, and I saw a shadow move along the side of the house. I put on my gun and went down there to see who was sneaking around."

"You walked into an ambush?" His eyebrows were high. "Really, Delaney?"

"I thought it was Xtelle. She is always snooping through the bushes. I figured she was trying to get away with going full pink unicorn in public again.

"A woman came around the corner and gave me some story about being at the lake and getting lost."

"Bullshit," he said. "She was casing the house, trying to get to you."

"Yeah, and I made it easy for her. I saw her glance at someone over my shoulder. I dropped, punched him in the knee—"

"I woulda punched him in his nuts," Jean said.

"Didn't have the angle," I said. "The woman jumped me. I didn't know two other people were out there. Frigg found them and knocked them both out."

"Thank you," Ryder said.

Frigg gave him a lazy salute.

"I pushed through the roses to give myself some room to maneuver. Once I got on my feet, I had my gun, and they both put up their hands and did what I asked. That brings us to now."

"You didn't call me," he said.

"There was a lot going on. Myra had Jean call you because she was bossing everyone around and told me I had to take a shower."

He exhaled and the tightness at the edges of his eyes and mouth eased just a bit.

"Oh, and Frigg figured out the people are demon touched," I said.

"What now?" he asked.

"You didn't know that yet?"

"We didn't get that far before he charged up the stairs to check on you," Jean said. "So butch, by the way, Ryder. Much hero." She gave him a thumbs up.

"Frigg caught the scent of a demon mark on them," I said.

"They are possessed by demons?" he asked.

"No," Frigg said. "That's a whole different thing."

"We think they made a deal with demons," Myra said.

"All right." He rubbed at his forehead for a minute. "How do we want to deal with the demon angle?"

"That's where you come in," I said. "Can you use your contract knowledge from Mithra on them? See what kind of deal they made?"

"We're pretty sure you're not a target," Myra started, but before she could finish saying whatever she was going to say, he cut in.

"Yes."

"Good. Let me get my shoes on," I said.

The chorus of arguments and discouraging noises was impressive since there were only four other people in the room.

"Of course I'm going. I'm the chief of police. It's my damn job. You are all worse than a bunch of mother hens. Move dragon-pig."

Dragon-pig growled and grew heavier, making it clear it wanted me to stay put.

"Please," I said. "You know this is my job."

It huffed, and moved off my lap.

I left the room, and noted that they all started whispering at each other as soon as I was at the top of the stairs. I sighed. It was good to be loved. Annoying, but good.

RYDER DROVE and dragon-pig came with us, because every time we took it back into the house and told it to stay with Spud, we found it waiting for us in the back seat of Ryder's truck.

Hatter and Shoe were still at the station. One of them, probably Shoe who was short, wide, and ill tempered, would pull the late shift and keep an eye on the people in holding. Our other reserve officer, Kelby, who was half-giant, should be on duty soon too.

"Hey, boss," Hatter called. "Ryder. Wondered when you'd show up." Hatter was the opposite of Shoe in almost every way. Tall, lanky, always cheerful, he gave off easy-going cowboy vibes. We'd stolen both of them from the Tillamook police up north, and they'd settled in quickly. I couldn't imagine taking care of Ordinary without them now.

"Evening, boys," Jean called out as she, Myra, and Frigg all strolled into the station.

"Looks like a party," Hatter said. "How's this going down?"

"Ryder," I said, "Frigg, just you two, with me."

Myra and Jean frowned, not liking my plan, but I strode back to our very small holding cell, unlocked the door that separated it from the bullpen, and stepped through.

All four people behind the bars watched us step into the small space. I didn't bother trying to keep the dragon-pig out. It was clearly going wherever it wanted to go tonight, and that was clearly with me.

"Evening," I said. "I'm chief of police, Delaney Reed. We met earlier when you tried to kidnap me." I paused for reactions, but only the gray haired man dropped his gaze. "Or maybe you were trying to kill me."

The older guy winced slightly. The man I'd punched shifted his weight, staring straight ahead past us like he was at parade rest. He was standing closest to the two women.

"Well, you've been advised you can call a lawyer, and I hope you've considered doing so. But until your attorney or attorneys show up, Officer Bailey here has some questions for you."

I moved back so Ryder could take the space in front of the holding cell.

Ryder didn't say anything for at least a full minute. In such a small room, in such a charged situation, it felt like that minute went on for hours.

"You all new to Ordinary?" he asked, low and easy, like they'd just met on the beach, in a grocery store, at a gas station and he was welcoming them to the town.

"I'm not trying to incriminate you," he went on when they remained quiet. "Or have you say something that could be used against you. I'm just curious if you've ever come to town before."

Silence. Ryder watched them. He had told me being connected to Mithra meant he could "read" the contracts and laws that bound people. He said it sort of hovered in view if he focused his eyes just right.

I didn't know what he was seeing now. To me they

looked like four people who were tired and angry about being behind bars.

"All right, let's do something easy," he said. "Have they given you dinner yet?"

The man whose knee I'd punched shook his head. The woman next to him reached over and pressed her fingers on his wrist.

"Okay," Ryder said. "We can change that. We'll get some food in here. Anyone vegetarian?"

The old guy snorted.

"Burgers it is," Ryder said. "Frigg, would you tell the officers to order baskets for our guests?"

She left, and Ryder threw me a look. "That okay with you, Chief?"

"This is a holding cell in a tiny town on the coast, not a maximum security prison. Food is provided. Especially since they'll be here overnight."

The old guy's gaze came up, and he sighed.

"Like the chief says, you'll want to get comfortable. We'll provide blankets, but it's not going to be the most luxurious bed and breakfast. Anyone need anything else?"

I wasn't sure what Ryder's play was here, how his questions had anything to do with the demon mark. Maybe he was trying to be chummy so they'd trust him.

Or maybe there was more to it.

A lot of contracts with demons were about agreeing to something, by voice or via writing, and Ryder was giving these people plenty of chances to agree with him.

I wondered if that would unlock more information on the demon contract. I had never seen him do...this. He was connected to a god, but I very rarely saw that manifest so clearly. He looked like a guy who could be your friend, someone who knew how to change a tire, or how to get a cat down out of a tree.

Agreeable, competent. He had one thumb hooked in his front pocket, was rocked back on his back foot, and had an easy smile on his face.

But all that was a lie. He was angry as hell.

"All right," he said, "we'll leave you for the night. Since no one needs anything."

"Bathroom," the woman said. "I need to use the bathroom."

That. That was what Ryder was looking for.

"Right. Of course," he said. There was a thread of something strong in his voice. Like a fishing line had hooked and caught, and he was now teasing and drawing his prey to him.

"Chief, do you want to take her?"

"Yep."

"If you gentlemen could just step back to the wall away from the door," Ryder said, "we'll get your friend to a restroom."

They shuffled backward, and Ryder smiled. He'd gotten them to agree with him and do what he said.

The guy I'd hit said, "I need to piss."

"One at a time," Ryder said. "Ladies first." He opened the holding cell door, but only a small crack. "Come on out," he said. "What was your name again?"

"Lori," she said.

"Ryder," he offered with a nod, and that was hook, line, and sinker. Even if it was just the exchange of names, it was an agreement given and taken. "Nice to meet you. Go ahead with Chief Reed."

She wasn't shackled and her hands weren't zip tied. I didn't have my gun on me. But the bathroom was a very short trip down the hall where the other officers, and the security cameras we had in the building, could keep tabs on us.

I opened the door, and let Lori step out first. Unsurprisingly, Myra was right there on the other side of the door.

"Bathroom break," I told her.

She nodded, gave the woman a hard look, then started down the hall to the bathroom. We walked that way, Myra in front, the woman behind her, and me at the rear.

"Wait here," Myra said. She stepped into the restroom, checked the stalls, then held the door open. "Come on in."

Lori walked in, I stayed outside.

A few minutes later, Myra and I took Lori back to the cell and traded bathroom escort jobs with Hatter and Shoe.

Ryder was waiting at my desk in the bullpen.

"Get what you wanted?" I asked him.

"Yes."

"You going to explain it?"

Jean and Myra and Frigg pulled close.

"They're just human," he said. "They made a deal with a demon, not highest level—not the king—but someone much higher than a foot soldier."

"Crossroads demon?" Myra asked.

"I don't think so," he said. "Those contracts are about granting someone's wildest desires in exchange for their souls. This contract is a more like some demon hiring them to snatch Delaney. In return, they were going to be paid some money."

"That's...disappointingly normal," Jean said.

"What?" she asked, when we all looked at her. "If I ever made a deal with a demon, I'd expect some sis-boom-bah, you know? Not just a few bucks."

"Were they supposed to kill me?" I asked.

"Kidnap you. Though if you were hurt in the process, that wouldn't have voided the deal."

"Terrific," I said.

"You don't know which demon they dealt with?" Myra asked.

He shook his head. "The contract that binds them is recent. They weren't in debt with the demon before-hand, and the stakes of them failing were low. If they failed, they didn't get the money."

"So boring," Jean whispered.

"Could you tell if the contract was aimed to lure in or trap the other demons in town?" I asked.

"I can't see all of it. But they just understood they were to get you out of town. Any way they could."

"That's more than we knew a couple hours ago," I said. "Maybe this isn't as bad as we thought."

"You are unreal," Myra said. "Things aren't as bad. Demons put a hit out on you and hired thugs to steal you."

"But we stopped them," I argued. "That's the point. I'm fine. The demons had terrible taste in hitmen."

"I want more intel," Jean said. "I want to know what the demons are planning."

"Let's ask our friendly neighborhood demons," I said around a yawn. "See if they can give us some insight. Tell us what strategies Vychoro or his underlings might use next."

I yawned again, and Ryder's hand came down on my hip.

"We'll do that in the morning," he said. "Whatever they're planning, I doubt they're going to launch into it before assessing their failure."

"No, we can do this now," I said. "Myra, ask Bathin to meet us at my place. Jean, tell Xtelle and Avnas to join us."

Both my sisters said, "No," at the same time.

"Bed," Myra said.

"You were attacked dude," Jean said. "Get some rest. We can do demon stuff in the morning, okay?"

I wanted to say no, but Ryder's hand was heavy on my hip and he squeezed gently, signaling he was on their side, which meant I was totally outnumbered.

"Fine," I said. The painkiller was keeping most of the aches out of my head and back, but getting some sleep suddenly sounded like heaven.

Kelby strode through the door and paused in the lobby. "Looks like the gang's all here," she said. "I heard about the attack. You okay, Chief?"

"I'm good, yeah," I said. "Headed home. Call if you need anything. You sure you're up for the night shift?"

"It's more interesting than staying home trying to find something new to stream. Here, I can at least beat Shoe at arm wrestling again."

"You're doing paperwork," Shoe grumped, without looking away from his hunting and pecking. "And I don't lose."

"Right," Kelby said, dragging out the word and shaking her head.

"Keep an eye on the holding cell," I said. "They're human, but there are demons involved in this somehow. No one is allowed to spring them except their lawyers."

"Got it, Chief."

Ryder was already walking toward the door, guiding me along with him, dragon-pig at my feet.

Out at his truck my sisters each hugged me, made dragon-pig promise to keep me safe, which Ryder complained about because what was he, chopped liver?

I told Frigg I didn't need supervision while I slept, I would be safe, we would be safe, and to just go the heck home.

They all—finally—listened and went their way while we went ours.

"Did you get dinner?" I asked Ryder, as he drove through darkness softened by a layer of fog that had drifted in with the night.

"I'm fine," he said, the words short and tight and very much not fine.

"Jump Offs is still open. Why don't we go there? Get a burger to go or something?"

"There's food at the house." Grumpy. He was grumpy.

"Frozen burritos," I said.

"We have eggs and ham."

"Oh good! I can make you an omelet," I said.

"No, gods. Please don't."

I made a fake shocked sound. "I'm getting good at omelets."

"Delaney, I love you. But I do not love you for your cooking."

"That's it," I declared. "The wedding is off! I don't even know who you are any more. Stop the truck. I'm walking home."

He slowed the truck, but hit the automatic locks so I couldn't get out.

"Hey, I already thwarted one kidnapping today. Don't get any bright ideas, Bub."

I was grinning, but he wasn't. He parked the truck on the shoulder of the road, threw on the hazard lights and reached for me.

"No. Not until you take back that cooking comment. How am I going to get better if you don't show any support... Hey," I said, catching the glisten in his eyes. Tears. He was crying. "Hey. Are you okay? Ryder?"

He unlatched his seatbelt and shifted so he could put both palms against my face. "Delaney," he choked.

I fumbled with my seatbelt, blindly trying to get out of it so I could get closer to him.

He kissed me, softly at first, tasting slightly of chocolate. It was an apology, a wish that he had been there when I'd been hurt, so he could have somehow stopped it, which was, of course unlikely.

I kissed him back, loving him, letting him know I was alive and whole and well.

The kiss deepened, became more needful, sending heat licking beneath my skin, and for a moment, I lost myself, let go of the world, my worries, my mind.

I rode the soft sensations of his lips, his tongue, his hands, still cradling me as if I were breakable. As if I could be swept away by the smallest shifting of sand beneath our feet.

An eighteen-wheeler rushed past us, rocking our vehicle like the waves at sea.

Ryder finally pulled back. I licked my lips, chasing the taste of him, and reached over to run my fingertips along his jaw.

"Are you okay?" I asked.

He drew a hand back through his thick hair. "I

thought you were going to be wedding dress shopping. Safe. Making a memory with your sisters and aunt. I thought...I thought everything was okay. I thought you were okay."

"Everything is okay. I am okay. I did make memories. Good memories. It was wonderful. Just because a demon throws some randos at me doesn't change that."

He narrowed his eyes. "I hate I wasn't with you. I hate I wasn't even in town."

"I know. But I'm tough. I know how to handle myself. That's the perk of dating a gal who grew up around gods and monsters and knew, at a young age, she was going to get into upholding the law. I know how to fight. I've been taught by all sorts of people how to fight. I know how to keep myself safe."

"I don't like it."

"What part of it?"

"All of it. It's our wedding soon, Delaney. In two weeks. We shouldn't have to be worrying about demon attacks."

"Sure, but it's better to know something is coming our way than to be blindsided. I don't know if you've noticed, but the gods are keeping a very close eye on me right now."

"Is that why Frigg and Hera insisted on going dress shopping with you?"

"Mostly. I mean, I think they like me and liked being there, but at least a part of it—Frigg driving me home— was to keep me safe."

He rubbed at his lips. "I don't hate that."

"Yeah, well, I don't love it, but the gods are aware of what's going on. I think stealing their weapons was a pretty genius move on Goap's part. It showed the gods they were vulnerable, and it showed them demons are willing to exploit those vulnerabilities.

"So the gods are paying very close attention to me," I said. "RIP Delaney alone time."

He sniffed and wiped at his mouth again. "Okay, I'm still not happy with the situation, but, yeah, I know. The gods have been paying more attention."

"Oh?"

"They have been all over the wedding plans, asking for timing, places, details. They weren't nearly as pushy about it a few months back."

"Shall we take it as a compliment?"

He chuckled. "Probably best." He flicked off the hazard lights, put the truck in gear, and eased back onto the road.

"Sure you don't want a greasy pub burger?" I asked.

His stomach growled, and dragon-pig in the back seat growled too. I chuckled.

"I think Chris has some nice rusted junk put aside for dragon-pig. I bet it would like a nibble."

It *oink*ed, and I glanced back. It was doing the adorable baby pig thing, wagging its tiny curly tail, mouth open in a silly smile.

"See?" I said. "It's starving."

"When isn't it starving?"

"You're hungry too. Let's get a burger, and I'll steal your fries."

He squinted at the road. "Fine. But we're ordering you your own fries."

"Even better."

Jump Off Jack's was our local award-winning micro-brewery, and the man behind it was Chris Lagon, our local gilman.

The brewery was still open.

"To-go?" Ryder suggested.

Just the thought of going into a crowded bar made me tired. "Yes."

"You wait here," he said, unbuckling and giving me a fast kiss before opening the door. "I'll be back."

"Don't forget snacks for dragon-pig," I said.

"I got it." He shut the door, and I watched him stroll into the building. Those legs. That ass.

"He is a fine looking man," I said.

Dragon-pig grunted.

"I think I'm an awful lot in love with him."

Dragon-pig grunted again.

"Don't tell anyone, Dragon-pig, but I think I'm gonna marry him."

Dragon-pig snorted, and smoke puffed into the air, filling the truck.

I grinned and rested my head against the seat. It was a good night, a quiet night, and the promise of Ryder and french fries was in my future.

What more could a girl want?

CHAPTER SEVEN

"For real?" I asked, as I finished tying my shoes. "You're still in bed?"

"It is five a.m.," Ryder grumbled into the pillow he'd pulled over his head. "Who gets up before the sunrise?"

"Healthy people."

"Thank gods I'm not one of those."

I threw another pillow at him. "I'm giving you fifteen minutes. Get up, Bailey. Socks and shoes. I'll fill your water bottle."

"I'll fill *your* water bottle," he mumbled.

"That doesn't even make sense. Get up. Spud wants his run."

I yanked the covers off him. He didn't even flinch.

"Quitter," I said.

"Me and the sun," he agreed.

I jogged down the stairs, pulling my hair back in a rubber band.

Spud was already at the door looking at his leash hopefully. Dragon-pig snored on the hoard of stuffed toys by the fireplace. Dragon-pig, like my fiancé, was not a morning creature.

"Let's go pee, Spud." I grabbed his leash and latched it to his collar. "Wanna come?" I asked the pink beast.

Dragon-pig opened one eye, which flashed red before it closed again and went back to snoring.

"Message received. C'mon, Spuddo, it's me and you."

August had melted into September and the mornings finally carried that crisp scent that meant cooler nights and days would be here soon. The Oregon coast's weather was mercurial to say the least. We'd had some rain over the summer, but I missed the cooler mornings of autumn.

Spud did his business, then pulled me back to the house and his food dish.

"Ryder!" I called, as I filled Spud's bowl with kibble. "Time's up!"

Ryder thumped down the stairs, looking grumpy and rumpled and generally pissed off with the world. He was adorable.

"There better be coffee," he mumbled.

I pointed at the full pot.

He was still scowling, which didn't deter Spud, who bounded over to his favorite person and circled his feet, dragging his leash that I hadn't unhooked yet.

Ryder bent, petted Spud, sidestepped the leash before he got tied up, then stopped in front of me.

"It's too early to jog."

I nodded. "We can walk."

He grunted and leaned in for a kiss.

He smelled like mint toothpaste and that lotion he put on his hands to keep the callouses from cracking.

"Walking. I can manage that," he said. "Coffee first." He poured himself a cup, and lifted the pot, offering to pour for me.

"When we get back. Did you sleep?"

He just grunted again and muttered something about someone stealing the blankets. I staged a tactical retreat to let that first cup of caffeine do its work. I wandered over to Dragon-pig and crouched in front of it.

Bruises on my legs throbbed with the movement, and my ribs didn't like it much either. Walking might end up being my favored pace today, too, but I'd at least try to get Ryder into a jog, just to see how grumpy he was going to be about it.

"Morning, Ruler of the Stuffies," I said to Dragon-pig.

It didn't move, its snoring soft and even and fake. It was not sleeping.

"You want to come jogging with me and Spud?"

Still no response.

I tugged on the flipper of the tie-dyed manatee toy I didn't remember either of us getting. It was about six toys down in the dragon princess-and-the-pea stacked bedding. I got it almost halfway out before it disturbed the toys and made them shift slightly.

"Morning, Dragon-pig," I said, tugging on a monkey tail. The monkey slithered free, and I set it next to me on the floor.

"Are you awake?" I Jenga'd out a stuffed hammer and a partially beheaded broccoli.

The dragon-pig's snoring became pointedly louder, annoyed.

"Because if you were awake, I might have a little

snack for you." I pulled on what was either a zombie, or the weirdest looking squirrel I'd ever seen.

The zombie squirrel was the linchpin. I yanked, and the entire mountain of toys avalanched, burying the dragon-pig.

"Oops."

The dragon growled.

"Uh-oh. Did I wake you? Did I disturb your slumber, oh, great one?"

The growl turned into a snarl.

"Would you like a treat? A little breakfast goodie?"

The half-buried dragon pushed its snout out, eyes and ears followed. It squinted at me, and I bit my bottom lip to keep from laughing. It looked an awful lot like Ryder.

"See what I have?" I produced the set of old keys I'd picked up at the junk shop and jingled them. "Delicious bunch of old, gross metal things. Mmmm. Look good?"

It *oink*ed begrudgingly and opened its mouth. I could feel the furnace heat coming out of its maw. I shuffled the keys so that only one was sticking out.

"Here you go, buddy. And you don't even have to go on the jog with us. You can stay behind and be grumpy with Ryder."

"Oh, no," Ryder said. "You made me get out of bed. I am going on this walk, no matter what."

"That's just the coffee talking," I teased.

"Yep. Coffee might be in a good mood, but I plan on complaining the entire time."

"Did you hear that, Spud? Is this what we signed up for? Grumpy-pants creatures all around us?"

Spud finished wolfing down his kibble and looked

between Ryder and me, trying to figure out who was going to feed him again or take him on a walk.

The dragon-pig lipped at the key, and I let go of the chain.

It slurped the keys into its mouth in small munching motions, then chewed and rumbled a happy rumble.

"Okay, that's one dragon sorted. How about you? Are you going to bite my head off?"

Ryder finished the last of his coffee. I could tell he was, if not in a better mood, at least more awake.

"You are disgustingly happy this morning. I am suspicious."

I shrugged. "Maybe it was shopping for my wedding dress. Thank you for setting that up for me."

"Myra and Jean did all the work. I just recruited them."

"Maybe it was watching you use your godly contract powers yesterday. Sexy. But did you have to be so nice to the people who stepped all over our rose bushes?"

"They stepped all over you," he said. "You were the one who stepped all over the rose bushes."

I waved a hand like it didn't matter. "What was the power move you pulled back at the station while you were acting like a super nice guy?"

"I am a super nice guy."

"Spill it, almost-hubby."

"Over the last couple years, Mithra's tried to find different ways to…I don't know…tempt me to take his side? He hasn't given me actual power, but he has made it so I can see how contracts connect things. People, the supernatural and the unmagical, follow rules and laws, both manmade and natural. Why are you staring at the coffee pot? Am I boring you?"

"No, I'm just trying to decide if I have time for another cup of coffee before we head out."

He grabbed the cup I'd used earlier out of the sink, ran water in it, then filled it about half full.

"Thanks," I said, as he handed it to me. "Carry on."

"After a couple years seeing how...*everything* is connected by some contract or other, I realized that if I talk to someone and get them to respond—an agreement is best, but any response works—I could see *how* they are tied into contracts. How they offer their word or intention or will. The construction of all the contracts we make, hour by hour, minute by minute is actually beautiful."

"So you wanted them to agree with you so you could see how they agreed with the demons?"

"Pretty much. I offered to get them something, and they said yes."

"The bathroom."

"Yup. When Lori agreed to go to the bathroom with you, and the men agreed to step away from the door, that was when I saw how they were tangled up."

"This better all be in your final report."

"I'll put it in the one Myra files in the magic library. It won't be on the public record."

"You're getting pretty good at juggling this reserve officer thing. But you're getting pretty good at juggling a lot of things. The job, your actual job, Mithra, our wedding."

"I like some of those things more than others."

"Wedding, I would hope."

"I keep telling you not to worry about that. I love working on it. No, don't make that face, I do. In case you were wondering, being tied to Mithra is the thing I hate. If I could find a way to break that contract, I would."

"We will," I said. "There has to be a way to break it, or make Mithra break it."

He nodded.

"It did come in handy yesterday, though," I said.

"Yeah."

"And you looked really hot working them over. Making them like you, getting them to do what you wanted."

He huffed a laugh. "Yeah?"

"Hot." I put down my coffee cup and took his hand.

He chuckled. "Does that mean you won't like me if I'm ever just an average Joe again?"

"Oh, you will never be an average Joe. Never were."

"Are you sweet talking me so I don't notice it's still dark out, but you're slowly backing us toward the door?"

"No? Wait. Is it working?"

He tugged me close and planted a kiss on my mouth. "No sweet talking necessary. I'd follow you anywhere, Delaney Reed."

"Back atcha, Ryder Bailey."

He snapped his fingers for Spud who plopped down in a sit next to us, waiting for Ryder to pick up his leash. "Beach or lake?"

"I'm thinking beach."

"Good."

We walked through the quiet neighborhood, past houses still dark, or with only single windows illuminated. The air was heavy and damp, the hearty evergreen bushes and trees in the yards spackled with dew.

It was just over a mile to the beach access we liked to use. We walked it hand in hand, stopping for Spud to get his sniff on. By the time our shoes hit the soft sand, my muscles were moving a lot better, my ribs weren't giving me as much grief, and the sun was just starting to rise up over the Coastal Range behind us to the east, slowly dragging back the long heavy shadows of night and replacing them with dawn.

We ambled toward the water where the sand was wet and packed harder, but instead of heading off in a jog, we strolled north.

"What's on the agenda today?" I asked.

"Which agenda?" he said.

"Any of them. Wedding?"

"Follow up. All the follow up. Two weeks sounds like a long time out, but there are still a lot of tentative agreements I'd like to nail down. Cheese is still an issue. What do you think about a DJ for music instead of a live band?"

"You were going to bring in a live band?"

"It was an option."

"I think a DJ sounds great. As long as there are some fun songs in there too."

"Like what, the Funky Chicken?"

"Sure. And the Time Warp."

"Just a jump to the left," he said. "Any other requests?"

"Check with Jean. She probably has a list of songs she wants to dance to."

"Already done."

"Look at you. You don't need me for this, do you?"

"Oh, I very much need you for this, but I don't need you to *worry* about it. I'm enjoying the process."

We were quiet for a bit, and Ryder bent and unlatched Spud's leash. We were the only people on the beach at this point, and Spud was trained to return at a whistle.

"Anything else today?"

"I have some drawings to go over with a client. Mr. Tabbs wants to build an ADU on his lot. He said it's for his mother-in-law, but the way his daughter keeps talking about it, she's going to move in there first, then give it to Nana when Nana's done going on cruises."

"Fun," I said. "Anything else?"

"It's not your birthday, not our anniversary. Am I forgetting something?"

I bumped into him and snaked my arm behind his back. "No. I just...we've been flying at different altitudes lately, and I don't want to lose track of you. Of where you're at. Of where we're at."

His arm came around behind my back. It was warm, strong, and I leaned into him before drawing back because walking that way over sand and rocks was tricky.

"We are good," he said firmly. "Even if I feel like I'm never home. I make plans for the day and by the time it's midnight I can't figure out where the hours have gone or what I've done."

"Mithra's calling you away a lot more. Do you know why?"

"There's nothing that connects it together. Sometimes it's one of those archaic laws he wants me enforce, which I don't, because no one is going to let me arrest someone for juggling without a license."

"Oregon City?"

"Hood River." His phone rang. He pulled it out of his pocket and frowned.

"Work?"

"Mithra."

"Speak of the devil. Can you ignore it?"

"No." He swiped the screen and put it to his ear. "Ryder."

He moved toward the ocean, one hand on his hip, annoyance in every line of his body.

The morning breeze and rolling hiss and thunder of the waves covered the rest of his words.

I knew he wasn't happy. I also knew he was going to head out to do Mithra's orders before he even turned back to me.

"It's okay," I said before he spoke.

"It's like a hook in my chest," he said. "I can say no for a while, but it gets worse the longer I resist."

"I know."

"I don't want to go. I was going to talk to you about the wedding. I was going to make you breakfast."

"I know."

He stared at the horizon, then back at me. "I'll be back as soon as I can."

I put my hand on his arm. "I know. It's okay. You're tied to a god, and gods are not reasonable. Do you want me to go back with you? We probably have time to toast a Pop-Tart before you leave."

"No, you should finish your walk. Or jog. I'll grab food on the way out of town." He took a step, then rocked back toward me and leaned in for a kiss.

"Sorry, Laney," he said again.

"Go. Do the jerk god's bidding. We'll catch up later today."

He nodded, then started back toward the house.

Spud took a step toward Ryder. I snapped my fingers. "Wanna run, Spuddo?"

Spud wagged his tail, and as soon as I took a couple jogging steps, he abandoned all loyalty to Ryder and bounded along beside me, then ahead of me, loving this game.

I worked on my breathing and stride, letting the worries fade as I fell into the rhythm of breath and footfall.

The sun had pulled most of the shadow off this stretch of beach. A few people were out now, searching for agates, shells, or starting their morning jog.

One figure was headed straight at me. I knew who it was before we drew close enough to speak.

Zeus.

The god wore dark blue shorts and a light blue, long-sleeve shirt that clung to his muscular chest, biceps, and lean waist.

I slowed just a little, because it wasn't every day I saw the cultured and chic owner of the fashion boutique jogging down the beach.

"Morning," I called out.

He slowed, then pivoted and began jogging alongside me back the way he'd come.

Spud thought that was the greatest thing that had ever happened, and bounced around Zeus, before jumping ahead to charge into a flock of seagulls standing around a half-buried piece of driftwood.

"Good morning, Delaney," he said, not a bit out of breath, which I thought had more to do with the fact he was a god than his exercise regime.

"Funny seeing you here," I said.

"How so?"

"I jog most mornings. I've run into you, what, twice in all that time?"

"We aren't on the beach at the same time," he said. "I run fairly often."

I mean, it wasn't a lie. But a god's idea of time was a little different than a mortal's idea. "Fairly often" in god-speak could mean once a century.

"Why today?"

"Why run?" he asked.

"Yes. Why today?"

We covered a little more ground, the wind at our backs, cool enough I was glad I was moving.

"I wanted to," he finally said.

"You got tagged with Delaney duty, didn't you?"

"Who have you been talking to? Crow?"

"Yes. And Than and Frigg."

"They never could keep a secret."

I huffed a laugh and slowed my pace. He matched me until we were down to a brisk walk.

"You know, you gods don't always have to get your way," I said.

"Oh, being here in Ordinary has made that very clear." He speared me with a look, and I was caught, as I sometimes was around gods, by how magnetic he could be.

He might be on vacation but he was still Zeus, god of the sky, ruler, protector, and so much more. His copper skin and dark hair made him look like he came from a land of sun and rich wine.

"But getting our way isn't why I'm here this morning," he said.

Spud nosed around a clump of rotting kelp, chomped on a stick, dragged it out of the mess, then trotted his way back to us.

"So what's it about?" I asked.

Spud stood a few yards away, tail high and wagging, waiting for us.

Zeus reached him just before me, and to my surprise, took the gross, wet, sandy, slobbery stick and gave it a hard throw.

Spud took off like a fuzzy brown bolt of lightning.

"Uh, oh," I said. "Don't let Bertie see you have that kind of arm. She'll make you pitch for the Ordinary Octopuses."

"Death would be preferable," he said, as we fell back into an easy walk.

"To answer your question, it is about keeping you safe, yes, but it is also about our weapons. The breach of our realms was not something that has ever happened before. Not like that. Not so easily. And to be able to transport our weapons and taunt us by delivering them to our doorstep?" His eyes tightened.

"Goap said he was trying to help us. Arm us against the king."

"They crossed our thresholds."

"Yes, but—"

"They took our weapons."

"Sure, but—"

"They delivered them to us in paper boxes. A mockery of our power."

"Okay. I can see how—don't give me that glare—I *can* see that it was a breach of things that shouldn't have been breached."

Spud reached the stick and picked it up. He trotted slowly toward us.

"You think the king of hell is going to attack Ordinary?" I asked.

121

We'd both stopped and were waiting for Spud to reach us.

"No."

Interesting.

"Want to let me in on your reasoning?"

"Demons don't follow rules, Delaney. They rarely follow a straight path to what they want. If he wants Ordinary, he'll find a better way to get it than a frontal assault."

Spud reached us. I bent for the stick, but he turned his head to the side and sat with the stick in his mouth. No more throwing.

I started walking back the way I'd come, the breeze stronger now, salted and cool against my face.

"Maybe that's the one thing gods and demons have in common," he mused.

"Frontal assaults?"

"No."

"Power hunger?"

"No." This time his tone was a little amused.

"Super massive egos?"

He chuckled. "No. They aren't always what they appear to be."

I hummed. "I know a few deities who are all light-ning bolt and thunder, inside and out."

"Yes, well, I didn't say we were *never* what we appear to be."

We'd made it back to where I needed to turn toward the softer sand and the wooden stairs that would take me to the road home.

"This has been fun," I said. "It was good to spend time with you. We don't do this very much, do we?"

His eyebrows went up as if he'd just realized that

truth. "We don't. I enjoyed it. We could make it a more regular thing?"

"I'm out here every morning," I said with a grin. "You are invited to join me any time. Spud would love it too."

The dog had worked his way under Zeus' hand and was enjoying the head-scratching Zeus was giving him.

"Tomorrow?" he asked.

"Sunrise," I agreed.

The breathing of the ocean faded as we made our way up the stairs and out onto the neighborhood street.

By the time we were passing the first houses, the ocean was a white noise in the distance.

"Have you decided who will officiate at your wedding?" he asked.

"Ryder's in charge of the details. I don't think he's asked anyone yet. Are you volunteering?"

A car rumbled by. We crossed the main street and started up into the neighborhoods to the east.

"It would be an honor to marry you and Ryder. But I don't think I am the god he will choose for that boon."

"Boon. Fancy. But why wouldn't we choose you?" I was curious how he saw weddings in general, and mine specifically.

"If you asked, I would gladly officiate. But I think...you know you have my blessing, don't you?"

"I didn't know I needed it," I teased.

"You don't, I suppose. But you have it. I have hoped for many years that you and Ryder would see how your hearts aligned. And now you have. Mazel tov."

"Thank you. Just curious. Who did you think we would ask?"

"Crow? You are very familiar with him."

"True."

"Perhaps Hera."

"You know there are humans who could do the ceremony."

"Why would you choose a human when you could choose a god?"

"I like humans."

He grunted. "I assume Ryder will have the sense to choose a god for your nuptials."

"We'll see. So, that's my house, and an overly-protective dragon is waiting inside."

"Perhaps I should go with you."

"Perhaps no." I gave him a sunny smile and a wave. "See you tomorrow morning, jogging buddy!"

I hopped up the porch stairs, strode through the door, and closed it behind me.

Finally. Alone.

"Good morning, Delaney!"

Gan, the god Ganesha, was a big man with burnished brown skin and thick, dark hair. His face was wide, his eyes bright and playful.

He'd recently come back to town to open a tea and florist shop.

"What are you doing in my kitchen?"

"Making coffee since you hate tea."

"I don't hate it."

He made a considering sound and placed one of our biggest mugs on the kitchen island next to a box that I didn't even have to read PUFFIN MUFFIN on to know it was filled with decadent breakfast treats from Hogan's shop.

"Breakfast sandwich?" he offered.

"I need to shower." But the coffee smelled wonderful, and I was already moving toward it. I took the cup and sipped. "What did you put in there? Magic?"

He waggled his eyebrows. "Maybe. Ha. Your face," he chuckled. "Not magic. I just know how to brew a really good cup of, well, anything."

"I'm taking this with me to the shower. Don't eat my sandwich." I jogged up the stairs, stripped, and showered.

I was dried and dressed when my phone rang.

"Chief Reed."

"You didn't come by last night," Bertie said. "I'm disappointed in you."

"Morning, Bertie."

"I'm a very busy woman, Delaney. There is only so much time in my schedule to accommodate you."

"I understand that. The job ran late."

"Your sister told me you went home after dress shopping."

"Yeah, well, there were some people waiting to kidnap me. You have no idea how much paperwork is involved in something like that."

"You were attacked?"

"More like wrestled. It's fine. They're in holding. I'm headed over there now. I can stop by your place later this morning."

"Yes," she said tightly. "See that you do."

She didn't immediately end the call. "Something else?" I asked.

"Has Patrick contacted you?"

"No?"

"He still wants to interview you over coffee."

"Yep. I'll get to it. Bye, Bertie."

She ended the call, and I thumped down the stairs.

Gan sat on the couch, feeding the dragon-pig pennies like kibble. "How did you end up being hoarded by a dragon?"

"I'm not hoarded."

"Oh, you very much are." He flipped a coin. Dragon-pig jumped and snapped it out of the air.

"It was in a cave. Jean and I found it. I told it that to stay in Ordinary, it would have to take a non-dragon shape."

"And it did so it could hoard you. Didn't you, you little pink fireball?"

The dragon-pig *oink*ed, its beady eyes focused on the penny in Gan's fingers.

"Not a hoard," I repeated.

The dragon-pig chuckled.

"I mean it," I said, pointing at my chest. "Not a hoard."

It snorted.

"You might think it's just hanging out for the easy eats," Gan flipped another penny and the dragon-pig gobbled it out of the air, "but I'm telling you it thinks you are a hoard. Therefore it owns you. No, that's not quite right. Therefore it *protects* you."

"It's gonna just have to un-think that. I'm headed to work now. Do you need a ride?"

Gan stood, gave dragon-pig a pat on its head and collected the pastry box before walking with me to the door. "Please."

"How are you settling in?" I asked, once we were driving south, and I had finished the delicious breakfast sandwich.

Gan messed with my radio, settling on a Spanish language station playing BAILANDO, Enrique's voice tempting us with dancing, dancing, dancing.

"Ordinary's changed since I was here."

"Has it?" He hadn't been gone for more than a few years.

"The penguin got famous," he said.

"True."

"Death is on vacation. I'd love to hear how that happened."

"Something about whipped cream and an ancient vampire he wanted to destroy."

"Sounds about right. Demons. That's new."

"Very new. I made them sign contracts. Unbreakable. Ryder looked them over. Ever since he pledged to Mithra, he's got a good eye for that sort of thing."

"That's new too. Ryder back in town. Tied up to a god. Not a very...kind god."

"He didn't know what he was doing. I tried to warn him."

"Your father being gone. That's different too," he said in a softer voice.

I nodded and swallowed. The pain was still there, I knew it would never leave me, tied too tightly now with my love for him.

But the edges of it were duller. Not easier. Different. Like I'd sustained an injury, broken my foot, dislocated my knee, and while healing had learned to walk around the pain that would never completely fade.

"Yeah. Not as new as it was."

"I heard you spoke with his soul."

"I did."

"This is good."

He sounded very satisfied. I thought about asking him if he'd had a hand in that, but decided I didn't need to know.

The song wound down just as I pulled up to Gan's shop.

"Looks good with the fresh paint," I said.

"Thank you. Come in sometime. We'll have tea. You'll love it. I promise." He opened the door.

"What?" I said, "No excuses to follow me all the way to the station? I thought you gods were trading off the watch-Delaney duty."

"I don't know what you are speaking of." His smile said he knew exactly what I was speaking of.

Crow tapped the top of the Jeep. "Hey, Boo-boo."

"No. Good-bye, Gan. Please slam the door before Crow can get in."

"Oops," Gan said. "Looks like it's too late."

Crow ducked into the Jeep and shut the door himself. "So how's our morning been?" he sing-songed.

"Annoying. The one man I wish would stick around had to leave, and all the other ones I wish would leave are sticking. Just sticking, sticking, sticking."

"We're a grumpy little bunny this morning, aren't we? Is it because of me? Sticking," he poked my shoulder, "sticking," another poke, "sticking?" Poke, poke.

I slugged him on the shoulder, and even with the odd angle of the blow that took all the sting out of it, he put his hands up in surrender, laughing.

"I could arrest you," I said.

"For what?"

"Harassment."

"Moi?" He pressed fingertips against his chest. "I thought you offered to give me a ride."

"I didn't."

"You gave Gan a ride."

"I like Gan."

"You like Crow too. You like Crow, Delaney. You love Crow." He batted his eyes and widened them.

My phone rang, and I answered: "Chief Reed."

"This is Than," he began, like he often did when he was on duty.

"Hey, Than. What do you need?"

"There has been a murder."

CHAPTER EIGHT

I DIDN'T HAVE time to kick Crow out of the Jeep. He wouldn't have left if I'd asked. I made it to the scene of the crime in about two seconds flat.

"Who would kill someone here?" Crow was no longer yukking it up and being a fool. His gaze was sharp, and I knew he was looking for danger lingering in the early morning shadows.

"A killer." I swung out of the Jeep, noting that Myra was here with her cruiser, and that Than's pimp-mobile was nowhere to be seen.

The Heritage Garden was an acre of rhododendrons and iris and other flowers that had all been planted by one very clever nature sprite who had a particular knack with greenery.

It had started as a little garden around her house, but then, over the years, it had become something quite beautiful. Beautiful enough, it drew tourists who could appreciate the cool, dappled space, the hint of fragrance and green, and the quiet paths, even though it was only a few blocks away from the main street.

This wasn't one of the things Bertie had to advertise. People were automatically drawn here to delight in the ever-changing watercolor quilt of bloom and leaf and earth and sky.

I strode down the narrow path through trees and bushes and flowering plants delicate as lace.

September meant many of the blooms had already put on their best show and bowed off the stage. But it was still lush and beautiful.

I found Myra first, her arms crossed. She faced me, shaking her head. "I told him not to tell you."

"That there was a murder?"

"I told him not to tell you *that way*," Myra said. "He decided to be dramatic."

"I did no such thing," Than said, his voice just a pinch high. Offended. He was offended. "I am *never* dramatic."

"What about when I told you I found that Belleek for five bucks?"

"Thief and rascal," he accused. "You did not pay five dollars for that teacup."

"No," Myra said. "I paid four ninety-nine for that tea cup *and* saucer."

Crow snorted.

She grinned like a cat who had gotten a second bowl of cream and was drinking it out of an antique four ninety-nine tea cup.

Than turned to me, dismissing Myra's existence. "There has been a murder," he intoned.

"Show me," I said.

He glided down the path that wended between trees and bushes and stopped at a clearing.

No, not a clearing. Or at least, it wasn't supposed to

be a clearing.

"Murder." Than pointed one long, boney finger downward.

"The plants?"

"They have been killed, harvested," he said.

He wasn't wrong. Whatever bushes and plants had been here—and just offhand, it looked like a few ferns, azalea, maybe some borage and daisy—had not only been hacked down in several spots, it looked like they had been ripped out by the roots.

"Messy," Crow noted.

"So." I glanced at Myra. "Someone cut the flowers, and this—this is the murder?"

"They have been destroyed," Than said. "Eaten."

"The plants," I said one more time just to make sure we were on the same page.

"Are they not living beings?" he asked.

"I mean, yeah. Living. But murder doesn't really apply here. You know: 'unlawful killing of a person' is the sort of murder that we respond to. Not harvesting flowers."

"It was done with intent to harm," he said.

"You can tell that?" And oh, the look he gave me. "All right, you can tell that. How did you find this?"

"Jimmy called it in," Myra said.

Jimmy was one of the volunteers who kept the garden going.

"Did you get his statement?"

"I did," she said.

"And you called me here even after that?" I asked Than.

"She was speaking to the volunteer when I called."

"I know you read through the manual before you

started this job," I said. "And while you might be able to see that the plants were distressed—"

"Are distressed," he said.

"—are distressed, because you are a god—"

That was when I heard the scuff of a shoe on the concrete behind me.

"—god danged lover of nature," I covered, "this isn't a murder."

Myra moved over to block whoever had just walked up on us. "This is a restricted area," she said.

I knew, I just *knew* who it was going to be before I turned.

"I was hoping I could get an action shot." Patrick Baum held his phone horizontally—already filming?

"Sure," I said, stepping aside so he could get a look at the crime.

"That's real Baum of you, Chief Reed," he said, working his catch phrase into the conversation. "What am I looking at?" he asked, as he panned the area.

"A garden," Than offered.

"But what crime are you investigating? Who got killed? Where is the body?"

"You're standing on it," Than said.

To his credit, Patrick kept the phone steady as he rabbit-hopped backward several feet. "What?" He scanned the ground, then his gaze came up to me.

It was not a happy sort of gaze.

"We're investigating who stole the bushes," I said.

"And flowers," Myra added.

"And flowers," I agreed.

He lowered the phone. "I thought there was a murder."

"Who did you hear that from?" I asked.

"From you. I was going to film here, and saw the cruiser and your Jeep. I wanted to see what Ordinary's police were doing in the garden."

"Policing," Than said.

"Most of our crimes are misdemeanors," I said for him, and for his audience behind the camera. "Ordinary is a safe place. We have a lot of visitors who stop in for our beautiful beaches and our wonderful festivals."

He lowered the camera and tipped his chin. "Nice advertisement you got in there."

"Was it real *Baum* of me?" I asked.

He shook his head. "I'm not here to hassle you. This is going to make a good segment. It's going to make Ordinary look good. Can I film you processing the scene of the crime?"

"No. It might be small, but this is still a crime scene," I said. "We aren't done taking our own pictures. You need to leave until we're finished."

"I'll be quiet as a mouse."

"Perfect." Myra tapped his arm. "All rodents are required to wait in the parking lot until we're done. I'll escort you. Right this way."

"You want to say that on camera, officer?" He pointed the camera at her face.

"Sure. We need you to step back to the parking area until we clear the scene. It's right this way."

He swung the phone toward Than and me, then settled on Crow. "Why is he here? He's not police."

"I am an expert on the native flora and fauna," Crow said, leaning a little extra hard on his accent. "I am also a native son of this land."

I didn't think he needed to lay it on that heavy, but

from the considering look on Patrick's face, he'd played it right.

"This way." Myra tugged his sleeve.

That finally got him moving, and the two of them walked off. Their voices mingled, then he chuckled. Myra was good at diffusing situations.

"Have you gotten pictures of this?" I asked Than.

"Yes, as has Myra."

"Okay, give me a minute." I studied the space, took a few photos of my own, and circled the crime scene with an eye for how someone would have arrived, and how they would have left with a pile of greenery—some of it large, heavy bushes—without anyone seeing them.

"Did Jimmy see anything?"

"He saw the missing plants."

"No security cameras?"

"No."

"Jimmy was the first one in this morning?"

"Yes."

"All right, let's walk the exits and see if we can find anything. Than, Crow, go that way, I'll cover the west exit."

Whoever, or since this was Ordinary, *whatever* had taken the plants had been in a hurry. The soft ground was churned up, as if there had been a lot of traffic. It was possible Jimmy had done his fair share of stomping around before Than and Myra arrived.

Bits of leaves and twigs scattered the otherwise well-groomed lawn, leaving a trail like breadcrumbs leading the way out of the forest. I stopped in front of the west gate. A smashed pile of freshly murdered daisies were clumped to the left, a few discarded fern fronds to the right.

And right there in the soft mud near the front of the gate was a footprint.

No, not a footprint. A hoof print. A very small, pony-sized hoof print.

Xtelle.

"You little jerk," I said. I didn't know why she would be mincing around stealing shrubbery, but it was exactly the kind of thing she'd do.

I snapped a few pictures of the print and found another print, this one from a cloven hoof. Avnas had been here too.

"Morning, Chief," Jimmy said from behind me.

Jimmy was the kind of old guy who still dressed the way he had in high school. For him that meant high-waisted denim cuffed at the hem, a plaid shirt buttoned all the way up and tucked behind a belt with a shiny buckle.

"Morning, Jimmy. Sorry about the plants. Looks like our vandals went this way."

"Yeah, I thought so too. This wasn't here yesterday." He pointed at the sad pile of daisies.

"Are those deer prints?" he asked.

"I think so," I lied. Jimmy was a human and wasn't going to believe that a demon pretending to be a unicorn pretending to be a pony, and her boyfriend demon pretending to be a miniature bull, had broken in and stomped on his flowers.

"Took out a lot of foliage," he said. "A darn shame."

"Might be elk," I said. "Maybe a herd. They've been around town lately."

"Sure, sure. That can happen. We just don't have fences high enough. I've been saying we should have fences high enough."

"At least they moved through before they did any more damage," I said.

He nodded. "We'll make do. It was time we thinned that area anyway. I just need to fix it up before we open for the day. Thanks for coming out, Delaney."

"Any time. Oh, and how much do you think it would cost to replace those plants?"

He sucked on his teeth and rocked back on his heels. "Couple hundred, I'd think. Why?"

"I'll talk to a few people I know. See if I can get them to pitch in some donations toward it."

"That'd be fine. Real fine. You think they would?"

"I can be very persuasive."

We made our way back to the scene of the crime where Than and Crow were waiting. Jimmy gave us a wave, and headed off to the tool shed, obviously wanting to get to fixing the area.

"Our cover story is elk," I said.

"Elk," Than said, "and not the demons."

"What about demons?" I asked.

"Xtelle and Avnas murdered the plants."

"Why didn't you tell me that when I got here?"

"You did not ask."

Crow laughed.

I inhaled, exhaled clinging to my calm. "You could have saved me some time if you'd just told me."

"And yet was this not good practice for the murder mystery?" Than said.

"No. I don't need practice. I'm a detective. I already know how to solve crimes, especially when my own officers don't withhold relevant data from me."

"Ah," he said. "I see."

I just shook my head. "Let's go deal with Baum."

Patrick and Myra were in the parking lot, Patrick's phone aimed in our direction, filming our approach.

"Looks like it was elk," I said. "Happens every once in a while. They come through, get spooked by traffic or something, and take refuge overnight here in the garden. Unfortunately, they had the munchies."

"I thought it might be something like that," Myra said. "Wasn't I just telling you about the wildlife that sometimes wanders through town?"

"You mentioned bears and cougars," Patrick said.

"Add elk to the list," I said. "That's it. Sorry to disappoint." I gave the camera a smile, and started toward my Jeep.

He dropped his phone into his pocket. "Look, I know I came on a little strong yesterday. But I really would like to have coffee with you. Sometime today would be great, but anytime you have free works for me."

"If you want to know more about Ordinary's history, or our events and festivals, you really should talk to Bertie. She's a spectacular organizer, and honestly, Ordinary wouldn't be the same without her. She's the reason our little town is such a fun place to visit."

"You don't have to hard sell me, Chief," he said. "I'll talk to her too. Of course I will. But I would like to hear what it's like to be a small town cop in a modern world. Small towns like this are sort of a...well, not a time capsule, but they are outside the normal world, or they seem to be. I'd love your perspective on how your town adapts or tries to resist forces so much larger than it is."

Was he talking about gods and demons? Was he talking about social unrest? The economy? Climate change?

I opened my mouth to ask, but my phone rang. "I'll let you know when I'm free."

"One o'clock? Lunch?" he pressed.

I held up a finger and put the phone to my ear. "Chief Reed."

"Hey, Delaney," Hogan said. "I'm sorry I didn't call yesterday, I got busy, like, really busy, and I didn't think about it again until now."

"No worries." I moved to my Jeep, ignoring Patrick, who was filming again.

Both Than and Crow headed to the passenger side of my vehicle and reached the door at the same time.

Crow grabbed the handle, and Than placed his hand over the top of Crow's. The two gods glared at each other.

"Than, you're with me," I said over the top of my phone. "Crow, could you show Mr. Baum your studio and explain our Find and Keep glass float treasure hunt weekends?"

Than didn't smile in victory, but he did look smug. Crow rolled with the punches and turned on the used car salesman charm.

"Happy to, Chief. Mr. Baum? Can I call you Patrick? Paddy? Pat? Have you ever blown your own balls?"

"Uh..." Patrick didn't have a quick answer for that one.

"Well, then," Crow said, "you are in for a hot, sweaty, glory-hole treat!" Crow slapped him on the shoulder hard enough it had to sting.

I got into the Jeep. Than was already buckling his seatbelt.

"Sorry, Hogan," I said, starting the engine. "What were you saying?"

"You asked me to tell you what Patrick Baum might be. What kind of supernatural."

"Right." I backed out of the parking space. "So what is he?"

"A leprechaun."

I glanced over at Patrick. Crow was gesturing lewdly with his hands, explaining his glass-blowing technique, but Patrick was watching me. He gave me a little half-bow, then held up his finger and mouthed: *one o'clock*.

"Did you hear me?" Hogan asked.

"Yes," I said. "Leprechaun. Are you sure?"

Patrick didn't look like a leprechaun. We'd had one in town once, Siofra, a lovely woman who hosted wicked poker games, but otherwise stayed to herself and her garden. She had been small of stature, not even five feet tall, had thick auburn hair, and a green glow in her eyes that meant she always wore sunglasses when she went out in public.

I'd never met a male leprechaun in person. So maybe they did come in tall, handsome, young-ish, blond, social-influencer packages.

"I am sure," Hogan said. "He's got some affect on luck too, I think. Good and bad. He was at my shop, having a good time, and then a guy showed up who had just won a small lottery. The guy bought everyone donuts on the house. The crowd who gathered cleaned me out."

"Okay," I said, slotting that information. "Thank you. How did the rest of his visit go?"

"Great. Best money I've made in a day all year. On a *Tuesday*. In September."

I drove away from little parking area and noted eight cars lined up to turn into the garden parking lot. Six of them carried out-of-state license plates.

Tourists. Half a dozen coming to the garden on a Wednesday. It wasn't unheard of, but we usually didn't see an influx of people until the weekends. Was Baum and his luck already drawing them here?

"Thanks again," I said. "Say, Hogan. Where is Xtelle right now?"

"In the yard at my house. Why? What did she do?"

"That's what I'm going to find out."

CHAPTER NINE

Hogan's house was long and narrow, which put his backyard a good distance away from the road and prying eyes. Just like he'd said, Xtelle was in the yard, staring over the fence like a normal little palomino pony.

What broke the illusion was the look in her eyes that made it clear she was sizing up the world to see how much of it she could sell for spare parts.

Xtelle didn't usually spend time in the yard, preferring the extra bedroom she'd taken over inside the house. But since she'd insisted on remaining in the shape of a pony—an odd choice for the ex-queen of demons —she was supposed to act like a pony.

She had, so far, been terrible at it.

Than and I made our way to the backyard. Xtelle's head stuck out over the fence, her body mostly invisible behind the wooden slats.

"Hey, Xtelle," I said, looking around for Avnas, who had chosen the form of a very small black bull with very wide, sharp horns.

He was nowhere to be seen.

"I need to ask you a few questions."

She flicked her ears back and showed me her teeth. "You said you don't want me to talk," she said through clenched jaws.

"We've been over this," I said. "A lot. You know the rules. And you know when it's okay to talk. Like right now when no one can hear us."

Her lips flopped over her teeth, but her ears stayed cocked back.

"I know why you're here, copper," she said. "I regret nothing. Nothing!"

"All right. Noted. Why am I here?"

"Because you know I..." Her ears flicked forward, then straight up. "Oh," she said, her tone contrite. "Delaney, you kidder you. I was just...acting. Yes. Acting. I've been given the starring role in the unsolved crime theater and have been practicing my part. End scene." She lifted a leg, and executed a bow, tail held high.

"Wasn't I wonderful? Of course I was! And you. You must feel so special to have seen my performance. This is the most awe-inspiring day of your life. All that you have known before pales in comparison. You realize your life has been nothing before this. Go ahead. Weep."

"You're in the murder mystery?"

"I am the star!" She tossed her head, and her shiny mane glowed in the sunlight.

"Uh-huh. Where's Avnas?" I asked.

"I'm sure he's around here somewhere." She minced away from the fence backward, keeping her eyes on me as she retreated.

"Good-bye Delaney. You are welcome for that life-changing experience. I understand how you must now go and reassess everything you've done with your years to this point. Good-bye. Good-bye."

She pivoted and trotted toward the back door.

"Xtelle! I'm not done talking with you." I strode over to the gate, then crossed the backyard. "Stop," I ordered. "Right there."

She paused on the patio, her hoof lifted to open the back door. Then she dropped her hoof, and I noted the mud on it, even though Hogan's yard was not muddy.

"Fine. One photo. But the autograph is fifty dollars. I knew fame would ruin my private life. Now I'm being harangued. Bullied. Ordered around by dirty photo-popping sharks out to make the glossy pages of every greasy celebrity magazine."

"I am not a paparazzi. Where were you this morning at sunrise?"

"I was in my bed. Queens such as I do not rise before the sun. It gives us wrinkles."

"Is there anyone who can attest to you being here in bed?"

"No. Hogan holds horrendously early hours at his shop. I was all alone." Her lip wobbled and fake tears glossed the bottoms of her eyes. "So very alone."

"Was Avnas not present?" Than asked. He had pulled out a little notebook that looked an awful lot like the one Myra kept on her.

"He was...busy. I'm sure." She inched toward the door again.

"What was he doing that early in the morning?" I asked.

"Oh, I don't know. Walking. Roaming. What is it humans do outside before dawn? *Jopping*?"

"Jogging," I told her. "Avnas was out jogging. In bull form."

"Really, Delaney, why are you asking me? It's like you're obsessed with him. Avnas this, Avnas that." She gasped, and her mouth fell open. She pressed her hoof to her chest.

"You're in love with him!" she said.

"I am not in love with him."

"You *are*. Why else would you show up here and demand of me, his one and only love, what he was doing in the morning? Was he with you? Did you lure my man away?"

She drew her head up and back, wrinkling her neck so it looked like she had triple chins.

"You floozy! You keep your Delaney mitts off of my man!"

I crossed my arms over my chest. "Xtelle. I have no interest in your man. You can drop the outrage. Where is he right now?"

"You *are* in love with him. You're going to take him and leave me alone. Bereft. And I will have no choice but to steal *your* man. Tell me, what size of wedding dress do you wear, because I am going to buy the exact same one and wear it to *my* wedding to Ryder..." she made a little gagging sound. "...Bailey." She shuddered.

"The demon, Avnas," Than said. "Tell us where he is. Now."

It wasn't loud. It wasn't even all that unfriendly. It was, however, a command.

Xtelle stilled, and the drama-queen facade fell away, leaving the shrewd, calculating glimmer of demon queen in her eyes.

"You think you can command me?" she asked.

"Having dropped your powers off to be stored on the shelf with other, cheap powers, like discount jars of pickles? You think you can command me to bow to your will? You are no god to me, Thanatos. Go fly a kite."

"Xtelle," he said, even more quietly. "Truth is required. These are Ordinary's rules."

He didn't have power to wield. Not god power. He could tap into magic if he wanted, but this wasn't that either. This was just...age, I thought. Aeons of him carrying the power of death, the finality of life.

It was heavy, weighting the air, as if the corners of the sky had been gathered into his fist and cinched tight.

"We're asking as law enforcement," I added. "You need to answer us."

She narrowed her eyes, and the heat in her gaze was all demon. Then she blinked and once again appeared as innocent as a unicorn disguised as a pony. "He's in the house."

Than leaned back, just a fraction, and the oppressive weight in the air lifted. A light breeze stirred the warming day, and I swear the sun got just a little brighter.

"Lead the way to him," Than said.

Xtelle tossed her mane again. "This is private property."

"Hogan told me I can enter his house any time I need to," I told her. "Open the door."

She snorted and grumbled, and I caught more than one creative curse word as she stomped over to the sliding glass door, opened it, then galloped into the house.

"Avnas!" she yelled. "Hide the weed!"

I got to the door before Than, and followed Xtelle

down the hall. She was making good time, her hooves clacking like canastas. She reached the room she'd taken over as her own and shouldered open the door.

I was right behind her. I thought she was going to slam the door in my face, but she left it open.

"This better not be a trap," I said, strolling into the room.

The scene was not what I expected. The last time I had been in Xtelle's room, it had been wall-to-wall mirrors and clashing tones of red and pink velvet and satin.

She'd done some interior decorating since then. So much so, that I had to pause just inside the door to orient myself.

The room had been divided into four quadrants. One section was familiar: the bed, the mirrors, the layers upon layers of pink and red velvet and lace. Another section of the room was set up in what looked like a tropical beach: sand on the floor, a hammock, fake palm trees, and the wall painted in what could be considered a sunset.

The other corner of the room was a sort of office: desk, chairs, and shelves all painfully white and clearly put together from flat packs.

But the last section of the room was a crime scene. It had been done up like a forest. That wall was painted dark green, sawdust was sprinkled across the rug, and a tree stump was propped up like a chair. Next to that was a stone—large enough I knew she hadn't gotten it in through the door without using magic. All around that were plants: some ordinary sword ferns and fir branches, a few clumps of salal, and one crooked-looking rose bush.

But amongst all that, planted and arranged so they created a throne out of the boulder in the middle of them, were heritage plants. Several rhododendron bushes, azaleas, lilies, ferns, and daisies.

All of them stolen from the garden.

It took me a minute to get a grip on what I was looking at—and I still wasn't sure that grip was all that tight. While I was staring, Xtelle and Avnas were shoving greenery into the closet.

"You can't catch us, copper!" Xtelle tossed over her shoulder. "We don't even know where any of this came from. Push, Avnas, push!"

"I am pushing, my queen."

"Okay, you two," I said. "Knock it off."

Both demons turned their backs on the closet and faced me.

"Delaney!" Xtelle said, in a sugar-drenched voice. "I didn't see you there. What a lovely surprise. Your hair is so…there."

"Have you become more youthful?" Avnas asked. "You look more youthful than last I saw you."

"You want to tell me why you have the plants that were stolen from the Heritage Garden in your bedroom?"

"This isn't my bedroom," Xtelle said.

"It looks like your bedroom."

"Have a little imagination, Delaney. This is my bedoffistudiocation room. They're all the rage. Work from home, play from home, vacation and create art from home."

"Bedoffistudiocation room," I said.

"All the rage."

"Yeah, I'm not calling it that. Why are the stolen plants here?"

"Where else would I keep them?" she asked. "If I put them in Hogan's boring bedroom, he'd ruin them."

"You stole them."

She scoffed. "I did no such thing."

"My queen," Avnas said, "as your bedoffistudiocation assistant, perhaps you will allow me to speak to the Reed on your behalf."

"Yes. Explain it to her."

Avnas took a few steps forward, tipped his bull head up, and met my gaze. "She did no such thing," he said solemnly.

"There were hoof prints at the scene of the crime. Hooves I believe will match Xtelle's. There were also prints left by a bull. A miniature bull. The prints were fresh. What were they, Than?"

"Fresh."

"Fresh. And we drove right over here. Only to find mud on Xtelle's hooves, mud on your hooves, and the exact plants which were stolen on display in this room. Unless you have some proof someone else did this, I'd say this case is open and shut. You are both going to be charged with trespassing and destruction of property, which carries a monetary fine, jail time, or both."

"You would dare lock up this magnificence?" Xtelle demanded.

"It was I," Avnas interrupted. Then, in a voice meant for stage, "I gathered unto my breast, the most precious shrubs, flowers of great beauty, and fragile blossoms to bestow upon my one true love. Even so, these rare plants fade to ash under the sunlight of my queen's beauty."

Xtelle made a little gasping sound.

"If I am to be jailed for love," he went on, "so be it. If I am to be pierced by debt, shackled, degraded for my devotion, then I offer my flesh, my muscle, my bone to your cruel mortal punishment."

He stretched one leg out and bowed over it, his head and horns sweeping downward.

"Bravo," Xtelle called, clapping her little front hooves together. "Oh, bravo!"

"No," I said over her, "not bravo. You just admitted to committing a crime, Avnas. This is serious. This is the kind of thing I can throw you out of Ordinary for."

He straightened from his bow. "I understand. Perhaps a bribe is in order then?"

"No." I rubbed at my forehead. "Bribery is another crime, Avnas. You're just digging yourself in deeper here."

"Huh. Well, I've admitted to the crime. Now how shall we proceed? Perhaps I will simply tip you a few hundred dollars to look the other way? Wink. Wink."

"Still a crime. Why did you take the plants?"

"I don't understand the question."

"Why did you steal these plants from the Heritage Garden?"

"Pardon?"

"Let me give it a try," Xtelle said, pushing forward. "Speak cleeer-ly, Deeee-laney."

"All right, if you won't talk to me here, I'll just take you both to jail and lock you up."

"The boring jail?" Xtelle asked through pursed lips.

"No. The magic jail. Which will hold you both. You might remember it, Avnas, since I've already locked you up there once."

"Perhaps you should also be reminded," Than said, "that there are only three chances one may have to 'misunderstand' the laws of Ordinary. And then one will be banished for all time."

Xtelle and Avnas both stilled. Then they looked at each other. I didn't know if they could speak telepathically, but it was possible since they both nodded and looked back at me in tandem.

"We would not speak of this in other circumstances," Avnas said. "You must understand our discretion is of the highest caliber."

"All right."

"The plants are for…the main event."

I shook my head. "That doesn't mean anything to me."

"Of course it doesn't," Xtelle said. "You have no culture. Just look at the trousers you're wearing. The main event," she trotted over to the rock and stump and greenery, "is my acting debut. Yes, you may applaud."

She set one hoof on the rock and lifted her head, striking a pose.

"The murder mystery?" I asked.

"In which I am the *star*," she said.

"Does Bertie know you are the star?" Than asked.

"I have sent her a memo," Xtelle sniffed. "I am the star. Let me give you a sample of my greatness. Neigh, neigh. Nicker, nicker." She flounced around between the greenery, throwing what were either suggestive glances or expressions of indigestion our way.

"I don't think you're supposed to say the words," I said. "Ponies don't say 'nicker.'"

"Line!" she yelled.

Avnas produced pages of a script from some pocket

151

he must have in his bull shape. I really didn't want to know where that pocket might be. "One lonely pony…"

"One lonely pony," Xtelle repeated, "stands in a field. Nibbling the greenery." Xtelle lowered her head to the uprooted rhododendron and made fake eating motions. "Nibble, nibble."

"You're not supposed to say—" I said.

"Nibble, nibble!" she repeated louder.

"If the pony had heard the murderer, she showed no signs," Avnas said.

Xtelle lifted her head and widened her eyes, giving a silly vacuous look, as if she didn't have a single brain in all the world.

"And scene," Avnas said softly, as if he were afraid to disturb her moment.

"For the love of—" I began.

Than clapped his hands twice. "Adequate," he judged.

"Adequate?" Xtelle lifted her nose. "You may leave."

Than did not leave.

"Okay, this is what we're going to do," I said. "I'm going to charge you both with trespassing and destruction of property. You will donate five hundred dollars to the Heritage Garden, so they can replace what you took."

"Five!"

"Which will not be stolen funds, but money you have earned here in Ordinary."

She made an offended sound.

"And if you do so in the next three months, I will not throw you in jail for what you did. Do you understand what you've done is wrong?"

Xtelle kicked at one of the plants. "If you say so."

"I say so. Do you understand, Avnas?"

"I do."

"You also owe five hundred dollars to the Heritage Garden. Money you've earned."

"Very well," he said.

"You stink," Xtelle said.

"I don't care what you say to me. The fine stands."

"No, you stink. You smell." She lifted her nose and made a big show of sniffing the air, then pulling her horsey head back and rolling her eyes. "Leprechaun. Eww."

"What do you know about leprechauns?"

"I'll tell you if you pay me five hundred dollars."

I couldn't help it. I laughed. "I'll give you my undivided attention."

She camped back on one foot, which pushed her butt out to one side. "You've been around one, haven't you?"

"Yes."

"Hogan was around one."

It wasn't a question, but I answered anyway. "Yes."

"There's one in town. I thought so. They bring luck. Good luck, bad luck, mostly luck that goes their way."

"They fall into contracts too easily," Avnas added. "They assume everything will always work out in their favor so they will sign anything you put in front of them."

"Do demons make contracts with leprechauns a lot?" I asked.

They both winced like I'd just squirted lemon juice in their eyes.

"No," Xtelle said. "Not because leprechauns are

smarter or stronger. But luck follows them. They stink of it."

"Also, everything works out in their favor," Avnas said. "They are very lucky. Even when they're unlucky."

Xtelle nodded. "They are not a good bet for the concerns of demons."

"Do most leprechauns know they're leprechauns?" I asked.

"Yes."

"Always? Is there a chance someone could be a leprechaun and not know it?"

They exchanged a look again.

"No?" Avnas said, then stronger, "No. Unless for some reason it is luckier for them not to know?"

"I don't think…" Xtelle mused.

"No," Avnas said firmly. "Leprechauns know their nature."

"Thank you, that's helpful."

"Who is it?" Xtelle asked. "Which leprechaun is here?"

"Patrick Baum."

Xtelle's mouth fell open. "Road Bomb? He's *here*? But he only goes to wonderful, amazing places. Why is he in Ordinary? Did you kidnap him? Oh, that is *so* like you, Delaney. Trapping a delightful man like Road Bomb in this dreary little town."

"One, I didn't trap him. I didn't even know who he was. Two, Bertie brought him here to give Ordinary some good press."

"He reviewed Boring, my queen," Avnas said.

Xtelle chuckled. "I see. This is a war between Valkyries. Isn't that so very… *traditional* of them? A battle over two terrible little towns no one wants anyway. Dead bodies everywhere."

"No, no dead bodies everywhere," I said. "This is for the publicity, for the fame. No blood will be spilled."

"If you don't think advertising kills, Delaney, dear, you obviously haven't played the game."

"Knock, knock!" Myra's voice called out from the back door. "Delaney, are you here?"

"In the guest room."

"Bedoffistudiocation room," Xtelle shouted.

I shook my head. "That's never going to catch on."

"What, like umbrella hats? Oh, yes, don't look so surprised. I heard about that little bet you lost to Crow. Tricksters are a lot like leprechauns. Things tend to go their way in the end too."

"Hey," Myra said, taking in the scene a lot quicker than I had. "So you found our plant murderers?"

"Yes. They've admitted to it and are going to pay a fine. What's up?"

"You need to come in and handle some paperwork on those people who attacked you."

"Attack?" Xtelle asked. "Was it because of your choice in trousers? It was because of your choice in trousers."

"My trousers are fine. Some people made a deal with some demons, and tried to kill me." I said it like this sort of thing happened every day. It didn't. But other weird stuff did happen every day around here. I was sort of immune to the stress of being attacked by regular people, demon contract or no demon contract.

"Which demons?" Xtelle asked. She was suddenly very serious, even if she still appeared to be a small pony standing among drooping stolen shrubbery in a bedoffis-tudiocation room.

"My guess? Your ex."

"Why would he want you killed? I mean...your trouser choices, maybe."

"I haven't had the chance to ask him, and the people he sent aren't talking. I suppose it has something to do with Ordinary being the kind of place that will stand between him and the mortal world if he decides to wage war.

"Or, it could be you divorcing him, Avnas abandoning him, and Bathin hiding from him for years. Oh, and maybe his other son, Goap, wanting to kill him and take the throne."

"Still," she said. "You?"

"I might have just been the easy target. Since I allow people in and out of Ordinary, it might have just been his way of making it easier to get to someone else."

From the very shrewd look on her face, she knew exactly who the king of hell was most angry with—the demons hiding out in town: Bathin, Avnas, and of course, her.

"So if you have any information on any of that, I'd love to hear it," I said.

"If I do, I'll tell you. They were human, though? Just human?"

"Yes. Contracted to demons, but just human."

"Very well. Do go away, Delaney. I have to finish decorating my bedoffistudiocation room so that I may take the social media by storm!"

"That's what this is for?" Myra asked. "You know you can't be a pony posting online," she said.

"Of course I can be a pony. I'll create a fake person

who 'owns' me and likes to take beautiful pictures of me being beautiful."

"And you're doing this because?" I asked.

"Apparently I need to earn money to pay the fines imposed upon me for temporarily borrowing common shrubbery. Go away. All of you." She waved her nose toward the door, then she and Avnas shoved at the bushes, moving them around.

Myra looked and me and raised her eyebrows. "Okay, so this is a thing now?"

"Apparently. Don't forget about the fines, either of you. And if you take anything from private property again, it won't just be a fine you'll be paying. Do you understand?"

"Go be boring somewhere else. You'll get your money."

We left them to it, and I waited until we were in the backyard. "Did you ask Bathin about the attack?"

Myra nodded. "He didn't know the people. As far as he can tell, they are just humans who stumbled into a deal where they thought if they kidnapped you, they'd get paid."

"Neat." We made our way around to the driveway where we'd both parked. I frowned. "Lots of traffic for a Wednesday," I noted.

"It's Patrick. Someone leaked a video of him saying he was going to be filming here. Ever since then, there's been a pretty steady stream of cars coming through."

"Do we need to put more people on traffic?" I asked.

"I don't think so," she said. "It's not that bad yet. You coming into the station?"

"I have to go see Bertie first. Angry Valkyries wait

DEVON MONK

for no man. Or woman, apparently." I gave her a wave and strode back to my Jeep, Than beside me.

BERTIE PERCHED BEHIND HER DESK, her sharp, bright orange nails clicking on the smooth dark wood.

"Sorry I'm late," I said.

She glanced up at Than. "You may close the door."

He raised one eyebrow, but turned and did as the Valkyrie commanded.

She waited until the door latched, then sat back with a small grunt. "You've seen the list of festivals already. I have made a few changes I want to run by you."

"All right." I sat in the only available chair, spinning the folder on the desk toward me. "I notice you're not asking my permission."

"Nor would I, as it is not your place to coordinate the events. Unless you would like me to create a larger role of involvement for you in the ongoing festivities?"

"Nope. I am all the involved I prefer to be."

"Mr. Baum has offered us the honor of sponsoring some of his videos. In return he would create extra footage."

I glanced over the events and didn't see any change drastic enough to get me involved with it. I pushed the folder away. "Why am I really here?"

"Have you seen his reporting on Boring?"

"No."

She nodded, her lips pressed tightly together. "Let me show you."

She typed on the keyboard next to her, then turned the screen so I could see the paused video.

She pressed play.

Patrick Baum had a snappy intro flashing pictures of him posing in all sorts of places, with all sorts of animals and food. He looked like he was having a rollicking time, and unlike some of the other people doing videos like this, it looked sincere.

Man might be handsome in person but he positively oozed charm over the camera. From the opening, it cut right to the ENTERING BORING highway sign. Patrick pretended to fall asleep as soon as he crossed the city line.

The rest of the clip or stream or whatever it was called was fun, funny, and over quickly, with a promise for more.

I immediately wanted to see the next one.

"That," Bertie said, "is our problem. He loved Boring. It's gotten more likes and hits and attention than any other series he's made."

"Boo?" I said. "Boring sucks?"

"That is not the point. The point is, if he likes our town, we will, for some time, anyway, receive a lot of extra attention. If he hates Ordinary, we will receive hate tourists."

I raised my hand.

"Yes, Delaney, they are a thing, put your hand down. And if we receive hate tourists, it is very possible we will lose tourists."

"Too many of the wrong tourists and we'll lose tourists? Am I following your logic?"

She flattened her palms on the desk and glared at me like I was just too annoying for words.

"I have a...wager. With Robyn."

I waited because this was why she had asked me here.

"By the end of the year, we will tally the attendance of our events. Whoever falls short will move."

"Move?"

"Yes. Move to the other's town. And work for her."

The way she said the last part, it sounded like a fate worse than, well, worse than whatever a Valkyrie hated most.

"If Robyn loses she comes here and works for you?"

"Yes." The glint in her eyes was a sword's edge.

"If you lose, you go work for her?"

"Yes." The sword edge dulled.

"For how long?"

"A year."

"Okay. So we really want to win this."

She hesitated, and that surprised me.

"We want to win this don't we, Bertie?"

"I'd rather not work for my sister. I'd rather not live in Boring."

"But?" I asked.

"But there is some risk of winning bringing too much attention to Ordinary. As you pointed out, the gods do vacation here."

"Sure, and there are plenty of supernaturals, some more discreet than others. But we've always made it work. We'll make it work this time too, win or lose."

"Hogan told me what Patrick Baum is," she said.

"Yeah, he told me too. A leprechaun."

She studied me. "That doesn't worry you?"

I shrugged. "I'd rather deal with a leprechaun than the king of hell. Patrick might have some magic and some charm. Some influence on luck—good and bad—but we've had our share of all of that and still managed to keep this place on its feet."

Bertie glanced at Than, and he made a low humming sound.

"You've never met a leprechaun, have you?" Bertie asked. "I forget sometimes how young you are." Then, to Than, "She's very young."

"Yes," he agreed. "Very."

I rolled my eyes. "Joke's on you. I met Siofra when I was a child. So I have met a leprechaun."

"Yes, but she lived in Ordinary," Bertie said. "She followed our rules."

"All right. Explain to the youngster why I should be worried about a leprechaun."

"Magic, most of it, nearly all of it, will not affect a leprechaun," Bertie said. "They are protected by their inherent luck."

"Is that a problem?"

"It will make him a very difficult enemy to defeat," she said.

"We don't need to make him our enemy. Look," I said standing. "I think you're getting ahead of the issue. If he loves Ordinary as much as he should, we're totally going to get more people attending our events than Boring. Robyn will come here, work for you, problem solved.

"If he hates Ordinary, then you will throw some fantastic festivals, and we will still beat Robyn. We have a wonderful town, exciting events, plus the ocean and other natural beauty that Boring simply does not have.

"If, for some reason, you do have to go to Boring for a year, we will keep the home fires burning. Robyn will be damn lucky to have you, and we will demand she give you back on the three-hundred sixty-fifth day at midnight, or we will launch a war against her territory."

Bertie's cheeks had gone a little pink as if she were overcome with emotion. She looked away and swallowed before answering.

"Yes," she said. "Of course. *I'm* not the one concerned for the outcome. But since you may not have understood what we are working with, nor what was at stake, I thought it best to bring you here and inform you."

"Sure," I said. She had to have been a little concerned about it all, from the tension draining from her shoulders.

"I appreciate you keeping me in the loop. Is there anything I can do to help with the upcoming event?"

"The murder mystery? No, that's fine. I have all the actors hired and the venues prepped. Really, Delaney, if you wanted to be helpful, you would have offered months ago."

"I did offer months ago. You told me it would be too close to my wedding, then said something like you needed people who would be focused and committed to the mystery, not daydreaming about a honeymoon."

"That does sound exactly like what I'd say," she agreed. "And my decision stands. Please leave. I have a lot of work to do."

I pointed at the open folder. "You sure you don't need me to sign off on any of that?"

"Good-bye, Delaney. If you make time to have coffee with Mr. Baum, please remind his viewers that we have weekly events, rain or shine."

She was already working on her keyboard, having spun the screen so she could see it again.

"Can do. Bye, Bertie."

Than opened the door and stood aside for me to walk through.

"That was…something," I said, as we walked down the empty hallway, our footsteps echoing back to us. "Did you sign up for the murder mystery?"

"Yes," Than said. "I did. Would you care to guess if I am the murderer?"

I shouldered open the door and shot him a look. "You're totally the murderer."

"Yes," he repeated, pleased. "Of course I am."

"You're lying."

"Of course I am."

"Be that way. Is she making you dress up?"

"Dress up?"

"You know, put on a costume?"

"She informed me that it would not be needed."

I paused at the driver side of the Jeep. "What part are you playing?"

"The coroner."

I grinned. "Please wear one of your brightest Hawaiian shirts with matching socks and sandals."

"From the delight you exhibit, I can only assume I should not wear such a thing."

"Oh, no," I said, getting into the Jeep. "You totally should."

Than shut the door. "I will consider it."

"The play is in a couple days, right?"

"It begins Saturday and is repeated Sunday."

"Huh. What's gonna keep someone from going to it several times and spoiling the plot?"

"I am assured the murderer will be different in each performance."

"So you really might be the killer."

"Murderer, Reed Daughter. As it is a murder mystery, not a killing puzzle."

"Noted. Maybe I'll be in the audience one of those nights."

"Perhaps. Or perhaps you will be preparing for your nuptials."

I sighed. "Yeah, probably."

"Are you not giddy with pleasure at your impending marital union?"

"So giddy."

"I sense sarcasm."

I sighed again. "There's a lot to do still, and it both feels like it's never going to happen and like it's been going on forever."

"You have chosen the dress."

"Yes, but there's the bachelorette party my sisters have been trying to keep a secret from me, and then we have to do the rehearsal dinner. Who needs a whole dinner to rehearse a wedding? And we're doing that this Friday, so by the time we get to the ceremony a week after, everyone will have forgotten their parts anyway."

He was silent, and I felt a little silly having unloaded on him like that. Than was, of all the gods, a little slower to adapt to human behavior.

Things, like a bride having herself a little bitch session—when she should be happy to have family, friends, and an amazing fiancé in her life who were all willing to put together the wedding of her dreams—sometimes took him a little longer to process.

"Perhaps one could elope?" he offered.

I huffed a laugh. "One could, but one's husband-to-be would likely throttle one in one's sleep."

"Then perhaps one shall have coffee and endure?"

Since we were coming up on Ordinary's only coffee drive-through, I hit my indicator and rolled into line behind one other car.

"You really are getting the hang of this human thing," I said.

He didn't even acknowledge that with an answer. He did, however, dig around in the inner breast pocket of his jacket.

"I'll pay," I said.

"Very well." But he was still digging in his pocket.

We moved up to order, and I rolled down my window.

"Hello, Delaney Reed," Talli said.

Talli had recently moved to Ordinary and had been trying different types of employment. From the moment she had arrived, it was obvious that there was some sort of history between Than and her.

I'd subtly and not-so-subtly tried to follow them around and get a look at what kind of relationship they might have. I thought they might be dating.

Myra, who spent more of her off time with Than, spelunking among the books in our family's magical library, hadn't had much luck getting info out of him either.

"Hi, Talli," I said. "I didn't know you were working here."

"Yes, it is a new position. I am enjoying it so far. Hello, Thanatos."

"Tala," he said.

"It is very nice to see you," she went on, leaning her forearms on the window ledge. The sunlight caught her dark hair, chasing threads of gold and ruby through it.

165

The sun also made her skin glow, and her burnt umber eyes go soft.

"I would like to order tea," he said. He wasn't leaning over me, but I slid my seat all the way back anyway so I could get the best view of this exchange.

Talli inched forward so she could better see him. "We have fresh strawberry and mint," she said. "Have you sampled it?"

"No."

"Would you care to?" The way she said it, the little blush that hit her cheeks and the twinkle in her eye told me there was something else being said here. Flirting. She was flirting with him.

"Yes. Please steep a full cup for me. For Delaney Reed, please prepare the drink with the most amount of whipped cream and chocolate in it. She has emotions that need soothing."

I laughed. "Hey. I don't need to soothe anything. Black coffee with cream is all I need."

"I see," she said. "Give me a moment."

She disappeared back inside the shop, and the sound of the coffee grinder covered the music playing inside.

"Perhaps you will reconsider the chocolate?" Than asked.

"No, but thank you for thinking about me. Or maybe this was just an excuse for me to drive you to see your girlfriend?"

"She is not, as you say, my girlfriend. I have said as much."

"No, you haven't. Okay, so I'll stop calling her that. What sort of relationship do the two of you actually have?"

"One you simply wouldn't understand, Reed

Daughter."

He was so prim about it, I had to turn my head to snort-laugh into my shoulder.

He grunted as if wholly unamused by my reaction. Then Talli returned to the window.

"Here you are. Would you like to pay by cash or card?"

I handed her my card, and she took it, then gave me the drinks. "Run a tip too, okay?" I said.

She nodded and got busy with the card. I handed Than his tea.

"Thank you," he said.

"Do you want to try it before we leave?" I asked.

"Why would I do that?"

"To make sure you like it."

"I am sure it will be pleasant. It has strawberries."

I didn't know that was a sure indicator of pleasant-ness, but nodded.

"Here is your card," Talli handed it to me.

"Thanks," I said. "You have a nice——"

"Light of the Dawn," Than said, and there was warmth in his voice, but it was also strained as if he were very new to the operation of his brain and needed to keep his eyes on the prize just to get the words out.

"Yes, uh," I said. "Have a nice light of the dawn."

"No," Than said. He bent just enough so he could easily see her, and she could easily see him. "Light of the Dawn." He extended his hand.

That man had arms. Long, long arms. He easily reached across me so that his hand was out my window.

In his hand was a very small, bright yellow, folded origami box. Sticking up from the box was a tiny green stalk and leaves.

"Oh," she said, eyeing the little plant. "Yes." She nodded and nodded, her eyes never leaving the offering. "Is it for me?"

"It is."

I'd thought I'd seen her smile before. But not like this. It was both delight and that little bit of awe when the gift is something that has been hoped for but never expected.

She very carefully lifted it from his hand and tried to get her smile under control without much success.

"It is very, yes," she said, "very alive."

Than didn't smile. I'd had yet to see him so much as smirk, but he did incline his head as if he were very proud of that acknowledgment. "As I said it would be."

She nodded. "Thank you. I will plant it. It will grow."

"Good," he said, drawing back. "Perhaps you will show me once it is planted."

"I will." She very carefully placed the tiny plant on a high shelf in the shop, a place where it wouldn't get bumped or hurt, then went back to work.

I waited a minute. "Is that it? Are we done?"

"We are done," Than said.

Talli gave me a short wave. "Have a good day, Chief Delaney."

"You too."

I rolled up my window and took a sip of coffee. "That's good. She's good at that. Coffee."

"Yes," Than agreed, as he lifted the cup lid and blew over the top. The air filled with the summer scent of strawberries. He closed his eyes and took a sip. "Yes, she is."

CHAPTER TEN

I STRODE into the station and found a dozen people crammed into our tiny lobby. Kelby, behind the front desk, nodded.

"Chief," she said.

"Hey, Kelby. Everything under control?"

Several people had phones in their hands. They lifted them to, I could only assume, film our conversation.

"All good, Chief. Lots of visitors today stopping in to see the little police station they heard Patrick Baum talking about. I've asked them to only linger a few minutes, take their photos and leave. So far it's been twelve people out, twelve people in kind of thing."

I gave the tourists a smile. "As long as we don't push the fire marshal's occupancy limit, that's fine with me."

I stepped into the bullpen, which was in clear eyeshot from the lobby. We were going to be working in a fish bowl today. It wasn't the best of conditions, but we'd handle it.

"Also," Myra said, addressing the crowd from where

she was seated at her desk. "Please respect that we are working. There may be confidential conversations we will not want recorded. If that happens, we will ask that you please leave quietly."

I settled at my desk and powered up my computer, ignoring the crowd. Things would have been fine if Road Bomb himself hadn't strolled into the place.

The gasps and excited babble were instant. Half the people stood and rushed toward Patrick, cameras out, the other half snapped photos as fast as they could.

"Hi there, everyone," he said, holding his camera—not his phone, but an actual camera—to give the room a slow pan. "First, I need to ask if you are all okay with me using your image on my channel."

The chorus of agreement was universal, everyone nodding, laughing, and squealing about the whole deal. He was filming, and they were taking pictures of him filming, trying to angle devices so they were in the frame with him.

"Morning, Mr. Baum," Kelby said, over the clamor. "Is there something we can do for you today? Preferably outside? I bet all these nice folks would love to get your autograph, or maybe be interviewed for your show?"

This time the gasp was synchronized. The silence was absolutely breathless with hope. One girl sat down hard and looked like she was about to faint.

"Outside is better light, and there'd be more room," Kelby pressed.

I liked how she was making the case to move the circus out of the building. She wasn't wrong about the light and room, but it would also move Patrick and his hangers-on out of the way so we could get our work done without so much attention.

"I'd be happy to sign autographs," Patrick said to the crowd, like that sort of thing happened every day, which for him, it probably did. "Unfortunately, I don't have time for interviews."

The crowd made disappointed sounds, but most of them were producing paper and pens with stunning speed.

"I know you are all my truest fans. Thank you for being here. Thank you for sharing the road with me. But you know how I roll." He winked. "I like to keep it natural. No script. Just having fun, interacting, you know..." he waved his hand between himself and the crowd, "...all of us adding our lives to the story, and all those stories connecting us, holding us tight while they set us free."

The crowd was absolutely mesmerized. Someone started clapping.

Man had charisma, and he used it like a weapon. Those people would follow him anywhere.

"Please do as the officer asked and wait for me outside. I just need a quick word with Chief Reed."

His gaze flicked to me. "Then I'll come out for photos and autographs. And hey, we'll stay away from the station from now on, right? Since this is a real working police department, and we don't want to get in the way of them taking care of the town we're exploring.

"Remember, Bombers respect the road, and all those upon it."

"And all those upon it," they repeated.

Sure, that wasn't creepy.

He gave me a look that said he could just as easily turn this crowd the other way. Tell them to stay, to do their own interviews, film, and generally disrupt us trying to get our work done.

"So, how about it Bombers? Meet you outside?"

They cleared out in seconds flat.

"If this is about lunch," I said, once the crowd was gone, "I'm open around one."

He blinked, and his eyebrows lifted. "That easy?"

"I don't know. Does one o'clock work for you?" I asked.

"No. I mean yes. That's great. Where?"

"Jump Off Jack's. It a brewery."

"I've heard of it. Perfect. I'll see you there."

He turned the camera on himself. "Hey, looks like I finally got a date with the chief of police. You know how I love a woman who can take charge."

He laughed like things always went his way, because apparently they did, and strolled out of the station.

"I'm beginning to dislike leprechauns," I muttered.

"Beginning?" Than asked.

"Tish still keeping an eye on him?" I asked Myra.

"Yep. They're outside." She pointed at the paperwork on my desk. "Finish that. As soon as the Bombers clear out, Hatter and I will escort our guests in holding out of town."

My attackers would have their day in court. But their sentencing was out of my hands. It would be taken up by the judge and court in Newport some other day.

Eventually Baum and his fans left, and Myra and Hatter got rid of the jerks in holding.

When one o'clock rolled around, I drove over to the brewery.

It was time to deal with the leprechaun.

. . .

Jump Off Jack's outdoor picnic tables were filled with tourists and the parking lot was packed. I jogged up the narrow staircase to the restaurant which was a long, rustic space above the massive brewery with windows facing the harbor.

The delicious smell of burgers and fish and chips, along with yeasty hops and something sweet, like pineapple, filled the air.

"Delaney Reed," Chris Lagon, proprietor of the establishment and our resident gilman, called out. "Pour you a beer?"

He was halfway to the kitchen, an empty tray of glasses balanced in one hand, a pitcher of water in the other. Those tattoos down his arms did a fabulous job of disguising the slight scaling of his skin.

I wasn't surprised to see him working the rush hour. He had always been hands-on with this place and his customers. It was part of what had put it and him on the must-see list of several regional magazines.

"Just a Coke, thanks," I said.

"You meeting with…" He tipped his head toward the far corner of the room and the table by the window. Patrick sat on one side of the table, Odin sat on the other. They seemed to be having a spirited, friendly conversation.

"Yep."

"Want me to throw a burger on for you?"

"Gods, please," I said. "Thank you."

He was on the move again, smooth and graceful like only a creature of the water could be.

I walked between tables occupied by unfamiliar people laughing, eating, and stealing quick glances at Patrick Baum.

Patrick stood and waved at me like I might miss him. Like I might miss the only person in the room everyone was there for. Like I might miss the camera he'd propped on a napkin holder, facing the harbor.

Footage for his show. The boats on the slips and the bay surrounded by the forested hills would be beautiful, I was sure.

I wondered what we would become once Patrick was done with us.

"Gentlemen." I pulled out the spare chair next to Odin and sat.

"Perfect timing," Patrick said. "Mr. Odin and I were just finished."

"No," Odin said. "I still have half a beer."

I knew exactly what Odin was doing. He had planted himself there to keep an eye on the leprechaun, but mostly to keep an eye on me.

"Plus I ordered lunch," Odin said. "And all the tables are full."

Patrick scanned the crowded room. The one table that had been cleared moments ago had five people sitting at it now.

"I'm fine sharing the table," I said. "Hey, Odin."

"Delaney," he said.

"Of course," Patrick said, not sounding very happy about it. "Chief Reed, may I call you Delaney?"

"Sure," I said. "I'm not on duty right now."

"Lunch?" he asked.

"Already ordered."

"Did you call it in?"

"No. Chris saw me at the door. Living in a small town does have some benefits," I said.

"I can see that. Thank you for meeting with me. I

know I can be a little pushy. Most of it is for the camera."

"Most of it?"

He leaned back and grinned. "All right, maybe I'm always a little pushy. What can I say? I'm a man who lives life like time's running out."

"I can see that," I said.

Odin picked up his beer. "Here's to following your dreams."

Patrick lifted his glass of water. "Cheers."

"Patrick was just telling me he's been over in Boring," Odin said. "Nice little town, I suppose."

"All of Oregon's towns are nice little towns," I agreed.

"Oh, that's good," Patrick said. "I am going to steal it. You mind if I film?"

"I assumed that was why I came here."

"Well, yes. But I did want to talk. To…" He threw a quick glance at Odin and seemed to change course. "To get to know the town through your eyes."

"Sounds good."

"Give me a sec." He busied himself adjusting the camera, checking what was going to be in frame. Then he held his phone in front of him and gave it a cheeky wink.

"I told you I'd hunt her down. I'm here at Jump Off Jack's, a nice pub attached to a brewery with a fantastic view. And with me today, is Delaney Reed, who is the police chief of Ordinary, Oregon. Say hello to my Bombers, Chief."

"Hey," I said.

"Okay, let's dive right in. What's the worst crime you've ever solved?"

"Worst? To anyone who is a victim of crime, that crime is the worst."

"No, no, no. I mean bloody. Horrific. The kind of crime someone would make into a movie."

"Well, it's pretty horrifying you're drinking water instead of one of Jump Off's award-winning beers."

He chuckled. "Beer later. I don't drink and film. Can't you let us in on a grim, gruesome murder? Please?"

I shrugged. "We're a small town. We have, statistically, the same kind of crimes as any other small town."

"Murder?"

"It has happened. It isn't common."

"Was it grim and gruesome?"

"No, someone was angry and someone died. That's horrible and sad."

He frowned, did something with the camera, then brightened, like this was take two.

"How about a weird crime? Something really out there."

"Weird?" Oh, the tales I could tell. But I wasn't going to blow Ordinary's cover for this guy. "Well, someone blew up a neighbor's rhubarb patch once."

"That's…uh…What kind of explosives?"

"Dynamite. We stick to the basics around here."

He laughed. It was a contagious sort of sound, one that made me feel more relaxed. It made a lot of people in the room lean toward him a bit too.

He was obviously magical. Very magical. He radiated it like the sun radiated heat.

I was naturally immune to most magics. It came from being the Bridge for god power entering into and exiting out of Ordinary. So if I could feel the pull of the guy, I could only imagine how much more irresistible he would be to other people.

"Nothing weirder? No severed heads? No alien sightings? No vampires and werewolves duking it out?"

"You telling him all our secrets?" Chris asked, as he stopped at the table with a burger for me and a double order of fish and chips for Odin.

"Well, not all of them." I moved back so he could more easily drop our food in front of each of us. He slid a small plate of tater tots and dipping sauce in front of Patrick.

"I know you said you weren't hungry," Chris said, "but Delaney and Odin stab people who steal their tots. On the house."

"Must be my lucky day." He waggled his eyebrows at the camera. Odin, Chris, and I all held our breath.

But he didn't say anything more, like: *I am a leprechaun, and I know I have magic and luck.*

"Anything else?" Chris asked to the table at large.

"I'm good," I said, as I dipped a tot in ketchup and stuffed it in my mouth.

Odin finished off his beer. "Another stout."

"You got it. Patrick?"

"All good."

Something large and metal landed hard in the kitchen, the clatter enough to stifle conversation for a second. Chris shook his head. "Excuse me. I gotta go check in on the new guy."

"What's it like to grow up here and become the chief of police at such a young age?" Patrick went on like we hadn't been interrupted. "What's it like to have your sisters on the force?"

"I like living in a small town," I said. "I had a pretty

177

normal childhood, school, friends, sports. Trained for law enforcement young because I knew what I wanted to do with my life. I'm very lucky that I get to do just that."

"You worked for it," Odin put in. "Don't let her fool you, she didn't just stroll into the job. It takes a lot to be the police chief. She did her time. Learned the laws. Did the grunt work."

"My job is to make sure Ordinary is as safe as possible, and that all citizens and visitors know that their voices will be heard."

I took a bite of burger.

"All right, hold on." He thumbed his phone, set it on the table. "These answers are boring. If you want me to use any of this footage to help your town, you'll need to step it up."

"Step it up?"

"Be…interesting. I'm doing you a favor here."

I took another big bite of burger and took my time chewing, then sat back.

"How I see it, Mr. Baum, is you are getting free content for your travel show, which may or may not grow your audience. We are getting the eyes of your viewers, which may or may not grow our tourist traffic.

"That's it. No favors given or owed. We don't owe you a show. What you see, is what we are. No big secrets, no weird crimes, just regular people getting through their days. We've got a great beach, a great brewery, and a lot of events run by our great events coordinator, Bertie. End of story."

"Okay," he said, slowly. "I like that. The direct approach. But can you do it without the glare? At least act friendly?"

Before I could answer, he had the phone in his hand again. "I'm here with the chief of police, Delaney Reed. She suggested Jump Off Jack's for lunch.

"Road Bomb: Ordinary has an award-winning brewery, and the food's great too. Thanks for the tip, Chief Reed."

"Delaney," I said. "I'd love to take credit, but that goes to Chris Lagon, our master brewer."

"And that's him right there." He swung the phone toward Chris, who raised a hand in a wave. The phone came back to me.

"So, Delaney, if you had a chance to talk to all the Road Bombers out there, what would you tell them about your town?"

"We have fourteen miles of beaches—all public—and along with the award-winning brewery, we have an incredible bakery, wonderful small shops, and fantastic artists." I pointed toward Odin, who offered a grumpy grunt.

"Our lighthouses are said to be haunted, our off-shore fishing and whale watching are always a good time, and it doesn't actually rain every day of the year."

"Sounds like a Bomb of a place," he said. "Does the town put on any unique events during the year?"

I laughed. "We have something going on almost every week. The event coming up this Friday is a town-wide murder mystery."

"Bombing," he said. "Are you going to be in it?"

"No, I have a wedding rehearsal on the same day."

"You're getting married?"

"I am."

"Congratulations! Who's the lucky person?"

"Ryder Bailey."

"Ryder Bailey," he repeated like he was setting that name to memory. "Is he from Ordinary?"

"Grew up here. We both did."

"Childhood sweethearts? Aw…Isn't that the cutest? So romantic."

I shrugged. "He's amazing. The love of my life."

"Oh? Would you do anything for him? Climb tall mountains, sail wide seas, follow him into heaven or he —h, e, double hockey sticks? We don't drop the curse bombs on the Road Bomb."

"Yes," I said honestly, and then, "We're very excited about the wedding, thanks."

"I'd love to see the wedding rehearsal, share a little of the small town love with my big-time Bombers."

I shook my head, but he didn't see it. He'd thumbed off the phone and was tracking someone who had walked into the room.

"I'd love a shot of you and Ryder at your rehearsal. It'd look fantastic in the show, and you wouldn't even have to talk. I'll do a voice over or some nice music."

"It's a limited space venue and a private event," I said. "Sorry."

"I hope you'll reconsider. I'd really like to meet the man who stole your heart." He handed me a card, his gaze sincere. "Text me. I'd really, really appreciate just a quick moment with you and Ryder. I think it will pull the entire series together."

"It's a rehearsal. Nothing fancy."

"Childhood sweethearts getting married in a small town? Trust me, people eat that up like candy. I could build an empire on that story."

He glanced over my shoulder again. I wondered who had caught his eye.

I scanned the bar. I'd know those wide shoulders and dark hair anywhere: Bathin.

"Let me know when you change your mind," Patrick said. "It really would pull the whole film together and be an amazing opportunity for Ordinary."

He stood, scooping up his equipment in one motion. "This was fun."

"Oh?" I asked. "Are you leaving?"

"At your beck and call, if you need me. But, yes, I have an appointment. See you later, Delaney."

"What about me?" Odin asked. "I thought you said you were going to interview local artists."

But Baum was on the move and halfway across the room. He only made it that far before several of his fans got up to intercept him, cell phones and paper and pens in hand.

"That was weird, right?" I asked.

"That he practically ignored me the whole time you were here?" Odin scratched under his armpit and belched.

"No, that as soon as Bathin showed up, he was in a hurry to scram."

"Who says 'scram' anymore? You should keep up with modern slang. Is yeet still a thing?"

"I think he recognized Bathin."

Odin shifted, his chair making a lot of noise across the old wood floor. "We could ask."

"I could ask," I corrected. "I don't need a babysitter."

"Four people who almost kidnapped you say otherwise."

"They didn't almost kidnap me. They attacked me. Which I handled just fine."

"Because Frigg was there."

"Sure, and not because I am a police officer and know how to handle myself if I'm attacked." I tossed money on the table.

"Where are you going next?" he asked. "Work?"

"Yeah. First, I'm gonna talk to Bathin."

Baum was almost at the stairs now. He poured on the charm, posed for a couple shots, then squeezed down to the door, his audience following.

The noise level in the place dropped. I could hear the music playing over the speaker system.

I tapped Bathin on the shoulder and swung onto the empty bar stool next to him. "You here because of Patrick?"

"Isn't everyone?"

"Probably." Bathin and I had been tied together long enough that I had a sense of his moods. His current mood was calm, like the sky right before a thunderstorm tears it apart.

"Do you know him?" I asked.

"No."

"He recognized you. Yeeted out of here as soon as he saw you."

Bathin squinted at the exit, then picked up his beer and drank. "Interesting. He's definitely been around demons lately."

"Really? How do you know?"

"Leprechauns are hard to pin down because luck always goes their way. I think a demon's pinned him down."

"But how do you know?"

"I smelled the soured luck."

"Your mom mentioned something about that. Leprechauns have a scent?"

"You can't tell?"

"He smells a little like Sunset Riot, or one of those high-priced Tom Ford colognes."

"No, he smells like soured luck."

"Now you're going to explain what soured luck is, and what it has to do with a leprechaun coming into our town and wanting to watch my wedding rehearsal."

"If his luck has soured, then he's either lost a very large and very terrible bet, or someone has pinned him to a contract he can't get out of. Soured luck means things may not always go his way."

"Think he's on the run?"

"I don't know. If so, he's not hiding with all those films."

"Do you think it's your dad? Can he use the leprechaun against us?"

"I…" He frowned. "My father wouldn't rely on someone so weak. Any leprechaun that can be caught by a demon wouldn't be strong enough to carry out a demon's orders.

"Besides, luck is luck. Even soured, it's gonna go the way of the leprechaun eventually. No demon's dumb enough to think using a leprechaun won't blow up in their face. Especially an angry leprechaun."

"How dangerous are angry leprechauns?"

"You ever met a werewolf with a toothache?"

A faint memory from my childhood—Dad looking grim and buckling on all his tactical gear—flashed behind my eyes. "Kind of?"

"That." He tipped his head considering. "More than that."

"Terrific. Just what we need right now, an angry leprechaun."

"Oh, he's not angry yet. You'll know when he's angry. Right now he's just trying to decide whose side I'm on. His or the demon's who trapped him."

"Maybe you're on our side. Ordinary's side."

"He wouldn't believe that if I swore to it under a truth spell."

"Okay, can you ask around and find out who trapped him? He might be here trying to find help with whatever trouble he's in, but if that trouble means he's working for your father, I'm giving Baum the bum's rush, influencer or no influencer."

"I'll look into it. So. Are you excited for the rehearsal on Friday?"

I pulled a coaster over and fiddled with it, playing it casual, though I knew he could sense my raised heartbeat. "Can't wait."

He pressed his hand gently over the back of my own, waited until I met his eyes.

"Ryder loves you, Delaney. I know this. You know this too. Everything else in the world can go to dust, and that truth between you won't change.

"I heard what you said to Patrick. That you would go into heaven or hell for Ryder. He knows that, too, and would do the same for you."

I swallowed quickly, surprised by the sudden rush of emotions: happiness, pride, love.

"I know." I cleared my throat and tried again. "I know. Thank you."

He withdrew his hand and picked up his drink. "Plus, if Ryder abandons you at the altar, I will kick his god-bound ass. Me and several other people in this town."

I scoffed. "If he abandons me, you're all going to have to stand in line. I can do my own ass-kicking, thank you."

"Ah," he said, raising his cup. "True love."

CHAPTER ELEVEN

THE WORD of Patrick Baum holding court in Ordinary had blazed through all the on-line sites. We were seeing license plates from California, Washington, Idaho, Utah, Nevada, Alaska, and Arizona. Traffic was a nightmare.

By sunset, all the motel signs were turned to no vacancy. The restaurants pulled extended hours to accommodate the larger dinner crowd, the bars were over maximum occupancy allowed. Even the grocery store parking lot was full.

It was good business, but made for a long damn day for all of us working with the public.

It was past midnight by the time I got home. The driveway was empty. Ryder was still gone.

I thought about making dinner and decided it was too late.

"Popcorn works, right?" I said as I wandered into the kitchen. I tossed a bag into the microwave, then headed upstairs for a quick shower.

I changed and settled on the couch, a warm blanket over my lap, dragon-pig on one side, Spud on the other.

I was slotted for backup on the emergency lines tonight. Jean was first, but with so many people in town, I kept my phone ringer up, knowing I'd get overflow.

So when my phone rang, I answered it without looking at the screen. "Police Chief Delaney Reed. What is the reason for your call?"

"Police Chief? I'd like to report a crime," Ryder said on the line. His voice was soft and tired, but there was humor behind it too.

He sounded wonderful.

He sounded like he missed me.

"What kind of crime? Violent?"

"There's a thief. She's stolen my heart."

"So cheesy," I said.

"No, you don't understand. It's a heart of gold."

I groaned.

"A heart of *gold*," he repeated. "Which is very valuable. And it's been stolen. So what are you going to do about it?"

"Can you identify the thief? Did you get a look at her?"

"She's almost my height, has the softest brown hair, and these blue eyes…have you ever seen the dawn sky in spring just before the sun rises?"

"You are really spreading it on thick."

"You wanted me to report the crime, didn't you?"

"Yes."

"And describe the thief?"

"Yes."

"These blue eyes," he went on. "Like a spring sky before daybreak when everything is soft and possible."

"Uh-huh. Eyes: blue. Hair: brown. Sounds like a fairly average description."

"Oh, she's not average. Do you want to know the best thing about her?"

"The best thing. About this thief who stole your heart?"

"Yes. The thief. Do you want to know the best thing?"

"I want all the facts. So let's hear it."

The door latch rattled, a key in the lock turned, and then the door opened. Ryder stepped into the little entryway. "She's a part of my life. I couldn't imagine my day, night, or whatever hour this is, without her."

I thumbed off my phone. He pulled his away from his ear and looked at it. "Hello?" he said, bringing it back to his ear. "Hanging up on the victim of crime is very unprofessional."

"I already heard everything I needed to hear."

He shrugged out of his coat, hung it up, dropped his phone on the charger on the little shelf by the door, then started my way. "Everything?"

"Guy must have been delirious. He was spouting poetry about blue skies and eyeballs."

"Maybe it was just blood loss?" He lowered himself beside dragon-pig, who grumbled and hopped over my lap to curl up with Spud. Spud stretched across me to give Ryder a lick across his face.

Ryder sputtered and pushed Spud's head aside.

"Blood loss?" I asked.

"No heart, 'cause it was stolen."

I smiled and cupped the side of his face, studying him for a moment. "Hey," I said, loving him for being here—late hour, corny jokes and all.

"Hey," he said.

"It's really late."

He nodded.

"Are you okay?"

"Tired." He turned his head and kissed at my palm. They he shifted around until his big boots were hanging off the arm of the couch, and his head was propped on my thigh.

"You need some blanket?" I asked.

"No. This is good."

"Popcorn?"

He opened his mouth, and I dropped a few kernels in.

"Mithra keep you busy all day?"

"I drove to Washington and back. There was a contract he wanted me to read. About a patch of grass and whether it was owned by the town, or owned by the family who bought the property."

"Grass."

"Just a small patch of grass."

"Where in Washington?"

"Up in the Olympic rainforest. How was your day?"

"Long."

He nodded, staring up at me, waiting. I ran my fingertips through his hair, marveling at the strands of copper and gold that wove through the darker threads.

"Patrick is a leprechaun with soured magic," I said.

"Soured magic is a thing?"

"Bathin says it is. Probably soured by a demon. Maybe Bathin's father."

"The King of the Underworld sent a leprechaun to…film Ordinary?"

"We don't know. Could be Patrick's here to get away from the king. Bertie's worried. She made a bet with

Robyn and is caught in a catch-22. Damned if she wins, damned if she loses."

He grunted, his eyes drifting shut.

I waited a few minutes, letting time slip and slip until I debated just sleeping on the couch with him. But I didn't want to wake up stiff and sore.

"Let's go to bed," I said shaking his shoulder gently. "Nice soft bed."

His eyes opened, bloodshot and glassy. "Sure. Sure."

I shook his shoulder again. "Come on, love. Bed." I pushed up, which left him no choice. He had to move.

Spud and dragon-pig rearranged themselves into our abandoned warm spots, and Ryder got on his feet, but just stood there, rubbing his head until his hair stuck straight up.

I caught his other hand and pulled him up the stairs to the dark and quiet of our room.

"You know we're throwing you a bachelorette party," Jean said, as she settled into the easy chair at the dress shop. "I mean, Myra thinks you have no idea, but you know, don't you?"

I glanced over my shoulder. Cheryl had asked me to come in for a fitting, just to make sure the adjustments she'd made on the dress were right. My wedding was one week away, and real, honest excitement fluttered in my chest.

"You haven't been subtle about keeping it a secret," I said.

She chuckled. "Yeah. Well, I wanted to do it this week. Before the wedding rehearsal. Maybe tomorrow."

"Friday? With the murder mystery and rehearsal

happening the next day, and the town stuffed with tourists?"

"I know," she sighed. "We'll still have it, but it's going to be next week, I think."

Cheryl stood from where she had been tugging on the hem. "Let's take a look at this now."

She moved behind me, and I stared at myself in the mirror. She'd pulled part of my hair back loosely and added a spray of flowers to it. I almost didn't recognize the beautiful woman in the mirror.

I'd thought about being married, but I didn't dream about it all my life like some girls. I hadn't been saving ideas for my eventual wedding in scrapbooks or shoe-boxes or storing online images.

But I knew that this moment, and my reflection in the mirror, was far better than anything I could have dreamed. I was going to be a bride. The certainty of that was like sunlight beneath my skin. I couldn't stop smiling.

"It really is perfect," I said, wonder caught in my voice.

"Finally," Jean cooed. "You can see how gorgeous you are. Ryder is going to forget the world exists when you walk down the aisle."

I nodded in the mirror, hoping so, believing so. "Thank you. This is more than I ever hoped for. Cheryl, you made it perfect." I swallowed back all the emotion that threatened to turn happiness into happy tears. "I don't want to ruin it before the wedding. Can I take it off before I spill coffee on it or something?"

Cheryl chuckled and cupped my shoulders. "Yes. But you are fine. If you did any damage, we'd find a way to fix it. Relax, Delaney. It's all on rails now. Tomorrow's the wedding rehearsal, then next week the bachelorette party, and then," she patted my shoulders, "then you'll be married."

"And that's going to be perfect too," Jean said.

I nodded, believing her. Believing both of them. Because the bride in the mirror was smiling, and there were stars in her eyes.

"HAVE YOU DECIDED WHO'S OFFICIATING?" Old Rossi, the head of the vampire family in town, asked me.

It was Friday morning, and clouds had rolled in. Patrick was still in town, and so was his ever-growing crowd of fans. I hadn't invited him to our wedding rehearsal and didn't plan to.

One would think the town being so crowded would deter even more people from flooding in. One would be wrong.

I felt a little guilty stealing a few minutes for my morning jog with how busy I knew today was going to be, but only a little guilty.

"Not yet," I said keeping my pace easy. Rossi's limp was almost gone now. His injured eye hadn't regenerated. I wasn't sure it ever would. But he was strong, healthy, and that made me happy.

"Ryder's going to decide," I continued. "Crow thinks he has a shot at it. But Crow thinks he has a shot at everything. Nice peace sign." I pointed toward his bright yellow eyepatch with the iconic symbol in red. "You going back to hippie life again?"

"Who said I ever gave up hippie life? But yes. I've relaunched the yoga studio. Seemed like the right time to do it. Peace, love, and breathe into the pain."

"Is that your vision statement?"

"That is my life advice."

"You should put it on a T-shirt."

"I might. With all the attention we're getting from Baum, I think I could sell a shirt or two…" Rossi's head jerked up, eyes facing the land. "Demons."

He ran. I was right beside him, but as soon as he reached the edge of where the beach met the rise of the cliff, he simply disappeared.

Vampires are fast. When they want to be, they were faster than the eye could track.

"Shit." I plowed up the stairs, crested the top, and glanced at the three-car parking space where four cars were currently parked.

No demons.

This parking spot was at the end of a residential street. Most of the houses were single-story types, with the occasional A-frame.

No sounds of struggle coming from the houses. No signs of demons.

I didn't even know where Rossi had gone. At the speed he could move, he could be miles away.

"Shit." I dug my phone out of my pocket just as it rang.

"Myra," I answered. "Rossi said there are demons in town. Where are you?"

"At my house," her voice was shaking with anger or fear. "You need to be here. You need to be here, Delaney. Bathin killed them."

I was running through the neighborhood, headed toward the main street where I could flag down a car. Before I got even half a block, Jame Wolfe, who was a werewolf, firefighter, and the boyfriend to Rossi's son,

Ben, pulled up in his truck. "Get in. Rossi told me I needed to get you."

"I'm on my way," I told Myra, as I scrambled into the passenger seat. Jame gunned it. "Are you hurt? Is Bathin hurt?"

There was a pause, then Bathin's voice came over the phone. "She's fine," he said. "But it's a mess here. We'll do what we can to keep it quiet, but you'll want to bring someone who can throw an illusion."

He hung up on me. I cussed my way through my contacts list, trying to decide who was the best with illusions.

"Jules," Jame suggested. "Or Rossi. Though Rossi's going to be more of a one-on-one thing with people. Jules is a witch, she'll have a spell."

I dialed her. She didn't pick up, so I tried her crystal shop. Nothing. She was either flooded with customers or had turned all her phones off to get away from them.

"She isn't answering."

Jame wove through the back neighborhoods as far as he could, avoiding the main street, which was clogged with traffic. "Rossi's there, he'll deal with it."

"I don't want Rossi to deal with it. It's my job." I dialed Jean.

"Hey, Boss."

"Myra and Bathin have a situation on their hands. Myra's house. Demons."

"What the fuck? I'm on my way."

"No. I need you to get Stevie and take him there."

"Shit. Be safe."

We hung up. Jame laid on his horn to get into traffic and across traffic to the street we needed, then he put on the gas to get us to Myra's house in a hurry.

Crime scenes are strange things. Most of the time, law enforcement gets there after the tragedy has already happened. Sometimes there's blood, or fire, or grieving witnesses. Sometimes there are injured who don't know they're hurt. Sometimes there's death.

But sometimes when rolling up to a crime scene there is nothing out of place. No signs of struggle. The wind is calm. The neighborhood is going about its business as if nothing has happened. Birds are chirping and the chitter of squirrels making haste for winter fills the air.

Those crimes scenes were always the hardest for me. Because it was clear there was one world, one reality where I could pretend nothing had changed, where I could hope it wasn't as bad as the call had made it out to be. That there had been a mistake, and the horror, the loss, the grief would turn out not to have happened at all.

And then there was the other world, where I knew that was all a lie.

I was out of Jame's truck before he'd come to a stop. Myra's house looked fine, like nothing had happened, like no one was even home.

Myra walked out onto the porch. Her hair was pulled back with a red kerchief, She was in tights and a sweater, and she wasn't wearing any makeup. "In here," she said. "Jame?"

"Rossi sent him to get me."

She nodded, her mouth a grim line. "We're going to need containment."

"I sent Jean to get Stevie."

"That will work. Come through."

She turned toward the door, but I stopped her and gave her a quick hug. "Are you okay?"

She hugged me back. "Angry. Otherwise, fine. I should have seen this coming. I should have been paying attention."

"No, you were right where you needed to be. Jean didn't feel doom twinges. So maybe this isn't as bad as it seems."

I stepped into her home which was always softer than most people would assume, with doilies and knit pillows and live plants in the windows.

"Out back." She took me through to the backyard, and that's when one reality definitely became another, much more grim, reality.

Three bodies lay on the grass, all male. They were dressed in formal wear, which was strange, and all appeared to be middle aged. There wasn't any blood I could see, but from the broken ways they were lying, they were all very much dead.

"What happened?" I asked.

"They tried to break into the house." Bathin stood over another man who was kneeling, hands behind his back. The man's eyes glowed red.

"Delaney Reed, you too, will die. Die!" he growled in a voice much too deep for a human.

"Okay," I said. "What are we working with here?"

"Demon," Bathin said. From his tone, he didn't think very highly of it. "Assassins possessing humans. Oldest trick in the book."

"Assassins," I repeated. "Why would they come to Myra's house if they want to kill me?"

"They don't like you." He snapped his fingers which made the kneeling assassin grunt with pain. "I don't think they're fond of me either. I might have been their original target."

With that came a very satisfied smile.

"The wards?" Rossi stepped out of the shadows by the edge of the property. "Did the demon alarms go off?"

"I didn't hear them," I said.

I should have. We'd set them up so I would know if demons were crossing into Ordinary. As the Bridge, I would be the one who could push back and make sure they didn't make it inside our boundaries. "Why didn't I hear them?"

"Because these assholes," Bathin snapped his fingers, and the assassin jerked again, "possessed humans. Not something any self-respecting demon would do."

"Human suits can get through the wards?"

"Apparently these can." He held my gaze. "These aren't living humans. The demons held onto just enough of their souls so they could pass the wards and register as human."

"A loophole," Myra said. "Damn it."

Bathin nodded. "We'll close it. But I thought you'd want to question this one before I killed it."

"Who sent you?" I asked.

"The one who will be, the bringer of doom."

"The King of the Underworld?" I asked.

Glowing red eyes narrowed. "Come closer," the demon snarled.

Like I'd fall for that. "Who were you here to kill besides me? Myra? Bathin?"

"Kill the prince?" The demon smiled, and it sent chills down my spine. "Come closer, Delaney Reed."

"Delaney?" Ryder jogged out of the house and into

the yard. And there, just outside the yard behind Bathin, was Patrick Baum, his camera focused on us.

Shit.

Several things happened at once.

Rossi spun to face Patrick, who jumped the low fence into the yard. Bathin glanced over his shoulder at that movement.

Ryder paused just a short distance behind me.

And the demon, the one on his knees, surged to his feet, the bindings holding his hands breaking in a shower of sparks as he rushed forward, fast, faster than any human thing.

I reached for my gun and came up empty handed. I was in my jogging sweats and had left my gun at home.

Myra threw something that was on fire. Smoke filled the air.

Ryder plowed forward, trying to push me out of the way before the demon reached me. But the demon jagged to one side, going around me.

That's when I realized I was not his target.

Ryder was.

I pivoted, trying to reverse my momentum to stop the demon before he reached Ryder. But I was off my footing, and the grass was damp from the morning dew. My running shoes caught, then gave, slipping out from beneath me, wrenching my ankle. I went down on my hands and knees.

"No!" I yelled.

Ryder threw his arms up to guard his face, but the demon came in low and tackled him. I pushed up, twisting back to get to them as they wrestled.

Ryder grunted in pain as the thing tore at him like a rabid wolf. He couldn't throw it off.

I scrambled forward but before I could fully gain my feet, the demon roared and then, was still.

Bathin stood above the demon and Ryder, smoke rising from his fists.

"Holy shit," Patrick said, from the edge of the yard. "He just killed that guy. He just killed him!"

I should be dealing with that. I should be protecting our town's secrets. But Ryder was still under the demon, and he wasn't moving. It seemed like he hadn't been moving for minutes. Hours.

"Ryder?" I heard myself say from somewhere at a long distance.

"I filmed it. I got it on film."

"Give me your phone," Myra said.

"Like hell. I just saw a guy die. He's been murdered."

"He," Myra insisted, "was part of our murder mystery."

"Do you see?" Rossi said in a hypnotic tone that made it feel like there was a buzz in my ears I needed to scratch out. "Do you see him sitting up now?" he went on. "Yes, he is fine. A very good actor."

"He's…it's an act?" Patrick asked.

"Yes, of course. The play. Practice for the play," Rossi said. "Just as Officer Reed explained."

"But…his eyes were glowing."

"We have an excellent make-up department," Rossi said.

"I need your phone," Myra said. "We can't allow any filming of the event until the actual day of the event. Which is tomorrow."

I was on my knees next to Ryder, and reached out to pull the demon off him, panic making my hands shake.

"Don't move," Bathin said quietly. "Let Rossi finish with the leprechaun."

That's when I felt the hum of magic: a sticky hot push and pull drifting across my exposed skin. Not sandpaper, but too many fingers that caught and tugged before letting go to catch again. A hundred sticky vines searching for purchase.

There was magic in the air: Patrick's. There was illusion in the air: Rossi's. There was dark power in the air: Bathin's.

It was a lot.

For a moment it was an nexus point, three colliding dark enchantments vying for dominance.

I waited, studying Ryder's face for any sign of movement.

"You want to give the officer your phone," Rossi said.

"I don't give anyone my phone."

"You trust her. You know her. She is the only person you allow to touch your phone," Rossi said.

"I don't trust anyone."

"You do. You trust Myra Reed. Give her your phone."

"This sounds like a trick."

"This is only the easiest thing you could ever do. Your arm is so tired, holding the phone. It is so heavy. You want to take a rest, just a small rest from holding it."

"I want to rest?"

"Yes," Rossi said. "You want to rest. You are getting sleepy."

I wasn't sure, but Rossi sounded annoyed. Like he had explained the color blue to a toddler for an hour and the kid wouldn't stop asking questions. Like he wasn't used to being argued with.

"Sleepy…" Patrick repeated. This time his voice sounded muzzy, as if he'd just drunk a couple shots too quickly. He handed to phone to Myra.

Ryder's eyes were closed, but I could see the pulse at his neck, could see—now that I'd shoved the panic back into a small room in my brain where it could scream itself out—that he was breathing.

I also saw blood. His arm was bleeding.

I inhaled slowly, exhaled in a tight stream, trying not to move too much and screw up Rossi's power over the leprechaun.

"And now that's done." Myra finished deleting the video and handed the phone back to Patrick. "Remember, this is just a play, a murder mystery. That's all you saw."

"You believe her," Rossi said, "because you trust her. You saw a play. Everyone is fine. No one is murdered. You want to take a yoga class," he added, and even through the panic and worry, I threw a look his way.

Rossi shrugged and waved his hand in front of Patrick's face. "You want to find a coffee and a donut, and will consider taking a free yoga class. Turn now."

There was slight resistance, a micro-level struggle in Patrick's face, before he did as he was told and turned.

"Hop over the fence," Rossi said. "Carefully."

Patrick did that too.

"Now I will accompany you to the main street, and you will find a donut." Rossi glanced at Myra who nodded.

Rossi was over the fence in one smooth movement, then they both started walking. A few steps out, I heard

Rossi say: "…yoga. Have you thought of taking it up, my friend?"

"What?" Patrick sounded confused, like he was waking up. "Yoga?"

"All those long days on the road," Rossi said. "Yoga does wonders for the body. I have a studio here in town. The first lesson is free. Why don't we get a coffee and talk about it?"

"Now," Bathin said.

I lunged for Ryder, shoving the demon away with Bathin's help.

"Ryder," I said, my hands on his face, his chest, my fingers already tugging his sleeve away so I could assess the damage. "Wake up, love. Let me see your gorgeous eyes."

The cuts on his arm were deep, as if claws had slashed him. Stitches. He'd need stitches.

Myra was next to me now, saying something. "…right here, Delaney. I got it. Let me apply pressure. Just…there you go. Good."

She pushed my hands to Ryder's chest where I could feel the rise and fall of his breathing, then clamped a cloth, a towel—When had she found time to get a towel?—over his wounds.

The world had gone spongy around me. Swallowed me up and made every movement, every thought slow, too slow.

"Ryder," I said again. "Please, love. Please."

His eyes fluttered, and he inhaled a soft, dragged out moan.

"Hey," I said, as his gaze drifted to me. "Hey, hero. You're okay. We got you."

His forehead wrinkled. "Hero?"

"You just fought off a demon."

He blinked a couple more times, then looked around, seeing Myra. "What happened?" he asked her. "Why are you holding my arm…" His hiss was loud.

"Don't move yet," she said. "Jame's taking over now."

"Good thing I had my kit in the truck," he said, exchanging places with Myra. "Hey, Delaney. You back with us?"

His words cleared the fog in my brain.

The day came into focus again. Bathin behind me, dead bodies on the green grass, Myra talking to Jean and someone else—Stevie, must be Stevie—Jame pulling the towel off Ryder's arm, his hands quick and sure and surprisingly gentle for a werewolf.

"Delaney?" Jean asked.

All the rest came into focus too. The breeze that was still cool with morning dew, the shift of light as clouds drifted over the sun, the scratchy call of a crow in the neighbor's tree.

"I'm…yes…I'm here. I'm okay."

Jean's gaze was sharp as she checked for any lie, and her mouth was tight. She was angry. Worried. "I didn't see this coming. Any of this. No doom twinge at all."

I nodded. "Your gift is just for the big stuff, though." My voice was getting stronger, clearer with each word, until I didn't sound as shaky, didn't sound as shocky as I had just moments ago. "This wasn't a big thing. No big damage, right Jame?"

Jame grunted without taking his eyes off his work. "Needs a couple stitches, but yes, no major damage."

Every muscle in my body relaxed. I took a long breath and let it out. "See?" I said to Jean, who wasn't buying my everything's-fine big-sister tone. "This isn't a big thing."

"It was a demon attack," Bathin said, before sneezing twice. "Gods, man. Do you have to throw the illusion so thick? You're killing me here."

"This is a quiet neighborhood," Stevie's lilting scholarly voice said. Stevie was a Will-o'-the-wisp, who could do more than make people wander and get lost. He could weave light into very realistic illusions.

Built like a twig wearing a tweed suit, he spent his days collecting various insects. He had quite the library now and had been tapped for information by various entomologists around the world.

"Quiet neighborhoods can cross the line from quaint to creepy if the light isn't woven just so," he said. "We want to establish a good base layer before casting the finer points. How long will this need to last?"

Bathin was sneezing, so Myra answered. "I think we can get this cleaned up in a couple hours at the most. Does that work?"

"Do you have any tea I might enjoy to pass the time as I maintain the light?" he asked.

"You name it, I probably have it."

"Two hours shouldn't be difficult. I will stretch it a bit longer, just in case. I'd suggest removing Prince…I mean, Mr. Bathin, from the yard, at the very least. He seems allergic to my magic."

"No," Bathin said, between sneezes. He pinched his nose and rubbed his arm over his watering eyes. "I stay. Who's in charge of the crime scene?"

"I am," Jean said.

"No," I said. "I'm processing the scene."

"You need to go with Ryder," Jame said. "Hospital.

These wounds need to be cleaned better. He'll need a tetanus shot and antibiotics. Are there other precautions we should take for wounds caused by the possessed?"

Bathin shook his head. "They didn't have enough time in the bodies to generate poison. These are freshly possessed." He nudged the toe of his boot at the guy who had attacked Ryder. "This whole plan is a joke. Poorly exe—" He sneezed again and swore. "Executed."

"Done," Jean said. "Delaney goes with Ryder, Myra keeps Stevie comfortable, and Bathin and I deal with the bodies."

I closed my eyes for a second, reminding myself I didn't always have to shoulder the burden of looking after this town alone.

"All right," I said. "That's...that makes sense. I'll go with him. My phone will be on. Let me know what you find. What you do. Anything you need."

"Tea would be nice," Stevie repeated.

"On it," Myra said. "Do you need help getting him to the truck, Jame?"

"Delaney and I got this. Chief?" He motioned me to help him get Ryder to his feet.

"I can stand," Ryder said, but it came out a little soft. He cleared his throat. "I can stand. My arm's hurt, not my legs."

"Gonna insist we do this slow," Jame said, at the same time I said, "We're helping. Don't argue. Ready?"

Jame and I didn't do more than stabilize him as he stood, but I stayed under his good arm, my other arm wrapped around his back.

"You got him?" Jame asked.

"Yes."

Ryder held his injured arm tucked against his chest.

It was wrapped in thick bandages Jame had applied with skill and speed.

"Let's get you down to the ER," Jame said.

"Keep me informed," I ordered.

"We will," Myra promised. "Okay, I'll brew that tea. Bathin, maybe if you step over here, it won't make you sneeze so badly…"

Jame walked ahead of us through the house and opened the front door for us.

"I'm fine," Ryder said. "Just got the wind knocked out of me."

"You were attacked by a demon. We'll let the doctor decide when you're okay."

"I don't think…"

"Doctor decides," I repeated, keeping my eyes on the porch stairs, then sidewalk.

He tipped his head so his mouth was nearer my ear. "I like it when you get bossy," he murmured.

"That's good, because I'm your boss." I shifted so he could step up into the back seat. Then shut the door to hurry around to the other side of the truck so I could sit beside him.

CHAPTER TWELVE

"DAY OFF," I repeated as I handed Ryder a cup of coffee. "Doctor Myrrhis said demon scratches infect easily."

Doctor Myrrhis was a caladrius, which was a mythical white bird of healing. Here in town, she took on a human shape and was a licensed medical doctor. She was our go-to person at the hospital for magical or supernatural injuries.

He took the cup and set it down next to the glass of water, glass of orange juice, saltine crackers, grapes, and yogurt that I'd brought, one after the other, out into the living room to where he sat on the couch.

"Again, I'm not sick. This is a scratch."

I raised my eyebrows.

"Fine, demon cut. Which is on my *arm*. I can do more than sit on the couch and binge shows."

"Sure." I moved to the guest bathroom and dug in the drawer for the thermometer. "Or you could take a day off, which you haven't had in months, and sit on the couch and binge shows."

I snagged a couple pillows from the spare bedroom and brought them with me.

"Really?" he asked eyeing the pillows.

"Really." I stacked them at the end of the couch, where I'd already gathered several other pillows.

"I want to know you're comfortable. I'll only be gone for a couple hours."

"A scratch," he repeated, raising his arm and wiggling his fingers. "Human fingernail scratches."

"Demon possessed."

"Demon possessed fingernails?"

"The whole body. You know what I mean. They have poison. Bathin said so."

"Bathin said the bodies hadn't been possessed long enough to generate poison."

"I heard him. But we're going to be careful because Dr. Myrrhis said so."

"I'm fine," he grumbled.

"You are now. But you were the demon's target. You, not me. I don't like that, not anywhere, but sure as hell not in my town in my sister's backyard. I'm going to reinforce our wards, I'm going to get all the information I can out of our local demons, and I'm going to find out where those dead bodies came from."

"I can—"

"No. Stay with a dragon-pig that can tell when there are demons around, and a dog that's been missing you."

The sigh was long, but not loud. He stared out the window, his jaw set.

"Please," I said softly. "I might be...I could be over-reacting. But let me have a couple hours to make sure things are as safe as they can be. Then, if you're feeling okay, I won't get in your way of doing whatever you want to do."

"It's already two o'clock," he noted.

"Yeah, I know this is going to eat up most of your day."

"I'll get caught up on some calls for the wedding," he said. "Try to settle the cheese problem." He was letting me off the hook, even though I knew he was still annoyed.

"Yes. Good. Yes. Thank you. I'll see you soon. If anything happens, call."

"If anything happens while I'm sitting on my couch in my house, guarded by a dragon."

"And a dog," I said.

He gave me a look of utter exasperation. I decided silence was a virtue, and it was time to leave before either of us changed our minds.

"FOUR BODIES WERE DUG up from graves in Astoria a week ago, and they just now noticed?" I looked away from the manila folder Jean had given me.

The station was quiet this afternoon, which should have made me more comfortable. Instead, it made me jump at every creak and bluster of wind. I half expected Patrick or his fans to come rushing in and catch all of us talking about possessed dead guys.

Jean shrugged and took a drink of her soda. "It's not monitored closely because it's mostly family plots from eighty-plus years ago. These guys were newly buried, and according to records, don't have anyone in the area who would visit the graves."

"Who looks after the graveyard? The city? The state? A private agency?"

"The state, but they don't put any resources into it. It's just been there forever. Every once in a while, someone gets out a weed whacker and cleans up around the graves."

"We can return them for burial," Myra said. "We have a couple people in Astoria who will smooth over the grave robbing and make sure Ordinary isn't involved."

"Okay," I said, shutting the file. "Are we transporting?"

"Yes," Myra said. "Kelby volunteered, and Shoe's going with her."

I turned to Stevie, who was perched on the edge of Myra's desk, nibbling on a square of white chocolate. "How did the cover up go?"

"Perfectly," he said. "I never cast cut-rate illusions. It will remain for another hour, just in case there is any other need to investigate the back yard."

"Is there?" I asked Myra, who was sitting at her desk.

She shook her head. "Bodies are gone, blood is cleaned, I even mowed the yard. It's good. We're good."

"And you're sure Patrick doesn't remember anything?" I asked Rossi, who was perched in lotus position on the bench in the lobby.

He tipped his head, the light catching the edges of his face and turning him into carved moonlight.

"He might. There's something off about him and his magic, his luck."

"It's sour," Bathin said, leaning a shoulder against

the wall near Myra, his arms crossed over his chest. "He lost to a demon and his luck is sour."

Rossi blinked. "That is…not common. Do we know who this demon might be, and why this leprechaun came to town at the same time demons are slipping through the wards?"

"Delaney!" a voice yelled from the door.

We all faced the intrusion, weapons at the ready.

Xtelle burst into the room, in human form, and it took me far too long to realize who she was.

The demon queen could choose whatever form she wanted. Why she chose a pink unicorn was beyond me. But I'd only seen her in a human form, a female form, a few times.

She was beautiful, because of course she was. Long black hair cascaded over her shoulder and accentuated a figure Betty Page would have killed for. She wore wide-legged slacks, a soft pink sweater, and bangle bracelets on both wrists.

Behind her was a tall, gray-haired, stern-looking man. Avnas wore a black shirt with high collar, and black slacks. His gaze, as he walked into the station, took in every detail, assessing threats.

Everyone in the station watched him right back.

"What?" I said. "What's wrong?"

She strode up to the front counter, and paused there, her fingertips on its worn edge. "I have information for the police."

"You're here. We're here," I said. "What information?"

"There is to be an attack on your boytoy, what's his name. Soon."

"Ryder?" I asked.

"Do you have more than one boytoy? Really?" She looked me up and down. "With your choice in trousers, I don't even know how you attracted one."

"He's not a boytoy, he's my fiancé, and you are too late. He was already attacked. This morning."

"Oh," she said, drawing her hands away from the counter. "I thought it would be later. Well, condolences on his death."

"He's not dead, Mother," Bathin said. "How did you know he was going to be attacked?"

The smile she turned on him was bright as a munitions blast. "Son. Look at you there with that other... Reed. And you look so...human, smelling of cat and sour leprechaun."

"Who gave you the information?" he pressed.

"A queen has her ways." She brushed her hair behind her ear and studied her nails.

"Spies." Bathin didn't look away from his mother, but bent slightly toward Myra. "She has spies working for her."

"Of course I have spies," Xtelle said. "I'm royalty. And yes, they told me there would be an attack. I hadn't realized it would be so soon. Apparently, my spies are getting sloppy now that I've been away. There will need to be a gouging."

"Not here," I said. "No gougings here. Did your spies come into Ordinary?"

All heads swiveled toward her.

"What? Me? Allow someone from the Underworld to sneak into Ordinary just so I can hear some juicy gossip?"

Myra groaned. "Really?"

"Xtelle," I said. "Yes or no. Did your spies come to Ordinary?"

"No. Unlike you, I can leave town whenever I want."

"I can leave town whenever I want too," I said. "Are you telling me the truth?"

"Yes."

I looked at Bathin for confirmation, and Xtelle made an offended sound.

"She's telling the truth," he said.

"Okay." I walked to the counter. "Thank you for bringing us the information, Xtelle."

"Late," Bathin added.

Xtelle narrowed her eyes, and there was a flicker of pink fire there.

"Still, I appreciate it," I said, hoping to avoid a demon-on-demon throwdown. "I also appreciate you coming here in human form. That was very thoughtful. Of both of you." I nodded at Avnas.

Both he and Xtelle froze, like I'd just aimed a gun at them.

"What?" Xtelle asked.

"The…uh…shape you're wearing so you can talk to us in a public space. I appreciate it."

"Appreciate," Avnas said, speaking for the first time since he'd come through the doors. "That's…good?"

"Yes, Uncle, it's good," Bathin interrupted. "This was the proper way to do what you did, and she's praising you for it."

"Praise? Of course we should be praised," Xtelle said, breaking from her frozen state. "We did it right. I know this rinky-dink town's rules. Now, if you'll excuse me, we have shopping to accomplish. The queen requires a camera."

"Wait," I said. "Do you have spies who can tell us what the demon king is planning?"

"My spies aren't that close to the king," she said.

I wanted to double check that with Bathin, but he spoke first. "What about Yiff?"

"No," she said. "He's relocated."

"Chaff?"

"Dead."

"You've recently spent time around the king," he said to Avnas.

Avnas raised his eyebrows. "Of course, my Prince. I was his advisor."

"Have you left him a plan for destroying Ordinary?"

"I would not be here, in this form, if that were true. To your question: No. I did not encourage nor offer any advice or plan for overtaking or destroying Ordinary. On my word, my Prince." He pressed one fist to his throat and the other to his stomach, in what appeared to be an uncomfortable salute.

"Do you have spies close to my father?"

"No." He hesitated, then offered, "Your brother may still be near enough he would know information."

"The guy who tried to kill Bathin?" I asked.

Bathin lifted one hand to brush away that detail. "Still, I wouldn't trust his word. There is nothing binding him to the truth. Unlike Mother's spies."

"Your brother could be crushed," Xtelle mused.

"No crushing," I said. "We want information, not bloodshed."

"Then we can cross Goap off the list of new hires,"

Bathin said. "All he has ever wanted is bloodshed and the throne."

"Someone from Ordinary could go see what's happening in the Underworld," Rossi said.

We all turned and looked at him. He gave an inscrutable smile. "Certainly, you don't think only demons can exist in the Underworld? There are all manner of creatures who walk those paths."

"Vampires?" Jean asked.

He shrugged in a way that said yes.

Bathin grunted, like he'd just had something he'd suspected confirmed.

"Badass," Jean grinned. "I didn't know that. Myra, did you know that?"

"No. I'll want details, Rossi," she said.

"Boring," Xtelle announced. "I regret wasting my time on this. Avnas, we have shopping to do." She spun on her toe and, like the queen she was, drifted past Avnas, who pivoted to follow her.

"Well, then. If you don't need me?" Stevie brushed his fingertips together, then stood from Myra's desk.

"You've come through with flying colors, Stevie," I said. "Thank you again."

"Happy to help my fellow Ordinary citizens, of course. Thank you for the tea and chocolate. Ta, Reeds and Reed-adjacents." He wiggled his fingers at us all, then was out the door.

"So, vampires, eh?" I said to Rossi.

He unfolded from the bench and strolled across the room. "Do you want me to see if I have any contacts down there?"

"Yes."

He tapped knuckles on the top of the counter. "Are we also still going forward with the murder mystery?"

"Like Bertie would give up on an event," Myra said.

"Good. I've been asked to play the starring role," he said.

"The detective?" Jean asked.

"No."

"One of the group guides?" Myra asked.

"No. I'm the dead body."

Jean laughed. "Talk about type casting."

"We could use the dragon," Bathin said.

"For a dead body?" I asked. "I don't think so."

"What?" He pushed off the wall. "No. I mean for getting information about my father's plans."

"Sending a dragon into hell would be a little obvious, don't you think?" Myra asked.

"It might be able to go undetected."

I knew the tiny pink pig wasn't really a little pig. I knew it was a ferocious dragon, practically indestructible, and feared by all manner of creatures including demons.

But just the idea of sending that little squishy piggy to the Underworld, made all my protective instincts kick in.

"I don't want to do that," I said. "I don't want to draw that much attention."

"Plus," Jean said, "it's just a sweet little piggy dragon. What if it got lost? What if it got hurt?"

"The sun going nova wouldn't hurt that sweet *piggy*," Bathin said. "It's a dragon, Jean. A *dragon*."

"But also a squooshy little oinkie oink," she said.

Bathin shook his head. "Well, if we're not sending it to hell, then we should put it to work here. You were worried about the wards keeping demons out. The dragon would have sensed the possessed had it been somewhere other than sleeping in your living room."

Myra gave him a hard look, maybe not liking his blunt tone, but I was nodding.

"I can't believe I didn't think about that," I said. "Maybe a patrol? Have it keep an eye on Ordinary's borders so we can strike before being attacked?"

"Aerial support?" Myra said. "It flies. It has vision, speed, and range."

"Oh, my gods," Jean breathed. "A flying pig!"

"No," I said. "No flying pig. We don't need another thing to have to cover up. It can take another shape."

Bathin grunted, and Rossi chuckled. "Good luck with that," Rossi said.

"What? It was a dragon in a cave just a couple years ago. It can be a…I don't know. A bird. A drone. A kite."

"A kite," Bathin nodded. "Sure, Delaney. Convince the dragon to be a kite."

"Hey, I can be very persuasive."

Both my sisters, the vampire, and the demon had themselves a good laugh about that.

RYDER STOOD near the sliding glass door, his phone to his ear, his arm resting on the frame above his head. "As long as you can get it there by Saturday next week, that's all I need."

I shut the door behind me quietly, and gave Spud, who had trundled my way, a soft rub behind the ears. "Hey, Spuds," I whispered.

The dragon-pig lifted its head and gave me a beady-eyed glare.

I pointed at it. "I need to talk to you Bridge to dragon."

It tipped its head and one pink ear flopped over.

"But first, I'm going to get food. I'm starving."

"Yep," Ryder said. "Sounds good. See you then."

"Who was that?" I asked from the kitchen.

"Our caterer. There's been a little mix up in the order, so we're shifting to plan G."

"We already blew through A to F?"

"Yep. So now all plans are G, for good enough." He strolled over to me and sat at the island. "You're home early."

"Am I?" I glanced at the digital clock over the stove and was surprised to see it was just after five o'clock. "I'm right on time, actually."

"Except you never are."

"Never?"

"You've been working a lot of overtime lately."

I grabbed the jar of olives and some cheese and put them on the counter. "Is that right?"

"Yes."

I twisted the lid and fished in the drawer for a fork. "I'm wondering how you know when I get home anymore, Mr. Bailey. You are rarely here, either." I popped an olive into my mouth.

"I have my ways."

"Spies?"

"Maybe."

"Surveillance?"

"Possibly."

"Did you install cameras?"

"I'll never say."

I sliced cheese and placed it on a cutting board along

with the jar of olives and set both between us. "Look at that! I made dinner!"

"Olives and cheese?"

"It's a charcuterie board."

"No fruit?"

I glanced around the kitchen, found a banana magnet on the fridge and plunked in on the board. "Fruit."

"No crackers?"

"You're crackers," I muttered, while chewing on a slice of cheese.

He leaned both arms on the countertop. "You haven't asked me how I'm recovering. You know, from the disfiguring injury I've endured."

"Sounds like you're feeling pretty full of yourself."

"I might be in pain. After staying home all day on the couch, napping."

"Are you?" I stabbed an olive, offered it to him. He opened his mouth and pulled it off the tines with his teeth.

"I wasn't even in pain when you left. Still good."

I glanced at the square of bandaging taped to his forearm. "Are you? You got stitches, Ryder."

"Like three. I'm good. Don't believe me?"

"No, I do."

He caught my hand. "I am fine. It's a little stiff. That's it. Want to tell me why you didn't have enough time for lunch?"

"Who says I didn't have lunch?" I said through a mouthful of cheese.

He leveled me a flat look.

"Okay, I didn't have lunch. It took forever to process the crime scene, arrange to have the bodies reburied, make sure the leprechaun wasn't live streaming the whole thing, and work out a plan to go on the offense against the king of hell."

"I still can't believe this town sometimes," he said. "Bring me up to speed?"

"You cooking?"

"I already cooked. Dinner's in the oven. Chicken and dumplings. Salad in the fridge."

"Have I told you how much I love you?"

"Not for a very, very long time." He leaned across the island.

"I love you," I said, meeting him in the middle for a kiss.

"I NEED YOUR HELP."

The dragon-pig was rooting around in the huge pile of stuffies near the fireplace, its head buried.

"It's about the demons that have been getting through our protections and into Ordinary. The ones that got through and hurt Ryder. The ones that sent those people to attack me."

It popped its head out of the toys and growled.

"I know. I know. But I'm fine. So is he."

The dragon-pig narrowed its eyes at Ryder, who was looking through one of his three-ring binders that contained the notes, samples, numbers, and everything else that was going into our wedding.

"I'm good," he said, holding up his bandaged arm, but not looking at us. "You didn't get a package recently did you, babe?"

"How big?"

"Bigger than a breadbox. Smaller than a car." He

flashed me a grin. "You could just say no instead of digging for hints."

"Digging?"

"You like that it's going to be a surprise."

He'd really leaned into the idea that this was a surprise for me, a secret, a gift he was giving me that I wouldn't open until I walked down the aisle. I loved him for that, so didn't remind him that he was having to deal with all this on his own because I sucked at this stuff.

"You remember that the rehearsal is tomorrow afternoon, right?"

"One o'clock," I dutifully repeated.

"Right. And you remember it's at the community center."

"Yes. Bertie has been cackling about us holding it in the old gymnasium for months. She likes to think she won the bid for where we were going to hold our wedding, but you gave her the rehearsal to keep her off the trail of where we're having the real ceremony, didn't you?"

"I will neither confirm nor deny. Wear something comfortable."

"Why? Are we doing jumping jacks? Climbing the rope?"

"No, but we'll be walking over to the restaurant for lunch, and it might rain."

I blew air through my lips. "Rain."

"Don't wear your wedding dress, is what I'm saying."

"What if I do? Afraid of a little bad luck?"

"No, but I might not be able to keep my eyes off you and then I won't pay attention to what we're supposed to be doing for the ceremony. Then I'll mess everything up on our big day and make our officiant angry."

"Who's our officiant?"

"It's a surprise."

"Fine. Be that way. I'm gonna talk to the dragon."

"Mmm-hmm."

"As I was saying," I said to the dragon-pig, who had found the toy it wanted, a screw with a shocked expression on its face. "I need you to help me out with the demon situation."

It grumbled and stomped around on top of Toy Mountain.

"Please."

It sat, and steam came out of its nostrils in a heavy sigh. It grunted.

"The people who attacked me were sent by demons, so I understand how they got through our protections. But the possessed bodies that attacked Ryder were actual demons. Demons in human clothing, but demons. Our wards didn't recognize them as demons."

It made a growly sound.

"I know you would have seen they were demons. Until we have better wards around Ordinary, which, yes, we're working on, would you patrol for demons? We were thinking since you fly, you could keep an eye on our borders."

The dragon-pig opened its little mouth and the ridges over one eye quirked up.

"Not in dragon form unless you go invisible."

It made an offended grunt.

"Or maybe you could be a bird, seagulls are…"

The growl was low.

"Okay, you could be a drone, if you like the idea of

metal...yeah from that sound I'm guessing that's a hard no. Maybe a kite?"

The growl became an almost subaudible rumble with an overlay of clicking. Every hair on my body stood up, and goosebumps riffled down my spine. That was the sound of a very big, very old, very dangerous thing, about to eat my face off.

"We could brainstorm. Toss around ideas."

"You could just be a pig," Ryder said, and the dragon-pig grunted in approval. "But if you fly, you'd have to make sure no one saw you."

The dragon-pig got a very cunning look on its little pink face.

"No," I said, "no, I don't think that's a good idea. People are bound to look up. And then they'll see a flying pig, and just my luck, Patrick will film it, and we will become the ninth wonder of the world, which is exactly what we don't need."

"Nobody looks up," Ryder said. "Well, kids do, but anyone past eighteen is too busy to wander around staring at the sky."

"I wander around staring at the sky."

"Sure. Because you know what kind of wonder is up there."

"Sometimes you say the sweetest things."

"Sometimes?"

I grinned at him.

"Wait until you hear the wedding vows I've written."

I went shock still. "We were doing that?"

"Writing our own vows? Yes. You said you wanted to. Don't you remember?"

"I...yeah. Heck yeah. I totally remember."

I did not remember. Should I panic? I was thinking I should panic.

He studied my expression and seemed to make up his mind about something. He set the heavy binder aside and came over to sit next to me on the couch.

He rested his arm behind me, his fingertips brushing the top of my shoulder. "We don't have to."

"But you already have."

He made a considering sound. "Just because I have doesn't mean you need to."

"It's both of us together or not at all. I know how weddings work."

"Sure," he said. "That's how most weddings work. But this is *our* wedding. We can make it anything we want it to be. Personal vows, no personal vows. Formal, casual. Just you and me and a couple witnesses, or the whole dang town. It's our wedding."

He gently turned my face so he could catch my gaze. "This is ours. Our promise to each other. We do it how we want to do it."

"No, I got this. We still have a week. I can write vows in a week."

He waited, I think, hoping I would reconsider. But I tipped my chin up. "Mine will, of course, be more romantic than yours," I said.

And there was that smile. The smile that had caught my heart when I'd been just a little kid. The smile that had teased me when I was a teen, the smile that had hooked my soul once I was grown, and whispered to me in my sleep, asking if I was there, asking if I was the one, waiting for my reply.

"We'll see about that," he said. "My vows are pretty

darn romantic. Jean says I'll have you crying before the first line is done."

"Jean? You told Jean? You...you *read* Jean my wedding vows? Jean knows what you're going to say to me?"

"Yes," he said, unrepentant. "I needed to get someone's opinion, and I can't ask you, can I?"

"You could."

"Nope. They're a surprise too. But if you need any help rhyming *handsome* or *charming* or *best man I've ever known*, just say the word. I'd be happy to help."

"If I can write amazing crime reports," I said, "then I am going to kick ass on wedding vows."

He laughed, and I loved the look of it on him, his head thrown back, mouth open, joy stretching all the lines of him. "Two things that are absolutely the same skill set," he said.

"What?" I said. "Writing is writing."

"Oh, I cannot wait for this."

I pushed his hand away from my shoulder. "You are going to be dazzled, Ryder Bailey. *Dazzled.*"

"I bet I am," he said, dropping his hand back in place. "Totally dazzled. I wouldn't expect anything less from you."

The dragon-pig grunted, reminding me that I hadn't sealed the deal yet.

"Sorry," I said. "Will you patrol Ordinary?"

It grumbled.

"Inconspicuously?"

It grumbled some more.

"She'll pay you," Ryder said.

I tried to elbow him, but he just laughed and pulled me closer.

"Fine. I'll pay you. In food."

It growled softly.

"Or in stuffies," I said. "How about one new stuffy a month and an extra snack every day?"

The dragon-pig *oink*ed and jumped off the pile to run down the hall to the spare room where Spud was sleeping.

"Thanks for bankrupting me," I said.

"I wasn't the one who set the terms."

I leaned my head against his shoulder and was quiet, resting in the warmth of him, in the even rise and fall of his breathing.

"I love you, Ryder Bailey."

"I love you too."

CHAPTER THIRTEEN

"YOU REALLY SHOULD RELAX," the dead body on the floor said quietly.

I glared at Rossi, who was supposed to be staring sightlessly at the gymnasium ceiling and pretending he was breathing but was trying not to.

"You should be dead," I replied.

His eye crinkled with the smug smile on his face. He whispered, "I am."

"The next group of people will be here any minute. If you screw this up, Bertie will have your head."

"She'll get over it."

"No, she won't. This isn't the rehearsal for the murder mystery. This *is* the murder mystery. Be dead."

The gymnasium door slammed open, and echoes clanged off the high ceiling. Rossi went unnaturally still, but it was just Jean. She sprinted across the room, glanced at Myra who was over at the refreshment table getting some water, and came to a halt next to me. "Sorry I'm slightly late."

She wore a pink skirt and had layered a lime-green

shirt under an orange sweater. But maybe the most shocking part of her appearance was her hair, which was a lovely pale *natural* blonde.

"What did you do to your hair?" I asked.

"Oh, I colored it. Like I always do."

"But it's…normal."

She laughed. "It's blonde. My natural hair is brown."

"Sorry. I'm just used to, you know, green, or pink, or blue."

"Well, I wanted a change for the wedding."

"All eyes should be on the bride," Rossi agreed.

"Hey, dead guy," Jean said. "Nice tux. Did Bertie tell you to wear it?"

"It adds to the mystery. Why would a refined man in his prime…"

Jean laughed, then clapped her hand over her mouth.

"…in his *prime*," Rossi repeated, "be found stabbed to death on a gymnasium floor?"

"Because he was talking when he was supposed to be dead?" I suggested.

Jean drew her hand away from her mouth. "Nice pitchfork, though. Looks real."

He lifted his hand away from the tines of the pitchfork, which appeared to be the murder weapon, stuck into his stomach.

"I was hoping she'd go for something a little more dramatic than a knife or a bullet," he said. "Still, it's not the first time I've been pitchforked. This one time in Romania…"

"And this, of course," Bertie called out, her voice projecting like she was either leading a tour group or trying to warn us not to miss our cues. "This is one of Ordinary's large, historic meeting places. It used to be the gymnasium, but now we often gather here for all kind of events. Why today, we have a wedding rehearsal going on. Please keep your voices down and be respectful of the event."

"Oh gods," I groaned.

"Hey, it's good," Jean said. "Smile and pretend we're talking."

"We are talking."

"See? It's all working out."

The doors opened, the loud mechanical bar releasing, and I snuck a quick look.

Bertie was swathed head to foot in peacock blue, her jacket and slacks pressed within an inch of their lives. She'd donned a ruby red fedora and set it at an angle so that it dipped over one eye just a bit. She didn't look like the dame in one of those old detective movies so much as the investigator ready to tackle the crime and criminal on her own.

She stepped aside to let the crowd move into the room ahead of her.

"Where's Ryder, anyway?" Jean asked.

"He got called out by Mithra. He texted." I checked the phone clenched in my hand and read his text for the hundredth time. "He should be here in about five minutes."

"Here's your water," Myra said. "Take a drink. Everything's fine."

"Oh, my god!" a woman called out. "They're having their wedding in a gym?"

"Look!" a man said. "She killed her husband! With a pitchfork!"

The crowd made gasping sounds, and a few people chuckled. Most of them shuffled forward to get a closer look at Rossi, who, I had to admit, was doing a great job of looking dead.

Phones were in hands and several people snapped pictures. A couple jokers knelt next to Rossi and took selfies with him.

Other people fanned out and started inspecting the gym, looking, I assumed, for clues, and a few brave folk beelined to the table covered in cookies and pastries.

"Hold it," Myra said, heading them off at the pass. "Those are for the wedding rehearsal."

"Please stay on this half of the room," Bertie said. "You can see the line right there dividing the space. As I said, we have a wedding rehearsal in progress."

"Where's the groom?" a man called out.

"He'll be here shortly, I'm sure. Now, as I said," she went on, "there appears to have been a murder."

"What the fork?" a teenager said.

"That's a forking travesty," a man added.

"We need to catch that mother forker," a woman said.

"The murderer," Bertie corrected. "Has everyone had enough time to look for clues?"

"Are the cookies clues?" a woman asked.

"Maybe we should ask the police chief. She's standing right there," another woman said.

"No, she's not a part of the mystery," Bertie said.

"But it says right here," a pamphlet was dug out of a large purse, "that we can ask anyone in town anything during the mystery, and they will answer."

"With the one exception of the wedding rehearsal," Bertie insisted, but I decided to jump in. After all, Ryder wasn't here yet, and almost anything was better than waiting around doing nothing.

"You may absolutely ask me anything, and I'll answer." I strolled forward. "Until my husband-to-be shows up and we start our rehearsal. How may I be of help?"

Jean just sighed. Myra walked up beside me with a plate of cookies and offered them to the crowd.

Bertie looked surprised, but she went with the pivot like a champ.

"What we have here, Chief Reed, is a group of very sharp-eyed private investigators," Bertie said. "They are looking into a murder."

"A murder here? In Ordinary? Well, I'm glad to have you all on the case. We don't get many murders in town. We can use all the help we can get."

A woman raised her hand. "Are you really the police chief?"

"Yes."

I man raised his hand. "Did you stab that guy with a pitchfork?"

"I did not."

"Can you tell us who did?" another guy called from the back.

"I cannot."

"Have you met Patrick Baum?" a woman asked.

"I have."

The crowed *ooooh*ed like I'd just told them I'd dined with a rock star.

"What was he like?" the woman continued. "In person. I mean, I'm one of his biggest fans. But what was it like to…touch him?"

"I didn't touch him."

"What did he smell like?" another, younger woman asked. "Everyone says he smells so good. How good did he smell? Did he smell delicious? Will you dream of his smell? Did he tell you what cologne he was wearing?"

"Um…he smelled okay, I guess."

"Oh." She looked like I'd just shot her pet hamster.

"But hey," I said in a cheery tone, "we have a dead body. And everyone who solves the murder gets a prize."

"That is correct," Bertie said. "A prize for everyone who participates—we all have our clue booklets?"

Several people held up something that looked like passport books.

"Excellent. List a clue from six or more places and you will receive a second prize. Those who solve the mystery, will receive cash prizes. Let's just move along. Has everyone gotten a cookie, yes? Good. Excellent. Are there any other questions?"

"Did the killer leave a clue here?" an older woman asked.

"Yes," Bertie said. "Several. Would you like a few moments to investigate the room?"

"Yes," another older woman said. Then the two of them took off with determined steps, pointing out scuff marks on the floor and posters on the walls.

Everyone else fanned out and ate cookies, chatting. The teens remained. They stood next to Rossi and ate cookies over him, purposely dropping crumbs on his face.

"You got food on your face, dead guy," the taller one said. "Hey, you think he'll squeal if I kick him?"

"Do not!" I started while Myra and Jean also shouted, but that wasn't what stopped the kid.

Rossi's hand whipped out so fast, it could not be seen

by the naked eye. His hand was on the floor, then the next instant, his hand was around the kid's ankle. I could see the points of his fingers, talons at the moment, digging into the kid's jeans.

His eye glowed and his fangs dropped.

"I know where you sleep, Jeremy."

The kid shrieked and backpedaled, trying to kick off Rossi's hold and getting all tangled up in the process. His friend yelled and tried to help, but instead he just pulled his buddy back harder, which made both of them land in a pile several feet away from Rossi.

Rossi was still. Dead still. I could see the difference now. He'd been trying to pretend to be alive acting dead before, now he was undead and acting dead.

The stillness was eerie. Despite having been raised around all sorts of people in various states of living, I felt chills roll down my arm.

"Naw," one of the teens said. "No way. Did you see that? It's a dummy. It has to be a dummy."

"That was so freaky!" the other said.

"Jeremy, Scott, come on," a man's voice called out. "We got the clue. It was a dropped glove."

He said that loud enough, some of the other people groaned, but most of them scribbled it down in their passports.

The teens got to their feet. "It's a dummy, right?" Jeremy said. "There's no way that's real."

"It's a murder victim," I said. "And let that be a reminder that messing with evidence is sloppy detective work."

"And could get you killed," Jean added.

I rolled my eyes, but both the boys went pale.

"Keep your hands to yourself around the actors, and you'll be fine," I said.

The boys rambled away from Rossi, throwing looks over their shoulders and shoving each other, like it was all a big joke. A roller coaster ride. A haunted house.

"Really?" I said quietly, not looking at Rossi. "Full vamp-out?"

His smile was quick and wicked. "I might enjoy this part more than I thought."

"No," I said. "No more of that."

"Unless someone tries to hurt you," Jean added.

"Yes. That."

Bertie guided the crowd out of the room and kicked the stop block under the door so it would remain open.

A few people in ones and twos or smaller groups wandered in, spotted Rossi, made notes, then eventually found the glove that had "accidentally" fallen behind the trash can. The mood was fun, easy, most people walking around with coffee or treats they'd picked up from various stops in town.

I also noted several shopping bags, which meant the event was bringing in money. At least we had that going for us.

"He'll be here," Myra said.

"What?"

"You keep looking at the door. Ryder. He'll be here."

I nodded, but she was staring at the doors too.

"Reed sisters!" Crow called out, as he sauntered into the room. "Are we ready to rumble?"

"You're not officiating," I said. "Are you?"

"I might be." He stopped next to Rossi. "Gruesome. Almost as ugly as when he was alive."

Rossi lifted his middle finger, then quickly put it back in place when a group of three came into the room.

"But aren't you the best man?" I said.

"I'm always the best man in any room," he said. "Are those cookies open for participants?"

"Yes," Myra said.

He hustled over to the table where Jean was standing, scrolling through her phone.

"He's on the way," Jean said.

"Ryder?" I asked.

"Huh?" she glanced up. "Maybe? I mean, yes. Of course Ryder's coming. But I was talking about Patrick."

"He's coming?" I asked. "Here?"

"According to his tracking app he is." She turned her phone so I could see the screen.

"He has a tracking app...no, never mind. Of course he does."

"How many people are with him?" Myra asked.

"I don't know. His last live stream was at Gan's tea shop. That was fifteen minutes ago."

"And he's live streaming," I said. "Great."

"We made it," Ryder said. "I am so sorry we're late." He crossed the room in long strides, his gaze on no one else but me. "Delaney. I'm sorry."

"No, it's good," I said. "I mean, if you think that was just five minutes, you really need to refresh yourself on how long it takes the big hand to go around the clock."

"I got hung up," he said. "Mithra, then some business stuff, and there are so many people out there, traffic is a mess—no, no, don't give me that look. We can let our volunteers handle traffic flow while we do this. It's fine. It's going to be fine. I even brought our officiant."

I finally looked at his companion.

"Hera," I said, smiling. "Thank you. This is really sweet of you."

"I would not miss your marriage for anything," she said with a smile. "So, we have the bridesmaids," Jean and Myra waved, "and the best man."

"He did pick you," I said.

Crow chuckled. "Yes. Because I'm the best. In any room."

"Don't you have some random construction worker you could ask instead?" I asked Ryder.

He shrugged. "They were all booked up for that day." He winked. "Weird."

"Where's your other groomsman?"

"He'll be here in a minute," Ryder said. "He said to start without him."

"I'm here," Odin said from the door.

Myra caught my elbow. "Come on, let's go see where we should be standing, and when we should come in."

"Wait." I looked at Ryder. "Here? We're having our wedding in the gym? Really?"

He grinned. "I'll just say this was the best place to practice, especially since everything else is booked up due to the dead guy. Thanks for dying today, Rossi."

Rossi gave him a thumbs up, and Ryder chuckled.

"Aren't you supposed to practice the ceremony where the actual ceremony is going to happen?" I asked.

"I figured this would be enough. Besides," he waggled his eyebrows, "maybe none of this is the way it's going to really go. It's a surprise."

I shook my head. "You are something, Ryder Bailey. It's a wonder I've agreed to marry you."

"Yes," he said. "I am a wonder, thank you for noticing."

He took my hand, and we walked over to get our directions.

I expected arguments between the gods, but they were all far more congenial and respectful than I'd ever seen them. They treated this practice event with humor, but also as if it were important.

We got our walk down the aisle cues wrong half a dozen times, but finally got the hang of it, Odin with Jean, Crow with Myra, and me, walking down the aisle alone.

I was so focused on doing the step-pause, step-pause, which wasn't as easy as it looked, that I didn't even notice Patrick walk into the room.

Jean did, though, because she went stiff like someone had just slapped her. She was standing next to Myra, Hera between them, then Ryder, Crow, and Odin. They were all watching me, so they saw Patrick behind me.

I turned.

"Don't mind me." He held up his passport clue book. "I'm just here for the murder."

"Delaney," Hera said. "You'll come down the aisle," she reminded me.

"Sure. Right." I went back to step-pause, step-pausing, but something was off now.

The room felt charged, as if there was a dangerous thing in the space that hadn't been here just moments before. As if a fuse had been lit, and the flame was chewing its way toward the bomb.

I was aware of a man and woman coming into the room to make notes over Rossi, and then walking straight to the garbage can to find the glove. It seemed word had gotten out about some of the clues. Now it wasn't so much a hunt, as just checking that it was still where people said it was.

They mumbled something that sounded like, "it's him," and, "he's even taller in person," and then they were gone.

Patrick remained. I could sense him in the room, moving around like he was casually looking for clues, but that felt fake. Planned. There was a tension in him too, and I wondered if I was sensing his soured luck.

I step-paused to my position next to Ryder, and Hera said, "Nicely done!"

Ryder offered his hand for a high five, and I slapped it.

"Dazzled," he said.

I knew my smile was tight, because my nerves were jangling. Was something wrong, or was it just wedding jitters?

"This is the part where I'll ask everyone to be seated," Hera said. And then both of you can, yes, just stand like that. Good. I'll give you a second to just breathe, and I'll inhale," she did so, "and exhale. Just follow me. After that we'll be off to the races. Ready?"

"Inhale, exhale," Ryder said. "We got that."

"Delaney?" Hera asked.

"Breathe. Super easy."

"This, then," Hera said, raising her voice enough to be heard by the back of the room, and still somehow feeling like she was only talking to Ryder and me, "is a beginning. A moment suspended in time to mark and hold a vow of love, of loyalty, of devotion."

Ryder's gaze was unwavering, and I could not look away from him.

The man I loved, had always loved for all these years was standing here with me, pledging to stay with me, to give me his life, just as I would give him my life, to build with me something only we two could share, no matter if there was sickness or health.

Hera's words blurred. The whole room blurred because there were tears in my eyes. If there were more than just Ryder and me in this bubble of space, in this very private connection, I could neither see nor hear them.

"Wait," Jean said from miles and miles behind me. "I feel sick."

A crowd burst into the room, screaming, cheering, chanting. I felt like I'd tipped over a great dreaming edge and had suddenly landed in cold water.

The room was chaos.

Two or three hundred people were running across the floor, pushing to get through the doors, a raging, smashing mosh pit.

I didn't know what was happening.

Then Patrick was there. "My fans," he said, wild-eyed. He grabbed Ryder, pushing Ryder in front of him like a human shield, while dragging him back and back away from us.

"No!" Jean yelled. "Delaney, stop him!"

Myra was in front of me somehow, running, but she tripped—Myra never tripped—and stumbled before reaching Patrick and Ryder.

Ryder shoved away from Baum, but Patrick was fast. He pulled a knife, held it to Ryder's throat, then gave me a wink.

"Surrender Ordinary to the King, or Ryder dies. You have one day."

I ran, Hera ran, Crow and Odin ran. We never had a chance.

Patrick disappeared in a snap, taking Ryder with him. They were gone almost before the last word left his mouth.

And just like that, the crowd slowed, quieted. They milled around for a moment.

I heard, "flash mob," and, "hope I'm in his video," and, "don't know where the cameras were," and, "great disappearing trick" and other variations of that, and knew Patrick had set it up. A crowd of fans hoping to be part of his show, and all they had to do was run into a room and act like a wild, cheering mob.

All they had to do was create enough chaos, Patrick could steal my fiancé, and drag him to hell.

My ears were ringing. I thought I was shaking, shivering. I didn't think I was breathing, wasn't even sure if I was still standing.

I clenched my fist, my gut going hot, and that heat spread over me. Anger. Fury. Rage.

The rage burned through me, until every inch of my mind and body felt alive, violent, pure, and just.

Then the fire subsided, leaving me forged, cold, and unbreakable.

CHAPTER FOURTEEN

IT HAD HAPPENED IN A MOMENT, just seconds at the most.

"Are you all right?" Myra was there now, maybe had been for some time, her hand on my shoulder. The crowd was gone, Rossi was on his feet.

"I'm fine." My voice was hard. It was mine, but I was beyond it somehow, still wrapped in fury and steel. "Get Bathin. I want him to see if there is a way to trace their escape."

Myra hesitated.

"That's an order, Myra."

She pressed her lips together and gave me a short nod. "I'll be right back." She left, her phone already dialed and at her ear.

Crow had his arm around Jean's shoulders.

"I'm fine, it was just a punch to the head," she said. "Fucking doom twinges never give me enough time to *do* anything about them."

"Do you want us to hunt him down?" Hera asked.

"Can you find him in the Underworld?" I asked.

Her vision sharpened, hawk-bright. "I can find anyone."

"If you take up your power, you're out of Ordinary for a year," I said flatly.

Two girls, who looked like middle-schoolers, jogged into the room. Rossi was just fast enough to drop back into dead-body mode.

"He's supposed to be dead?" one of them said. "He looks like a vampire."

"Totally," the other said. They trotted across the room and stared down at Rossi. "Vampire," the second girl confirmed.

Rossi lifted his lip just enough to show fang, and both girls jumped, squealed, and ran, laughing, from the room.

Rossi sat and glared at me. "You're not going alone to save him."

"Did I say I was going alone?"

He held my gaze like he knew I was lying. "Delaney. You are not going alone."

"I'm not going anywhere until I have weapons and a plan." Voices in the hall grew closer. "You have a job to do. You're supposed to be dead. Do your job. I'll do my job."

I could hear it, how harsh my voice was. I knew Rossi wasn't to blame for Ryder getting kidnapped—

—*a knife at his throat, his eyes wide as Patrick dragged him backward*—

—stolen from me, his life reduced to a bargaining chip. But the anger in me was coal burning hot, and until I got Ryder back, until the King of the Underworld paid for what he'd done, there was no space in me for mercy.

"We should take this somewhere else, Delaney," Crow said.

There were footsteps coming down the hall, and Rossi was prone, dead again as the happy people, sipping sodas, eating caramel corn, strolled into the room.

"Oh, look!" said a man who probably hosted all the barbecues on his block. "Someone has been killed. Murdered, even. Shall we search for the murder weapon?"

"The pitchfork isn't enough, Carl?" a woman asked.

"We can't jump to conclusions," he admonished. He took in the surroundings, and startled a little when he saw me, Jean, and the gods.

"Is there…" He took a couple steps our way. "Is there a problem? A real problem? You're a police officer, aren't you? You look like the one from Baum's video."

I had done this before. Shoved all of my emotions down to deal with police business, to uphold the law, to keep the people in my town safe.

I'd certainly shoved my emotions and needs to the side to make sure that Ordinary's secrets remained secret.

But today, I could not.

"That's your murder victim." I pointed at Rossi. "The dropped glove is behind the trash can. You figure out if it's a problem."

"Sorry," Crow said, stepping forward, all smiles. "There isn't a problem, well, other than the," he made air quotes, "dead body. We've just had a little upsetting news about the upcoming wedding. The flowers are on back order."

"Fuck this," I said, starting across the room.

"She really wanted those flowers," Crow fake whispered.

He had done a good job. Made the visitors feel comfortable, made them feel like everything was normal. I was the one who was supposed to do that kind of thing, but I could not give a damn.

"Jean, tell Myra I'll be at my house. I want to see you all there within the hour."

Footsteps followed me, but I didn't look back. I wanted out of here, wanted out of this reality, of this place, this crime. If I could do it on my own, I'd march into hell right now, and demand the king give Ryder back to me.

But first, I needed weapons.

"You need a plan," Odin said, strolling up beside me.

I pushed out of the building into daylight. It was sunny and beautiful, only a few puffy white clouds in the sky. Cheerful. Happy.

How could the weather be so happy? I wanted rain. I wanted hail. I wanted tornado and wild fire.

"I'm driving." Odin opened the driver's door to my Jeep. I wanted to fight him for it. I wanted to yell.

"I'll take you home," he said, in a fatherly rumble I hadn't heard in years. "We'll make a plan. We'll need weapons. We'll need coordinates. I'll drive." He didn't wait for my answer, but shoved up behind the wheel and started the engine.

I got in. I didn't remember closing the door, didn't remember putting on my seatbelt. Most of the drive went by in a haze of anger.

There were too many people in my town. Brought

here by an asshole leprechaun who had kidnapped Ryder.

Taken him away from me, right in front of me, in front of gods, in front of a crowd of people.

I hadn't kept him safe—

—I shoved that away, breathing through the tightness in my chest. I hadn't kept him safe. But that didn't mean I wasn't going to save him now.

"Myra's here," Odin said. "Let's go."

There was another blink of time, and I was out of the Jeep and walking through my front door.

Spud greeted me, tail wagging, his favorite shark stuffy in his mouth.

"Not now, Spud," I said, pushing past him and rounding on my sister who was in the kitchen. "Where's Bathin?"

She placed two mugs of something hot on the kitchen island, then wrapped me in a hug.

"Don't—"

She squeezed tighter. "We'll get him back," she said. "We will kill the leprechaun, we will kill the Brute of all Evil. We will get him back."

"I know," I said. "Let go."

"You didn't do anything wrong."

"Don't," I said.

"You didn't fail him."

"I—" Words dried up in my throat, but I crushed the rising wave of sorrow under a mountain of rage. I did not have time for tears.

Myra held me tightly, her hand warm on my back. She didn't say anything else, but she didn't have to.

Sounds of the house came to me, Odin taking something out of the fridge and walking to our sliding glass doors. The crackle of the fireplace.

Sensations came to me, Myra breathing slowly and evenly, Spud leaning his head into my leg, pressing there, his doggy version of a hug.

Smells came to me, Myra's perfume of flowers and vanilla, the scent of cream and honey, and strong, black coffee.

But rage was all I could feel.

She patted my back, then stepped away.

"First, coffee." She reached for the cups. Spud tried to give me his toy again, whining softly.

I bent and rubbed his ears. "Good boy."

His tail wagged uncertainly, and he leaned harder against my leg.

"Bathin's checking the area where they disappeared." Myra pressed the coffee into my hand. "He'll be over after that."

I sat on a kitchen stool and set the mug down, too angry to drink. "What did you hear Patrick say when he took him?"

"You don't remember?"

"I want to hear it from you."

"He said surrender Ordinary to the King, or Ryder dies. You have one day."

"King of the Underworld. Vychoro."

"Maybe," she said. "Or that was a lie. We'll see if Bathin can tell. Drink."

I pulled the mug back into my hands, but didn't drink.

Myra studied me, the frown carving hard lines at the edges of her mouth. I stared right back at her.

She sighed. "You aren't in this alone, Delaney. You

need to remember that." Then she took her tea and walked away to talk to Odin.

Jean arrived, bringing Hogan with her. Hera and Crow showed up, too, as did Than, who must have gotten out of his coroner's duties for the play.

Bathin finally strolled in, looking as angry as I felt.

"Was Vychoro behind it?" I asked. "Is your father the demon who owns Patrick?"

"I couldn't find any trace of my father in the gym," Bathin said. "But he has plenty of lackies who could be pulling the strings for him."

"How did Patrick disappear?" Myra asked. "Was it a demon vortex?"

"It wasn't demon magic," Bathin said. "Leprechaun magic, I think."

"Can you track him?" Crow asked.

Bathin hesitated, then shrugged one shoulder. "Luck will be on his side. Always. But I know the Underworld. I know my father's kingdom. If that is where Patrick's taking Ryder, I can find him."

"They'll know you're there," Odin said.

"Yes. Eventually."

"If you guide us through hell, will that make us more of a target?" Myra asked.

"You're not going," Bathin said to her.

"You aren't in the position to say if I go or not," she replied.

"No," I said, "but I am. You're staying. I'm going with Bathin."

"Nice try," she said. "If you're going, I'm going."

"And I'm going," Jean added.

"Babes," Hogan breathed, his whole heart in that one word.

"Like I'd stay behind while my sisters go to hell to save Ryder," Jean replied.

Hogan nodded, even though he looked a little sick. He pulled her closer, his arm over her shoulder. "Then I'm going too," he said.

"No," Bathin argued. "We can't take everyone."

"Sure," Hogan agreed. "But I'm going."

"Delaney," Bathin sighed. "You need to talk sense into these people."

I didn't have time for this. Didn't have time to argue. "We need a small group. Bathin, you're coming because I need your directions. Myra, Jean, you're staying."

"The fuck I am," Myra said.

"Bullshit," Jean said.

"Which means," I raised my voice, "Hogan stays too. Me, Bathin and…" I glanced at the gods gathered.

"Any of us will come with you," Hera said. "You know that."

"I'm going," Crow announced.

"Only if you want to get them killed," Odin said. "Demons and gods have warred before. Humans rarely survive."

"This is a rescue mission, not a war," Crow said. "They don't walk into hell alone."

"Perhaps," Than said, "we should consider the most capable rescue party, not the most willing."

There was a moment of stunned silence.

"The demon king has not remained in power by making idle threats," Than said. "He has not remained in power by telling the truth. Who would he expect to follow Ryder Bailey? How would he expect Delaney to 'surrender Ordinary?'"

I shook my head. "I can't give anyone Ordinary. I don't own it."

"No," Odin said, "but you are tied to it. You allow the coming and going. He wants that."

"Which is why you shouldn't go," Myra said.

"If not me, then who, Myra? Do you think a god's going to go down there and save Ryder? If they leave Ordinary, they'll have to pick up their powers and won't be allowed back into Ordinary for a year. No one's going to volunteer for that."

Hera made a sound, and Than shook his head.

"We don't like leaving Ordinary," Odin said. "But it doesn't mean we won't. For things like this. For life, for love, for battle or rescue, of course we'll pick up our powers."

"Accurate," Than said. "But the question is *should* a god go into hell to find Ryder?"

"No," Hera said. She pushed her hair back. Her eyes were bright, hard. "Not unless we want to declare war on the Underworld and engage in what may be years of battle.

"If this is to be a rescue mission, we would only draw attention. Our power would draw attention. Even Hades would be known by the king. So, no. Unless we want to battle all of hell's forces head on?" She waited to see if any of us were down for that plan. "Then no. No god should try to sneak into the Underworld."

"I repeat," Crow said, "I'm going."

Hera tipped her head, like she was listening to far-off thunder build. "Even Raven will be seen," she said. "This was a *very* specific attack. This was a *very* specific kidnapping. The demon king wants you, Delaney. Because he thinks you will give him Ordinary."

"Only because Ordinary will stand between him and taking over the rest of the world."

"Yes," she agreed.

"How much time do we have before we leave?" Jean asked, pocketing her phone.

"Time is...fluid between the Underworld and here," Bathin said. "We have until midnight tomorrow night, our time."

That was good information to know, but I wouldn't need it. I wasn't going to wait that long.

He snapped his fingers. A map appeared in the air, glowing with lines in red, yellow, and purple. Other features beneath those lines were blurry from my angle.

"This is the Underworld," he said, "or one representation of it. There are as many entrances and exits as could be imagined, but the king's court is here." He pointed to the upper right corner of the map.

"Higher ground, more closely oriented to the power of the place. Secured by far fewer entrances."

"Is it a fortress?" Myra asked.

"Usually. It doesn't follow the rules of reality that are followed on Earth. The king and other forces can change the buildings, terrain, air, and power sources. Everything."

"Like a god realm," Crow said. "It shifts to the desire of the ruler. To their power."

"I suppose," Bathin said. "I've never been in a god's realm."

"What are the weaknesses?" Myra asked.

"There aren't any. Which is why we'll need intel from Mother's spies. And why we'll need someone on the inside guiding us."

"You'll guide," I told Bathin.

He nodded. "It won't be easy, but I think I can keep us hidden long enough. It will depend on where Ryder is being kept and by whom."

"You aren't leaving me behind," Myra insisted. "Or Jean."

"You'll need more firepower," Odin said. "If not a god then another powerful being should go with you."

"Or," Than said, "perhaps certain gods should leave Ordinary long enough to carry their power and use it for the most effect. If I were to leave Ordinary, I would once again wield the power of death to my desire."

"To kill the king," I said.

"Yes."

"No," Bathin said. "Only a first-spawned—first-born—can kill the king. That's me. It doesn't take a god of death to make that prophecy come true."

"But it takes the demon axe," I said. "Bunny Kisses."

"It does," he agreed.

"Is that still locked in the library?" I asked Myra.

"Yes. With the demon sword."

That was going to be the difficult part of my plan: how to get the axe out of the library without Myra knowing. I was not letting my sisters walk into hell with me.

"Okay," Jean said, "but killing the king won't help us find Ryder. This is still a rescue mission, right?"

She was looking at me, so I nodded. "Killing the king isn't our priority. We don't need firepower, we need stealth. You said we have until midnight tomorrow?" I asked Bathin.

"Yes. We'll be able to travel quickly through the stones I've left in the Underworld."

"Bathin, tell your mother to have her spies find out where Ryder is being kept." I swallowed, hating this next part. Demons were liars, and that deadline might never have been real. "Tell them to find out if he's still alive."

"Delaney," Myra breathed. "He's not…"

I put a hand out to stop her. "Jean, Hogan, get some sleep, and get prepared. We're leaving at dawn."

Jean narrowed her eyes, and I met her gaze. "Now," I added.

"Don't go anywhere without me," she said.

"I know."

"Don't go anywhere without us," she insisted.

"Jean. I'm not stupid."

"No one goes anywhere until we have intel and weapons," Bathin said.

"Get the intel," I said. "Get the weapons. Go."

They finally left, throwing grim looks at me, which I ignored.

"He is still alive, Reed Daughter," Than said. "I would know otherwise."

I swallowed and nodded. I should take that as comfort, but just because he was alive right now, didn't mean he would be alive by morning. "Do you want applause?" I asked.

Than's eyes went flint cold.

"Can I talk to you a minute?" Crow interrupted.

I turned my glare on him.

"This way." He headed to the stairs, then changed his mind and walked instead to our spare room.

Dragon-pig and Spud usually hung out in this room, but besides the random stuffies, the two extra-thick dog beds, and the water bowls, it was still set up for guests.

I followed Crow into the room, and he shut the door

behind us.

"I know you're angry," he said.

I crossed my arms over my chest and leaned against the dresser.

"But I need to know that you're thinking clearly right now."

"You," I said, my voice hard, "are asking me if I'm thinking clearly? When am I ever not thinking clearly, Crow? I'm the one who keeps this place on an even keel. I'm the one who makes sure gods and demons don't screw things up so badly we get wiped off the face of the earth. So, yes, I'm thinking clearly. I'm thinking I'm going to get Ryder back, and you aren't going to talk me out of it."

"Like you don't even know me," he sighed. "Of course you're going. I want to give you this." He pulled a necklace out from under his shirt. I was pretty sure it was the same necklace that was supposed to be locked up in the magic library so it didn't fall into the wrong hands and accidentally start Armageddon.

"Your god weapon? How do you even have this? It was supposed to be locked up in the library with the other god weapons, Crow."

"Well, I might have held onto it a little bit. The point is, I am giving it to you."

"Bathin said you'd stick out like a sore thumb in hell."

"This is my token, Delaney Reed. It will remain hidden. But if you need me, if you need my power, you will be able to access it with this stone."

"Sure. And what happens if I drop it?"

"It cannot be dropped."

"Lose it?"

"Can't lose it."

"What if someone or something takes it, breaks it, steals it right out of my hands? I am not batting a thousand when it comes to holding onto valuable things at the moment."

My voice had gotten rougher and louder. I wasn't yelling at the end there, but everyone in the other room probably heard every word.

Crow stepped up to me and looped the necklace over my head. The stone was heavy and cool, even through the cotton of my shirt. "No one will see this. No one will take it from you. You cannot lose it. Through it is my power, and through my power, the power of the other gods here in Ordinary, stored together in Death's image.

"This," Crow said, "is my wings around you, my eyes for you, my talons sharpened. This is my protection." His eyes glittered with quiet power as he spoke those words. A blessing, a prayer.

"Come home to us, Delaney Reed, with Ryder beside you."

His hands lifted from the necklace, palms resting gently on my cheeks as he tipped my head down so he could kiss my forehead.

"I bought a tux for your wedding," he murmured softly. "I'll be damned if I'll let it hang in the closet unworn."

I coughed. It was a sob. The mountain over my sorrow shifted, crumbled.

Then Crow's arms were around me, and my face was buried in his shoulder so I could cry and yell and trust him to keep my body attached to the world while my soul blew apart.

CHAPTER FIFTEEN

THE INTEL CAME IN.

Yes, Patrick had taken Ryder to the Underworld.

Yes, Ryder was bound and imprisoned.

Yes, he was still alive.

Yes, Vychoro would kill him by midnight tomorrow.

I sent the gods home, telling them I needed some time alone. I knew some, maybe all of them, were outside watching.

Dragon-pig came home, and from the stomping and steaming, it was angry at me for not telling it to eat the leprechaun.

"Ordinary is still a target for demons," I told it. "I need you here while I'm gone. I need you looking after Ordinary, keeping it safe until I bring Ryder home."

The dragon snarled. It was still in pig form, but I could see a full dragon shadow behind it like an after-image from staring at the sun too long.

"I know you can find demons. Every demon I know has been terrified of you. But that's *why* you can't come.

They'll know you're there. We have to be fast, quiet, and invisible."

The dragon-pig popped out of existence and made a little growl telling me it was still in front of me.

"I know you can be invisible. But I need...I need to know Ordinary is going to be safe from attack while we're gone. This could be a diversion to try and lure us away from Ordinary so they can attack. You can't let them get into Ordinary. You have to keep everyone safe."

There was a small *pop*, and the dragon-pig was visible again. It sat on the couch next to me, sighed, then bumped my hand with its snout.

I rubbed its soft little ears.

"It's going to be okay," I said to the empty room, as the dragon-pig pushed up onto my lap, making room for itself along with Spud, whose head rested on my thighs. "I'm going to get him back."

Bertie stopped by. Her event was done, the winners announced, the prizes given.

She handed me a beer.

"No, thanks," I said.

She waved it at me. "Chris insisted. It's a new berry and juniper blend he's testing."

I took the bottle and held it between my palms. "Did the murder get solved?"

"Yes, the butler did it. Of course." She lowered herself into the armchair, looking as tired as I should feel.

She twisted off the cap of her own beer and took a long drink. "I brought the leprechaun here," she said.

"Robyn shoved him in your face." My anger had

gone cool and strong. A thrum in my bones, waiting for the trigger.

"You should blame me," she said. "It is my fault."

I rolled the beer. Chris had outdone himself with the label. It showed the ocean and the curve of Road's End, with Wizard's Rock spiking out into the waves.

There was something lonely about it, and something inviting. As if this one place was magic, untouched, unreachable. But you were going to get sand in your shoes trying to get there anyway.

"I blame Vychoro," I said. "I blame Patrick. I blame myself. But that's it. If you came here looking for forgiveness, it's yours. But I don't blame you."

"I should have known," Bertie said. "She was so...*excited* to tell me how Baum's followers had brought so much attention to her town. If she'd really thought he had done her any good, she would have never told me."

She was staring at the beer label, running her thumb over the edge of it.

"Think I'll ever meet Robyn?" I asked.

"I doubt it," she said thoughtfully. "I plan to kill her anyway."

"Grim."

"Deserved," she replied. She took another drink, then placed the bottle on the table, pulling one of our rarely used coasters over first.

This whole thing: Bertie talking with me like we were at a bar sharing our sorrows, her attitude one of weary acceptance instead of sparking like steel on flint threw me a little.

"Why are you here, Bertie?" I put my beer on the table too.

She frowned at it, retrieved another coaster, and placed it under the bottle.

"Who have you chosen to retrieve Ryder?" she asked.

"I'm going." I waited for her to argue like everyone else, but she just nodded. "Myra and Jean think they're going."

"You won't let them?"

"I want them safe. I want them to stay behind. If I can make that happen, I will."

She hummed. "Who else then? The gods?"

"Crow wants to go. We talked him out of it. Bathin will guide me. Also, he's the first spawned, so he can kill the king."

"Which will automatically make him king."

I frowned. I'd forgotten that part. He didn't want to be king. He had even told his younger brother, Goap, he would step aside so Goap could become king.

"We'll figure it out. I want the king dead, but the main goal is to bring Ryder home."

"I should come," she said quietly. "If you'll have me. I am very good at retrieving souls from dark places."

I thought about it. Bertie wasn't a god, so she didn't have to pick up or put down her power to stay in Ordinary.

"We have to move fast," I said. "And we won't know for sure where we're going. Bathin can take people into rocks to move through the Underworld unseen. I don't know if he can take a Valkyrie into those spaces.

"Ordinary may become a battlefield if demons attack. I want you here if that happens. I trust you to protect our town."

She tipped her chin to the side, thinking that over,

then spread her hands. "You may be correct. But this is not something you have to fight on your own, Delaney. I hope you understand that."

I nodded. I understood what she was saying, even if I very much disagreed with her. This was my fight.

"When do you leave?" she asked.

"Dawn," I lied. "It gives everyone time to gather what they need. Get some sleep."

"And you?" she asked.

"What about me?"

"Do you have what you need?"

My body burned hot with rage for a moment, before I wrestled it back down to lock it behind cold steel.

"Yes," I said in a soft monotone.

"Ah," she said. "I see." She reached over and touched my wrist, just one finger, gentle and cool, soft as a feather. "You should sleep, too."

I nodded. "I will. Soon."

She didn't believe me, but didn't say any more. She just sat there, holding space, holding time while I tried hard not to think of anything. She finished her beer.

She rose and took my hand, helping me to my feet. Then she walked with me, and it was like the floor was made of clouds. Following her, step-in-step, wasn't walking, it was flying, but as effortlessly as if I were the wind, wild and free.

Then I fell, but it was floating, into soft sheets, a pillow beneath my head and a quilt pulled over my shoulders.

"Sleep now," she said, in the kindest tone I'd ever heard her use. "For tomorrow, the battle begins."

Bertie left, just as quietly as she'd arrived. I felt Spud join me on the bed, felt the dragon-pig settle in on my other side. I wasn't in our room, but in the spare bed, and I had a moment to be grateful that Bertie hadn't taken me into the bed Ryder and I shared.

Then sleep took me down and down.

I woke to my phone alarm going off in the living room. It was nearly midnight, and whatever sleep I'd gotten was going to have to be good enough.

I petted Spud, who rolled over to claim where I'd just been sleeping, sighing as he snuggled into the lingering body warmth.

The dragon-pig opened its eyes, then watched as I changed into the clothes I'd grabbed earlier: black jeans, black combat boots, and a layering of shirts.

I changed quickly, Crow's stone resting cool against my skin. I pulled my hair back in a braid, gave Spud another petting, and glanced at his automatic feeder and automatic water system.

I had left our neighbor, Mr. Stein, a message asking if he could take Spud out on walks and check on him for the next couple days while I was out of town dealing with a family matter. I knew he'd do it, because he'd been happy to do it many times before.

I grabbed my coat, and hesitated before also strapping on my gun, and adding a few knives to my boots and belt. I had a backpack with water and food, and first-aid gear in the Jeep. No need to pack more heavily than that.

The dragon-pig was already in the passenger seat when I got to the Jeep.

"You can't go with me," I told it, as I got behind the

wheel and started the vehicle. "You promised to stay behind and look after everyone."

The dragon-pig gave me a serious side-eye, then proceeded to ignore me.

I thought about leaving messages for Myra and Jean, but they'd check their phones. Unless I scribbled a note and slid it under their doors, they would be onto my plans too quickly.

I couldn't let that happen.

There was no way in hell I was going to let my sisters follow me to the demon king's lair. They were staying home, safe. They were staying here so I didn't have to worry about them getting hurt. Or killed.

I'd said we'd all go together. I'd agreed we'd all go at dawn.

I'd lied.

THE FAMILY magical library was supposed to be passed down to me, along with the ability to be the Bridge for the gods, when Dad died. Dad had instead willed the library to Myra, a decision I'd always agreed with.

Until tonight.

The god weapons were in the library vaults. So were all our other most deadly magical items.

I needed weapons. Powerful weapons. I needed that axe that could kill the king.

I parked in front of what looked like a little pump-house, and turned off the engine. The night was dark, and here, in the hills on the east side of town, among the tall cedar and spruce, there was almost no light.

The moon and late summer stars were hidden

behind thick, dark clouds that had rolled in at sunset and hadn't moved on to the valley.

"What do you think my chances are of convincing the library to open for me?" I asked dragon-pig. "Fifty-fifty?"

The dragon grunted, but it didn't sound like an encouraging grunt.

I got out of the Jeep and used the light on my phone to guide me to the ring of mossy stones that formed the outer barrier of the space. If I were the key, all I'd have to do was stand there, maybe touch one of the rocks, and the entire library would unfold into this space and time.

"Library," I said, positioning myself between two stones that acted as a gate. "I am Delaney Reed, eldest born daughter. I know you respond to Myra, because she is the key. I am her sister. I was going to be the key once too.

"You know me. You know my heart. Please open, just this one time, and let me in."

Nothing.

I waited. Wind stirred and hushed through the trees.

"Please."

The air shimmered, and a soft song of chimes drifted on the breeze.

"Just this once."

The library appeared, a hodgepodge of a building that had been built and added to by generations of Reeds. Its patchwork nature somehow made it more wonderous, gave it a sense of whimsy, a bit of the fairytale.

I couldn't believe it had worked. I couldn't believe the library had showed up for me.

"Thank you," I breathed.

Then Myra walked out the door. "Delaney," she said. "Like I wouldn't know you'd try this."

She wore black, from boot to jacket, and had a knit cap pulled over her hair to keep her bangs out of the way. "Looking for weapons?"

I could lie. But not really. Not to her. My sisters knew me too well.

"Yes."

"I can't believe you thought you could go to hell without us," she said, shifting the straps on her shoulders, which were attached to sheathed weapons—the demon axe and the demon sword.

"Yeah," Jean said from behind her. "Totally rude, Delaney."

She was also in black, her hair French braided back from her temples and finished in two long plaits. "I brought snacks." She strolled past Myra and stopped in front of me.

"You—" I said.

"Nope," she said. "There's no more talking this over. No more tricks. You are not going to rescue Ryder without us. You're welcome."

Myra stepped up beside her and checked her watch. "Bathin will be here in a minute. You *were* going to ask him to take you weren't you?"

"I...fine. Yes."

Myra scoffed. "I knew it. Like he wouldn't have told me when you contacted him. This was always going to be us with you, no matter what you tried. So here, swallow this."

She opened her palm. In it were three very small pebbles. "These will make it so Bathin can keep track of all of us, and so we can find each other if we get lost."

"Cool." Jean grabbed one, popped it in her mouth and swallowed.

Myra pushed her hand toward me. "You too."

"This is gross," I said, picking the smaller of the two pebbles.

"If you hide that in your pocket or cheek, or under your tongue, I'm gonna kick you in the shins," she said.

She popped the rock in her mouth, waited for me to do the same.

The pebble tasted faintly of river and dirt and salt. It also tasted of magic: a sweet, honey spark.

Myra unscrewed her water flask, drank, and handed me the flask.

I swallowed and chased it with water. "So you have this all planned out?" I asked.

"We follow the plan we agreed we'd undertake at dawn. Except we do it early, because we have to."

"Because you knew I'd go without you," I said.

She dropped her hand on my shoulder and bent her head until she caught my gaze. "Because we have to. We have to save Ryder. Waiting around for the sun to rise isn't going to help. Did you sleep any at all?"

I nodded. "A couple hours. Did you send Bertie?"

"No, but she talked to me. She wanted to come with us."

"I know."

"Why did you tell her to stay behind?"

"Fewer people involved, fewer people I can lose," I said. "Which is why you and Jean should—"

"Are going with you," Jean said firmly. Myra nodded.

Before I could find some other way to argue them out of their decision, a voice called out. "Reed sisters, are we ready?"

Myra lit up at the voice, and Bathin strolled over to us. Behind him were four people I did not expect: Xtelle, Avnas, Hogan, and Old Rossi.

"So ready," Jean agreed. "Hey, Rossi. Did you bring my money?"

"No," he said. "Delaney, you lost me lunch money."

"What was the bet?" I asked.

"That you'd try to leave town without us."

"Beer *and* a burger, baby," Jean said. "Pay up."

"I will pay as soon as we kick the king of hell's ass."

"Don't aim for his ass," Xtelle said. "Aim for his head." She was in pink pony unicorn form, her horn glowing without any moonlight, sparkles wafting around her, creating a billowing cloud.

"Or his neck," Avnas said. "He also has a bad knee."

Avnas had decided to remain in his compact black bull form. His horns were extra wide now, curving into a very sharp, very dangerous looking arc. Black electricity snapped from the tip of each horn as he moved.

"So is this all of us?" Hogan asked, moving next to Jean to drop his arm over her shoulder. "You look badass, babe."

"Same," she said.

"No," I said, "this is too much. We can't all go."

"Yes," Bathin said, "we can. And we should. In this, I hate to admit, three demons are better than one. Also, the vampire refused to stay behind, and I don't see you talking your sisters out of it."

"I tried."

"You failed," he said.

"Hogan could stay behind," Jean suggested.

"Hogan could not," Hogan informed her.

Bathin gave me a look. "Waste more time arguing, or get the damn job done?"

"Get the damn job done," I said.

"Then leave your gun in your Jeep. Those bullets will only injure or kill mortals, which will do you no good in the Underworld. The portal stone is this way." He started off into the trees.

"Walking?" Xtelle complained. "But I just painted my hooves."

I gave Myra a look. "Leave the gun?"

"Bathin's right. It isn't a weapon down there, it's a liability."

"Okay," I said as everyone followed him into the forest. "I'll lock it up and tell dragon-pig to go home."

I jogged to the Jeep and opened the door. Light flooded the interior. "Hey, I'm sorry, but I gotta—"

But there was no dragon-pig. I guess it had seen me with my sisters, with the demons, with the vampire and then, knowing I was safe, it had popped back home.

I locked my gun away in the gun safe, then picked up my backpack from the back seat and slung it over my shoulders, adjusting for the unexpected weight. I didn't remember the food and water I'd packed being that heavy.

I shut the door and locked it.

"Just," I said, in case the dragon-pig was still in hearing range, "look after everyone, okay?"

Nothing but the wind in the trees answered me.

CHAPTER SIXTEEN

THE PORTAL STONE turned out to be a massive moss agate Bathin had stashed in the hills.

"What if someone had found it?" Jean asked.

"That dirty thing?" Xtelle sneered. "You want me to get in that dirty thing?"

"No one would have found it," Bathin said. "That's not how it works."

"Are you sure the stones you left behind in the Underworld are still there?" Rossi asked. He was also dressed all in black, including his eye patch. His clothes cut close to his body, but I had a feeling he had multiple weapons hidden on him.

"No. But there are options."

"The king wouldn't have destroyed them?" Myra asked.

Avnas snorted.

"What?" I asked.

"The king doesn't care if Bathin left stones behind," Avnas said. "The king doesn't…it is difficult to explain."

"He's blinded by his own power," Xtelle said, with

something that sounded a lot like a dreamy sigh. "So much passion. So much force." Another sigh. "But unfortunately, even an explosion gets boring after a while."

"That's...not helpful," I said.

"He doesn't see me," Bathin said, "my stones, or any of you, or any of this," he waved generally at the world around us, "as a threat."

"What about gods?" Jean asked.

"He sees them as minor inconveniences," Bathin said. "Something to bargain with to get what he wants. Which, in this case, is good for us."

"We're not bringing gods," I said.

"We won't need to," Bathin agreed.

"Time," Myra said, "is slipping. We need to go."

"But a moss agate?" Xtelle whined. "Couldn't you have used rubies or diamonds? Something more suited to my status?"

"Status as the ex-queen who's hiding as a pink pony with a horn in a podunk beach town in nowhere, Oregon?" Bathin suggested.

She huffed. "Be that way. A semi-precious gem would have been adequate."

"Moss. Agate," Bathin said. "Take it or stay behind, Mother."

"Why are you even coming along, again?" I asked. "Bathin can show us where Ryder's being held."

"Well, it's not because I left some of my favorite jewelry behind," she said. "Really, Delaney, how shallow do you think I am? As if a mere fortune in treasures, when I have a totally unfair outstanding fine I've been charged to pay, would convince me to trot back to the realm I once ruled. Shame."

She pushed past all of us to Bathin.

"Take me first," she demanded. "I despise group-rate travel events."

"Everyone at the same time," Bathin said. "We begin in this stone, then I'll take us to the Underworld. I should be able to get us close, very close in two or three jumps."

Hogan raised his hand.

"Yes?" Bathin asked.

"Any advice for a first-time demon stone traveler?"

Bathin grinned. "Don't fight it. You're not the first Jinn..."

"...half," Hogan said.

"...half Jinn I've transported, but the experience is different for each person. Some people," he said, giving Myra a smoldering look that could melt iron, "find it rather pleasurable."

Xtelle made a very juvenile "ooooh," sound, and loudly whispered: "He means sex. Kinky, dirty, you-bet-your-moss-agate-they-did-it-in-a-rock sex."

"Thanks for that," Myra said.

Bathin gave her a wink. "Everyone take a deep breath," he said. "One, two, three."

The world slipped, turned inside out. Then the world went blurry, trapped behind yellow windows with panes of green.

"Moss agate," Xtelle said, like she'd just stepped in a pile of slugs. "So pedestrian."

"And beautiful," Jean said. "This is gorgeous."

"Of course you'd like it," Xtelle said. "It suits your...uncultured style."

"I watched you eat weeds the other day," Jean said.

Xtelle scoffed. "That was an act. For the mystery. Of

which I was the star. I had to pretend I was an innocent pony, about to have her first love affair."

"Wow," Myra said. "That was not at all your part in the play."

"Well, I had to improvise, didn't I? Create a back story? Become the character? And after Pan, the darling, visited to give me his notes—if you know what I mean— I realized it was the juicy, really sink-your-teeth-into-it- and-leave-a-mark role I was born to play."

"Not sure what that had to do with you licking the dirt and muttering, 'nibble nibble,' when you didn't think the tourists were looking," Hogan said.

Jean laughed and gave him a high five. "I knew you'd be good for this quest."

"It's not a quest," I said. "We are *literally* walking into hell. Do you think this is a joke?"

"Walking?" Bathin said. "We're transporting. Hopping rocks to hell."

"Would you all focus?" I said. "This isn't a game." My fear of being too late to save Ryder mortared together with anger and a thin slurry of panic. I couldn't breathe. There wasn't any air.

"Look at me, Delaney," Old Rossi said, as he pressed one finger under my chin.

I was sucking thin air through my clenched teeth, drowning in a sudden spike of fear.

"Ah," he said.

Then his arms were around me, and the light of the moss agate, the sounds of voices, the echo of laughter were gone.

"Listen to me, Delaney Reed," Rossi said, his voice flowing like lightning-stitched moonlight. "You are not fighting this war alone. You are not fighting for Ryder alone. We are here. Your family. Your friends. The gods are watching.

"The lands we will enter are filled with deception. Know our hearts. Know Ryder's heart, and your own. We are connected in love, and that cannot be broken.

"We will all walk out of the demon realm together. With Ryder at our side."

The panic settled and cooled. It was still there, but didn't feel like a wild thing burning all the oxygen out of my lungs. I didn't know what Rossi had done, but it helped.

"Okay," I said, meeting his dark gaze. "Yes. All of us together."

"Excellent. Now," he said, "let's go find your man."

Light returned, sound, sensation. No one seemed to have noticed our exchange. It was as if we'd spent several minutes inside a split second.

Vampires had lots of abilities, and an old vamp like Rossi could apparently bend time if he needed to.

"...it isn't a game," Myra said. "We *are* focused on getting Ryder. That's why we're here. This is just jitters."

"We're taking it seriously," Jean said. "Going to the Underworld? That's heavy." She rolled her shoulders and tipped her head to each side to loosen up her neck. "Not saying I won't crack some jokes, but I know what's at stake."

"Was that a time trick?" Hogan asked Rossi.

Everyone narrowed their eyes at the vampire.

"You saw him do something?" Jean asked. "A time thing?"

"We just took a few extra moments to catch our breath," Rossi said.

"Okay," Jean said, pointing at her boyfriend. "That was totally cool. Keep doing that stuff."

He waggled his eyebrows. "Oh, I plan on it."

"Are you sure you want to do this, Delaney?" Xtelle mused. "It would be better if you stayed behind. The rest of us are less likely to be an emotionally manipulated liability. What?" she said, when Rossi glared at her. "She loves him. Love is one of the best weapons to use against someone."

"Really?" Rossi growled. "I just told her that her love for him is what will make her strong."

"Vampires," Xtelle sniffed. "Always the optimists."

Jean laughed, then pulled her lips down in an unsuccessful frown. "Sorry," she said, still failing to make her expression serious. "It's just, you know. Vampires. So optimistic."

"What's that about vampires?" Rossi asked, a dangerous edge to his voice.

"You do tend to get the mopes," she said.

"The mopes?"

"You aren't always the sunniest people," Hogan said.

"Don't reduce my people to a stereotype."

"Or what?" Xtelle asked. "You'll brood in your castle, wear black, and write sad poetry? This is fun," she added. "See how well I fit in?"

"Are we ready?" Bathin asked.

All eyes turned to me. I set my shoulders and nodded. "Do it, Bathin. Take us to hell."

"As you wish," he said with a slight bow.

He raised his hands and snapped—

—*blues and sparks of crystal white, turquoise shifting into midnight velvet*—

—and snapped—

—*greens, deep and lush, threaded with gold*—

—and snapped—

—*orange burning sunset bright, violet shadows*—

—and snapped—

Red. Everything was red. I breathed and breathed, my heart out of rhythm, thumping and skipping against my ribs.

"Fricking shit," Jean said, panting. "That was. A thing."

"You okay, babe?" Hogan asked, resting his hand on her hip.

"I will be. It felt fast."

"Time is not relevant," Bathin said, "but it was a lot of distance."

Myra was bent, hands gripping her knees.

"Myra?" I asked. "Are you all right?"

"Dizzy," she answered. "Just give me a second."

Rossi didn't seem fazed by all the rock hopping, nor did Hogan or the two demons.

My heart was still flopping like a fish, so I just kept breathing slowly.

"Delaney?" Bathin asked, checking in on me.

I lifted my finger asking for a moment.

"How many stones have you buried in hell?" Xtelle asked.

"More than will ever be discovered," Bathin said. "But I don't have any in the king's chambers."

"No, of course you don't," Avnas said. "He doesn't let anyone or anything into his chambers."

"There is always a way into any place," Xtelle said. "But that's not where he's keeping Ryder."

"The dungeons?" Avnas asked.

"You'd think so, wouldn't you?" Xtelle mused. "But

according to my spies, he's keeping him in the sunroom."

"Huh," Avnas said. "That's rather…open."

"You mean it's a trap," Bathin said.

"Of course it's a trap," Xtelle said. "He knows we're coming for Ryder. Well, not us." She pointed a hoof at Bathin and Avnas. "But he knows *she's* on her way." She jerked her head toward me.

"How does he know I'm coming?" I pressed my palm against my forehead to stave off the headache building there. "Did your spies tell him?"

"No, dear," she said, like I was a three-year-old. "He knows you love Ryder. He knows you'll try to rescue him. You are a very predictably *human.*"

"Good," I said. "Let him set a trap. We'll still kick his ass."

"Again with the ass?" Xtelle said. "Head. Kick his head."

Myra straightened and adjusted the weapons on her shoulder. "I'm ready."

Jean capped the water bottle and dragged the back of her hand across her mouth. "Aim for the flat top," she said. "Got it."

"How close can you get to the sunroom, my Prince?" Avnas asked.

"Not as close as I'd like. I can get us into the corridor. We'll have to walk from there."

"More walking?" Xtelle whined. "Really, Bathin, you should be fired. You are a terrible tour guide."

"Not a vacation," he said. "We're rescuing Ryder."

"Yes, yes, murder, rescue, is it too much to expect some scented lotion? All this walking is ruining my cuticles."

"How far is it from the corridor to the sunroom?" Myra asked.

"Unless it's moved, I'd say a half mile?"

"The rooms move or the corridors move?" Hogan asked.

"Both," Bathin said. "It's what the king wants it to be, and his wants are ever changing."

"Oh, they most certainly are," Xtelle said. "I've never met a creature more fickle."

"Pot, kettle, let me hand you a mirror," Jean said.

Hogan gave her a high five.

"What should we expect?" I asked.

Bathin, Xtelle, and Avnas all turned to me. "What do you mean?" Bathin asked.

"What should we expect we'll have to deal with? Demons? Ghouls? Other creatures?" I asked. "Will there be guards?"

"Yes," Bathin said.

"No," Avnas corrected. "It has been some time since you've been in the Underworld, my Prince. Your father's ego has grown."

"It's always been the biggest thing he's had," Xtelle muttered.

"He'll be alone?" I asked.

"*If*," Avnas said, "the king is in the sunroom with Ryder, he may have an attendant with him."

"They'd leave Ryder unguarded?" Myra asked.

Avnas shrugged, which looked a little weird on a stocky black bull. "If it's a trap, someone will be watching. If they simply are holding him for…other amusements, there will be no need for guards. It is one of the inner chambers of the Underworld. Very few could survive the journey, much less know the way."

"All right," Myra said. "I like the odds being on our side for once. Let's deal with weapon disbursement. We've all swallowed one of Bathin's stones already."

"I'll be able to transport any of you, even if I'm not with you," Bathin said. "It will be less pleasant than this." He indicated the red stone we were in. "But it is survivable and will leave you with no permanent injuries."

"Whee," Jean muttered. Hogan took her hand in his and bumped her shoulder.

"Avnas and Xtelle have their own weapons," Myra went on.

I looked at the unicorn and bull, both of whom were giving me innocent wide eyes, which I didn't believe for a moment.

"I have mine," Bathin said, touching his hip where for a moment, I thought I saw a scimitar shimmer into existence before it went invisible again.

"You're not going to take Bunny Kisses, the king killer?" I asked.

"If I behead the king with that axe—tempting—I will have to take the throne."

"Because you're first born," I said.

"First spawned, but yes, basically the same thing."

"So who's going to take the axe?" I asked.

Myra put her fist out. So did Jean. They looked at me.

"What?" I asked.

"Rock, paper, scissors," Myra said.

"Of all the ridiculous…fine." I made a fist.

We pumped our fists: one two three.

I threw paper, Jean threw paper, Myra threw scissors.

"Huh. Now that I think of it, you always win this game," Jean said to Myra. "Are you using your family gift to know what to throw?"

"Me?" Myra said. "I've never even thought of such a thing. I get Bunny Kisses." She shifted the axe to her other shoulder.

"Fine," I said. "Just Jean and me for the sword."

Fists again: one two three.

Jean threw rock. I threw paper.

"Dammit," Jean said. "So what's left?"

Myra slid the sword and sheath off her shoulder and held it for me. I took it, surprised that it was far too light, but it grew in weight until it was what I would expect in a blade. I took off my backpack, which was still heavier than I remembered packing it, set it at my feet, and worked with the sheath and straps to fasten the sword at my hip.

"You get a gun with demon-killing bullets," Myra said.

"Hells, yes," Jean said. "Gimme."

"Hogan?" Myra said. "Gun?"

"I'm a lousy shot," he said. "I thought I'd just use magic."

We stopped and stared at him.

"Half Jinn right?" he said. "You know I have magic."

"You can grant wishes," I said. "And you can see the true form of a person. You've never said you had any other magic."

He spread his hands. "Like I need to use magic in Ordinary? I can take care of myself. Don't worry."

"I need a little more than that," I said.

"Wishes. I can grant them, twist them, force reality

to break against them," he said. "I can tear them out of a man's heart, rip them from nightmare. It's not…you know, *nice*, but I am not here to be nice."

Then he gave me a smile that had an edge to it I'd never seen before.

"Babe," Jean said, taking his hand now that she'd settled the gun and ammunition into place, "that was so hot. I am gonna do so many dirty things to you when we get home."

"You haven't asked about me," Rossi murmured.

"I never worry about how deadly you can be," I assured him. That got me a smile with a flash of fang.

"Bored," Xtelle announced. "Are we done with our little games now? I, for one, would like to kick head."

"It just doesn't have the same punch as kick ass," Jean noted.

Bathin's gaze caught mine, burgundy in the red light around us. "Are you ready to get your man, Delaney?"

I picked up the backpack and shrugged it over both shoulders. "Hell, yes, I am."

He held up his hand, fingers pressed together, and snapped.

The red extinguished, leaving us in shadows.

It stank like cool stones, water, and something slippery and meaty.

"Gross," Jean whispered.

Hogan hummed.

There was no wind, but the air was cold. Stone beneath our feet, stone over our heads. The light was wan, as if coming from a great distance, moonlight breathing through the cracked ribs of the earth.

"Which corridor are we in?" Myra asked.

"The North," Bathin whispered back.

"We'll be walking for two miles," Avnas said.

"Then let's get to it." I grasped the sword hilt, but Bathin grabbed my wrist, stopping me from pulling it from the sheath.

"It will be noticed," he said. "Only draw it in battle."

I shoved it back down.

"Me first!" Xtelle pushed past me and trotted down the stone corridor. "Would it hurt them to add a little paint to the place? Pink. This should all be pink. Make it so!"

Nothing happened.

The corridor was just wide enough for Avnas to lope along at her side. "You have exited such things, my Queen. As you have exited your contract with him."

"Yes, yes," she said. "Contracts are easy. But this realm still bows to me. I was its queen, and there is no other."

Avnas hesitated, which worried me, then said, "Always, my Queen."

"Does she have influence here?" I asked Myra, who was walking on my left. Jean and Hogan were in the middle. Bathin and Rossi brought up the rear.

"She was the queen of demons for a very long time," she said.

"So...yes?"

Myra nodded. "I don't know how much. I don't know how many demons or other things are still on her side, but she didn't give up her power when she broke her contract with the king."

"Good," I said. "As long as she stays on our side."

Myra grunted. "Here's hoping."

The first mile went by in tense silence. Even Xtelle

kept her mouth shut. We were all expecting an attack. I didn't like that the corridor had no side exits I could see, no escape hatches above or below. Our only exit plan was Bathin and his hop stones.

"A little less doubt," Bathin said, moving sideways against the wall to come up next to me. He walked ahead of Myra and me, but behind Xtelle. "It's just a short way ahead."

"A mile," Myra reminded him. "It's another mile."

He spun on his heel so he was walking backward, his arms out to his side, his smile wide. "Space is also startlingly malleable here. There are more exits—"

It happened so quickly, my brain couldn't register the order of things. It took me a heartbeat, two, before the sequence of events made any sense.

Bathin's arms were seized by rock oozing out of both sides of the tunnel, pouring over his hands, and solidifying up to his elbows.

His mouth dropped open in shock.

Light filled the tunnel, a hot orange that burned afterimages into my retinas.

A drumming beat shook the ground beneath us, sifting dirt down from the ceiling, covering us in a layer of grime that tasted of mold and stagnant water.

"You *dare!*" a voice bellowed.

The sword was in my hand, glowing with neon green fire. I heard the click of a gun clearing its holster, a whispered wish that brushed the scent of rosemary and yeast through the air, and a quiet, "*Huh,*" from Myra.

Myra, next to me, had not drawn the axe.

That should have meant something. That detail was important.

"We don't dare," Myra said. "We're here to take back what is ours."

I frowned. She'd caught onto something before me.

Then I realized who the voice belonged to.

"Goap," I said. Myra nodded to the tunnel behind Bathin, ahead of us. "Show yourself. No," I said, changing my mind. "Get out of our way."

"Brother," Bathin said, "help or get out of the way."

Goap solidified out of thin air behind Bathin, a wickedly serrated short sword in one hand, a flashing dagger in the other.

The muscles in Bathin's arms bunched, but the stone that held him did not budge.

"Hello, brother," Goap sneered, then he stabbed Bathin in the back.

CHAPTER SEVENTEEN

I DUCKED AND RUSHED, moving under Bathin's outstretched arm, pivoting to face Goap, the sword pressed in his belly.

He was Bathin's opposite. They were both dark-haired, but otherwise, he was thin to the point of being emaciated, his eyes much more alien, less *human* than Bathin's.

He wore a tunic and trousers such a dark plum they were almost black. His long hair flowed free but did nothing to hide the hard angles of his pale face.

In each hand, he held a blade, but only the dagger had blood on it.

"Drop," I demanded, "the weapons."

Goap raised an eyebrow. "Why would I do that?"

"You stabbed him."

"Of course I stabbed him."

"Of course he stabbed me," Bathin said, shaking free of the stone bindings as if they had never been solid enough to secure him.

"Delaney," Rossi said. "You can lower the sword."

"Sheathe it," Goap corrected. "Before we're all seen."

"He's right," Bathin said. "Sheathe it."

I shifted my weight and reluctantly—very reluctantly —drew the blade away from Goap's stomach and sheathed the sword.

"Someone better explain this to me," I said, "or I'm going to stab him just because I'm in a bad damn mood."

"You'll do no such thing," Xtelle said, coming up behind me. "Goap." She lowered her head, and skewered his shoulder. His blood was just as red on her horn as Bathin's was on his blade.

"Mother," Goap gritted out. He poked at the leg she delicately extended, barely leaving a scratch.

"My Prince." Avnas drew a horn across Goap's forearm, a very light scratch.

"Uncle." Goap jabbed him in the shoulder.

"What is going on?" I demanded.

"Family greeting," Bathin explained, before he turned and punched Goap in the shoulder so hard, it sent him stumbling into the stone wall.

Bathin was wearing a ring I hadn't noticed. A ring that was actually a blade, which was now covered in Goap's blood.

"What the hell?" I demanded. "Stop stabbing. There will be no more stabbing."

"And she says I'm the drama queen," Xtelle said. "We're here for the human."

"Which one?" Goap asked.

"Boytoy whatshisname," Xtelle supplied.

"You're not here to take the throne?" Goap asked.

I was still trying to figure out what all the bloodletting had been about, but I did not miss the calculating look in his eyes.

"We are here for Ryder Bailey," Bathin said.

"And you brought Feather Duster and Bunny Kisses with you for that?" he challenged.

"We're not expecting Father to hand him over if we ask nicely," Bathin said. "So we're not going to ask nicely."

Goap's eyes flicked to the sword at my hip, which he instantly dismissed, then, hungrily, to the axe still sheathed over Myra's shoulder. "You should be carrying the axe, Bathin."

"No," Bathin said coolly. "I should not. I won't kill the king with that weapon. I won't take the throne."

"But you are the eldest. It would be easy for you," Goap pressed.

"If you want the throne, you'll have to find another way to get it. I won't stop you, but I won't use the axe either."

"We need to go," Myra said. "We need to be there, Bathin. We need to be there now."

Myra's family gift worked in the Underworld too. Good to know.

"Let's go," I said.

"Are you joining us, then?" Bathin asked Goap. "Rescuing the human?"

I was close to Goap, so I saw a whole movie of emotions roll across his face. An awful lot of it was anger, but there were other things: shrewdness, fear, and something that looked like vindictive satisfaction..

"Where do you think they're keeping him?" Goap asked.

"The sunroom," Bathin said. "Mother's spies are still Mother's spies."

"Yes," he said. "Of course they are. Since you have it all figured out," Goap said, "by all means, after you, brother." He stretched his arm out and executed a half bow that moved him out of the way for Bathin to pass.

"Nope," Bathin said, grabbing his brother by the arm and forcing him to march next to him. "I already gave you my back once because I was being *nice*. I'm not giving you it again."

I looked at the group behind me. Hogan and Jean just shrugged. Rossi tipped his head to one side, watching the demons go.

"It's a blood greeting," Rossi told me, though I hadn't asked. "Blood is difficult to disguise. If any of them had been imposters, their blood would have revealed the subterfuge."

"Did you know they would do that?" I asked Myra.

She patted the bag hanging off the side of her belt. "No, but I brought bandages and other first aid. I knew there'd be blood."

We were walking again.

In general, I tried not to use my sisters' gifts like tools I could pull out anytime I wanted to know something. But Ryder was down here, trapped.

"What else do you have in the med kit?" I asked.

She frowned, then the tightness around her eyes eased, and her eyebrows rose.

"No splints," she started with. "No tourniquets."

"Pretty sure I asked you what you'd packed, not what you hadn't packed."

"Sutures, smelling salts, forceps, goggles. You're asking me if he's going to be hurt. You're asking me if any of us are going to be badly injured. I know you, Delaney. Don't lie."

"Is he? Are we?"

"I don't know the future, but I didn't pack any morphine or a defibrillator if that helps."

I nodded, the bands around my chest easing. "It does help."

We hadn't walked much farther—it didn't seem like we'd covered another mile—but the demons in front of us stopped.

"Ordinarians," Bathin said quietly. "The sunroom is just ahead. Prepare."

"Wait," Goap said. "You can't just stroll in there."

"I go where I please," Bathin said.

"You never do what I say, do you? And yet you expect me to fall at your feet." He twisted out of Bathin's grip and whispered. "You are my shadow." He snapped his fingers.

Rossi was fast enough to skitter *up the side of the wall.*

I would have moved, too, but I did not have the speed of a vampire.

"Wait," Bathin loud-whispered, but it was too late.

Goap planted his hands on his hips and nodded. "I'll be able to see you, but to other demons you are invisible. It is one of the skills I have that no other demon here can do as well."

"It's a child's trick," Bathin sighed. "I taught it to you when we were kids."

"And your rock hopping is anything more? Please. Can you make the earth tremble? Can you raise the demon dead? No? I can. You have always underestimated me."

I studied my hands, which looked the same to me. "We don't look invisible."

"You do to demon eyes," Goap said. "Don't they, Bathin? Or would you rather they walk in there in full view, to be seen by anything that has eyes?"

Bathin cut his hand sideways, annoyance in every line. "Fine. It's not a terrible idea."

"It's a far better idea than just strolling into the sunroom. Without a plan."

"We have a plan," I said.

"Do you?" Goap glared at me. There was fury in his gaze, hatred. He might be on our side for the moment, but it was not where he would stay.

"This is a rescue, not a fight. But we do have weapons," I said.

"You don't have enough weapons for the kind of fight hell can bring. You have no plan," he repeated.

"Enough weapons?" Myra asked. "How many should we have? How many demons are in the sunroom?"

"Demons? One. But that's not who you should be worried—"

A beam of light ignited at the far end of the tunnel, a small sun shining in the distance.

I pressed up against the wall, the stone at my back warmer than I'd expected. Everyone else in our party did the same.

The light swung upward, illuminating the stone ceiling, then down one side, across the floor and up the other side where Jean, Hogan, and I were pressed.

The light crawled up my boots, pants, shirt. When it hit my chest, a sudden spark of heat bloomed there, the stone Crow had given me a small ember against my skin.

Before I could decide how long I could stand the heat, the light slid up to my face and winked out.

My heart was beating too hard. That light had to have seen me. It had to have known I was hiding in plain sight.

The light glowed again, wider, stronger. The tunnel looked like it went on for at least another mile. But much closer to us, a curtain of blue light rained down from ceiling to floor.

"Now," Bathin whispered. He jogged forward, following Xtelle and Avnas who were already stepping through that shimmering wall of light.

Bathin waited for Goap to catch up with him, probably not trusting his brother at his back, but Goap shook his head. "As you said, this isn't my fight."

"It could be," Bathin said. "Help us get Ryder out safely, and I'll do what I can to make sure you sit on the throne."

"Without the axe? Promises don't fall sweetly from your lips, brother," Goap said. "I know the poison of your words. I've done you a favor and hidden your mortals. But that is all you'll have from me so long as our father wears the crown."

Goap snapped his fingers and disappeared.

I exchanged a glance with Myra.

"Is he really gone?" Jean asked.

"For now," Bathin said. "Hurry."

We jogged to Bathin, and something tickled the back of my brain.

"He said something," I said, just before Rossi walked through the shimmer with Jean and Hogan on his heels.

"Who?" Myra asked. She settled the items on her body, fingers quickly checking the placement of each.

"Goap. He said demons on the other side weren't who we should be worried about—"

"He lies," Bathin said. "Through. Now." He was looking back the way we came. I knew demon eyes could see more than I could here. I knew he was tracking another danger I didn't sense.

Myra bumped her shoulder with mine. Together we stepped through the shimmer.

The temperature went up by several degrees, and so did the humidity. It was hot, but not unbearably so. I felt like I'd just stepped into a greenhouse or a jungle.

Jungle was right. The mass of green was every-where: a tangle of trees, bushes, and slick, hungry-looking flowers with fangs that blocked out the sky.

"*Sun room?*" I mouthed at Myra. She nodded and pointed to the barely visible trail where Jean was waiting.

Jean gestured at us and mouthed, "*Hurry.*"

We reached her quickly, then dove into the jungle after the others.

What I'd thought was a trail was actually just Xtelle ripping things down as she bulled forward.

"I hate that," she muttered, and the sound of plant matter tearing and tinny screams rolled back to us. "Hate that, hate that. That? Oh, well, maybe just a nip…"

"My Queen," Avnas said, "are you certain taking such…libations is prudent when we're on a rescue mission?"

"Loosen up, Avvy," Xtelle said, her words a little

slurred. "If there's one thing I know how to do, it's kill when I'm lii-ber-ated."

"We are here to rescue, my Queen."

"Save, slaughter. 'Sall the same thing. Oh, look at that! I hate it." The rip of roots, and, yes, definitely a scream, filled the air.

"Jungle," I said to Myra. "Did we know there'd be a jungle?"

"Bathin said it was a garden. Try not to touch the plants."

I tucked my elbows in and stepped over strewn plant matter, ignoring the crunching and little groans of pain. We finally caught up with the demons in front.

They'd all stopped on the edge of the jungle, looking out through the small space Xtelle had cleared. Bathin's hands were planted on his hips. Xtelle and Avnas had tipped their heads together, whispering furiously.

Jean and Hogan eased around to stand next to Bathin.

"Oh," Jean whispered, as she saw what was beyond. "Shit."

The stone heated against my chest again. I slapped my free hand over it hoping it would calm down.

I tapped Bathin's shoulder. He shifted to one side so I could see the scene before us.

The clearing was almost beautiful. White marble columns and arches created a grotto where streams of what I hoped was water rippled and flowed.

The jungle did not encroach on the clearing, except for delicate tendrils of vines that wrapped up the arches. Flowers that looked way too similar to red lips with human teeth, hung in silent screams from the green.

Golden fountains were scattered along gemstone

pathways, and the sky, because yes, there appeared to be a sky, was surprisingly blue.

It looked like something out of a painting. It looked like a garden where gods would linger.

"Fuck," Myra whispered behind me.

That's when I noticed two figures sitting on thrones behind the marble columns of a Roman-style temple.

The demon on the right could only be Vychoro, the King of the Underworld. He was wide—massive—his skin a collision of wart-covered greens that drew the eye. He had three mouths, two eyes, and a nose, but those features were fluid in their position and number.

His hair was dark and long on an oval head, his body a bulk of muscles that was only vaguely human under a black toga made of fur and scales.

It was difficult to look away from him, but I did.

Because on the other throne sat the god, Mithra.

The god sprawled, the very image of a bored judge who'd been pulled away from a nap to deal with petty complaints. He hadn't bothered to brush his hair, which was gray and stuck up at all angles from his blunt-featured face.

He had on a silk shirt, but it was misbuttoned, and the cuffs were undone. His breeches were dark and gathered at the ankles like sweat pants. He wore sandals on his feet.

He didn't look dangerous or clever. He looked like someone who would be easy to dismiss or ignore.

That was a lie.

Myra tapped my shoulder and pointed to one side of Mithra.

I shifted so I could see between the columns.

My heart stopped.

Ryder.

He was alive, he was here, he was whole.

And then my heart beat with fury.

His back was to us. He'd lost his shirt, but still had on his jeans and boots. They'd forced him to kneel. Shackles around his wrists, connected by chains that ran to heavy iron loops in the marble platform, trapped him in place.

His head was bowed, his hair a sweaty mess. I could see the muscles of his back shift and bunch as he moved his weight slightly.

He'd been on his knees for a long time, but not willingly. I could tell by the slight tremor in his arms, from the dried blood on his wrists and hands. I could tell he was furious.

Good. So was I.

Cold washed over me like endless fog. The same cold that had gripped me when he'd been kidnapped. I could taste the salt of the ocean on my lips, could smell the clean green of kelp and sea life.

Ordinary was with me, in my blood. And we were going to take back what belonged to us.

"Mithra?" Xtelle blew raspberries through her flappy unicorn lips. "What's that lowlife god doing here? Sucking up to the king?" She shoved a leafy branch into her mouth and chomped loudly.

"They're negotiating for Ryder," Bathin said.

"Who?"

"The human we're here to save, my Queen," Avnas said, as he tried to kick away a small pile of branches that looked like the one Xtelle was chewing.

"An...an...*and*," Xtelle enunciated. "Why is Vychoro negotiating with the god? Are they dating? Getting the boom boom on? Can I sell tickets to watch?" She swayed forward. Avnas caught her by the mane and tugged her back into the cover of jungle around us.

I didn't know how the demon king and Mithra hadn't heard her yet, but at the same moment, I realized we couldn't hear the king and god either.

Someone, probably Bathin or Avnas, had cast a silencing spell.

"They're not dating," Jean whispered. "Ryder's bound to Mithra. He signed a contract. Now Mithra thinks he owns him."

"Wha?" Xtelle asked. "What? A contract? Avvy, darl-ling. I am outta nibs-nibbles. Fetch me more."

"You've had enough, Mother," Bathin said.

She spun in place. Avnas countered the spin to keep her on her feet. He looked up at Bathin, a twinkle in his eyes. He nodded.

As if this was about to get good.

As if maybe this was all a plan between the demons I hadn't been in on.

Bathin crossed his arms over his chest, looking stern.

"You can tell me...wait. *Can't*," she corrected. "Can't?" she asked Avnas.

"As you say, my Queen. He can't tell you what to do. You still have the appearance of power."

"Appearance?"

"Even if they did give you the smallest part in the murder mystery: Unnamed Livestock," Avnas added.

"Unnamed?"

"Yes."

"*Livestock?*"

"I'm afraid so."

"But I am the star. You know. I am so much staaar."

"You were a background character," Bathin said. "You didn't even have any lines."

"Because my magnifi-magni-muchnificence was too muchness to witness."

"No," Bathin said. "The gods were the real stars of the mystery. Everyone knew it. Zeus was the murderer. He got all the applause."

I opened my mouth to tell them to stow it for later so we could find a way to get to Ryder, but a slight pressure on my forehead, like a fingertip pressing there, stopped me.

Bathin had possessed my soul for over a year. I knew his mental touch. He was asking me to wait just a minute more.

"The gods?" Xtelle laughed, but it was dark and cruel. "Stars? They know nothing."

"They know contracts," Bathin said. "They made very good deals for very juicy parts in the murder mystery. Didn't they, Delaney?"

He didn't look my way, but Xtelle did, her eyes narrowed, her lips already pulling back from stained green horse teeth.

"They did," I said. "They all had speaking parts."

Xtelle gasped.

"Some of them were even actual clues," Myra added.

She gasped again and pressed a hoof to her chest. "Assholes."

"Yes," Avnas said, as if it were the saddest thing he'd ever heard. "All because they made excellent, unbreakable contracts."

Xtelle huffed, and glitter-filled smoke puffed out of her nostrils. "Contracts. Gods know noth-*nothing* of how to make a contract. They are insects—no, smaller—bakt-bacteria when it comes to making contracts. *Am-a-teurs.*"

"Sure," I said, "now can we—"

Myra grabbed my sleeve. She shook her head.

"Amateurs!" Xtelle yelled. "I will destroy!" She dropped her head and scanned the ground. "Ah, here it is." She lipped up a small branch Avnas had missed and masticated it.

"I will de-*stroy* your stupid little contract!" She stepped away from the cover of the jungle and posed, head high, tail raised, wind that hadn't been there a second ago waving through her mane and making her pink coat shine.

"Stella?" The king said from one mouth while another screeched, "Betrayer!"

"What is this?" Mithra demanded, though he hadn't moved out of his bored slouch. He obviously didn't fear demons, no matter what shape they took.

But then, he'd never met the wrath of a pink unicorn.

"This-*sss*," Xtelle hissed, "is not a no-name *livestock*! This is a *staaar!*"

She raised her front leg and slammed her hoof down.

Mithra shot up onto his feet. Gone was the boredom. Gone was the illusion of unkempt slouch. Standing there, swathed in gold, he was one hundred percent pissed-off god.

"What have you done?" he bellowed. "What. Have. You. Done?" His voice was a roar, thunder, the sky breaking free of ancient bindings and crumbling to dust.

Xtelle lowered her head, then rotated it in a circle.

"This no-name livestock without any lines just broke your constra-*contract*, you bloated, egotistical, wrinkled-up old *has-been*! Now who's the damn star?"

Ryder's head jerked up, then back toward Xtelle. I could see the anger burning in his gaze. He pulled on the chains, his arms curling, but could not break them.

"You will not move!" Mithra pointed at Ryder. "I own you!"

Ryder held the god's gaze, then opened his fists, giving the god both middle fingers. "Fuck you."

Bathin chuckled. "That's our cue people. Show-time!" He clapped and strode forward, drawing his scimitar.

The sky flashed with lightning.

And all hell broke loose.

CHAPTER EIGHTEEN

WE RUSHED OUT from under the jungle protection. I thought Jean had tripped, but she straightened from her bent position, shoving what looked like a little green twig into her pocket.

She pulled her gun. "Kick head!" she yelled, a bright, wild smile transforming her face with such joy, I felt an unexpected sliver of a smile of my own.

If my sister who knew when doom was going to hit, who knew when we were going to take damage we simply couldn't survive, was smiling, then I took it as a sign.

A sign it was time to kick some head.

I strode out into the grotto and pulled the sword, which hummed and dripped green flames.

Demons appeared from the ground, from the air, from everywhere. Small, tall, humanoid, insect, animal, bizarre shapes that stretched logic until it snapped.

I slashed with the sword and it seemed to jump in my hand, guiding me for the best angles, the best killing strikes through mass and bone.

Myra swung the axe like a lumberjane, hacking off heads and limbs as if they were nothing but smoke.

Hogan stood in front of Jean, who now had a gun much larger than the one she'd pulled from her hip. She balanced the gun on Hogan's shoulder and fired, timing the shots with the tumble of words he was reciting.

Every bullet struck true and dissolved the demons into bloody steam.

Wishes and fire power: a very deadly mix.

The vampire was so fast, he was invisible. I only saw Rossi outlined in the blood spray of demons falling like dominos around him.

Xtelle had already made it to the open temple, and past the columns to the god who stood there. She squared off against Mithra, her now flaming and extra-long horn parrying the god's sword. Avnas had a ball and chain attached to his horns and was mowing down the waves of demons flooding into the grotto.

Bathin plowed a path through the monsters, his scimitar dark, cold, and hungry as empty space. He paused in front of the columns, just out of the king's reach.

"You have crossed the last line," Bathin yelled. He lunged, attacking the monster that was his father.

I was running, had already been running, to Ryder, always to him, this my only reason, my only need.

The Ordinary demons were keeping the god and king busy, just as we'd planned. It was up to us other Ordinaries to carry out the rescue mission.

I dropped down beside Ryder, sheathing the sword in a hurry so I could put both hands on him, on the chains, trying to find a way to free him.

"Laney," he said, his voice cracked like he'd been screaming for days.

Cold, my fury, the salt and the sea a storm beneath my skin.

"It's a trap," he croaked.

"Of course it's a trap," I said. "We're getting you out of here before it's sprung."

He shook his head and smiled. There was so much damn sorrow in that smile, my heart skipped a beat.

"I love you," he whispered. "Run."

The world stopped.

This was familiar. This had happened to me once before when Goap had come to Ordinary and attacked Bathin and Bathin had used his mother's ring to stop time.

Everyone around me was frozen, but just like the last time this magic had been used, I was free.

Crow's stone burned cool against my skin and I wondered if it was his power keeping me mobile. But just because I could move didn't mean I wanted to yet.

From where I knelt next to Ryder, I watched Patrick Baum walk out from behind the temple. He wore fine linen, woven from green, copper, silver, and looked rich, relaxed, and handsome. I wanted to stab him in the throat.

"This is what you wanted, wasn't it?" the leprechaun asked.

I had a wild moment to think he was talking to me.

But then Goap came into view, following Patrick. And on Goap's hand was a ring, much like his mother's, that could stop time. He was in charge of this magic.

"When you locked me into a contract even I couldn't get out of?" Patrick said pleasantly though the fury in his voice was barely hidden. "When you sent those humans, those demons to Ordinary, and then forced *me* to kidnap Ryder Bailey? This is what you wanted.

"You promised your father that you would give him Ordinary by stealing Ryder and bringing the Reed sisters to him. All three of them so he could devour them.

"You made a deal with Mithra that you would give him Ordinary by luring Bathin here to behead the king. Then once you had killed your brother, you would become king, and you would give Mithra Ordinary. This is what you wanted. You have double-crossed demon, god, and leprechaun."

"How have I double-crossed you?" Goap sneered. "You wanted fame. I gave you an entire year of fame."

"*I* did that," Patrick snarled. "I built my audience. I grew my fame. You didn't give that to me."

Goap laughed. "I very much did. A child's trick. Even a Crossroads demon could have pulled it off. You wanted fame, I gave you fame. You wanted fortune, I gave you that too. And now I *own* you. I own your luck.

"You will do as I say. That," he pointed at Bathin, "must have the axe in his hands. He must cut off my father's head."

"If I refuse?"

"Do you?" There was vicious glee in his tone. Toxic hope.

"Do your own dirty work, demon," Patrick said. "You don't control me."

"But I do. You aren't the only one here I control, puppet. You aren't even the best. Don't think yourself so precious." He snapped his fingers and the leprechaun went still, as frozen as everyone and everything else in this grotto.

Goap turned and surveyed the field. He and the leprechaun were about halfway between the temple where the gods and demons were frozen in battle, and where Ryder and I knelt.

Behind us, on the pathways with fountains, were the rest of our crew.

Goap snapped his fingers again. Ryder groaned.

Oh, fuck no.

"Rise," Goap commanded Ryder. "Now that your contract with the god is broken, I will make good use of you."

Ryder moved in a trance. He stood, the shackles melting off his wrists, chains falling to the stone with the slap of heavy metal.

"Stand in front of that Reed," Goap commanded. "The one with the axe. Bare your neck to her."

Ryder fought the command, a spark of his fury flashing through the trance, before his features slackened, and he was moving again. He took a step away from me, then another.

He was going to stand in front of Myra, who was frozen in mid-swing. Then Goap would start time again, and Myra would cut off Ryder's head.

"If your death doesn't inspire my brother to kill the king," Goap said, "then I will force each mortal to cut the other down in front of my brother's unblinking eyes."

Like hell I was going to let that happen. But I didn't know how to turn this to my advantage. One snap and Goap could kill everyone.

I had the demon sword, the brother killer. That would have to be enough. I would have to be enough.

No choice. No time. I reached for the sword.

The stone against my chest flared hot.

Wait, a voice said in my head. A very familiar voice.

Crow? I thought.

You didn't think I'd let you go into that cesspool alone, did you?

He's controlling Ryder. Goap is going to make Myra cut his head off.

Stand up, Crow said.

You don't know. You can't see...

Little Bridge, he said, using a name I hadn't heard in years, *trust your Uncle Crow.*

I surged to my feet and turned to face Goap and Patrick, Mithra and Vychoro behind them.

A wash of wind stroked gently across my skin, as if wings had flown past me.

My eyesight changed, shifting under Crow's power. The grotto filtered into primary colors. Hidden symbols beneath the paths, across the temple columns, cracking through the sky, glowed.

I could see the magic and power lashing this space into place. Could see how it could be pushed around and changed by the will of demons. We were in a gods damned bear trap and one wrong move away from triggering the jaws.

Patrick's eyes widened for a moment. Maybe he wasn't as frozen as he pretended to be.

"What is this?" Goap said. "Does the Reed have a will of her own?"

You need to repeat everything I say, Crow said. *And pretend you're me.*

Pretend I'm you?

Yes.

I loosened my stance and squared my shoulders, tipping my chin up.

This is very pretty, the cross, the double cross, Crow said in my mind.

I swallowed to get spit in my mouth,_then smiled with what I hoped was a Crow smile. "This is very pretty, the cross, the double cross," I repeated.

"But now I'd like to throw my feather into the ring."

Goap looked me up and down and sneered. "Raven. How did you get here, god? In that form?"

"The same way I always do, demon," I repeated with as much bravado as I could. "Do you think your kingdom has no entrances for a trickster? The leprechaun found his way in, didn't he?"

"You have overstepped by showing yourself," Goap said. "Be gone."

Kill Bathin, Crow said.

I almost choked. I didn't think I could say that, Crow or no Crow.

Delaney, he said gently. *We can do this. Just say it.*

"Kill Bathin," I said, my voice shaking, but strong.

"As if I hadn't thought of that years ago," Goap said. "There are precautions our parents put into place so I cannot kill my brother with my own hand."

"I know," I repeated for Crow. "I am offering to kill Bathin for you."

Goap held very still. He looked like a starving man who had just been offered a turkey leg. "I don't recall you being charitable to demons, old god."

Crow laughed, but my heart was beating too hard to do the same. So instead I smiled wider. It was fake, a rigor, but I hoped whatever illusion Crow was casting over me through his stone would cover my mistakes.

"This is not charity. This is my bid for who shall rule hell." These words were easier to repeat. "I lured your brother away from the throne with lies about Ordinary's strength. I lured your mother away as well, and your uncle. When you become the elder prince, the *moment* you become the elder prince, you will behead your father with the axe. And assume the throne."

"Why would you care if I took the throne? What do you get out of it?"

"I want the leprechaun and his magic."

"Fuck off, Raven," Patrick said.

Goap flicked a dismissive look at Patrick, not terribly surprised the leprechaun was no longer frozen. Then he glared at Bathin and the king with hunger in his eyes.

There was nothing he wouldn't do to see his father and brother dead. There was nothing he wouldn't do to be king.

Still, he was not foolish enough to take the bait.

"What is the leprechaun to you, Black Feather?"

"He owes me a debt as one trickster to the other. I intend to crush the payment out of his bones."

That last bit made Patrick squint, as if he were trying to remember something.

There was more to what Crow was saying, more history I didn't understand. Maybe Crow and Patrick had met, trickster to trickster. Maybe there was a debt to be paid. But I thought if that were true, Crow would have told me about the leprechaun and how dangerous he could be.

I was pretty sure Crow was lying about the debt between them.

"As I said," Patrick repeated, buying into Crow's ruse. "Fuck all the way off." Then he smiled sweetly. "From one trickster to the other."

"Make your decision," I said for Crow. "Your hold, demon, is slipping."

The ground trembled, shaking like a low, slow earthquake.

"Tick tick tick, Prince," Crow said, I said. "Your little time trick is about to explode. What do you think will happen next? You've made your father very, very angry."

Goap shrugged, as if he weren't afraid of the king of hell. "Do it, Black Feather. Kill Bathin for me. Show your loyalty to the true king of the underworld."

Bow, but not low, Crow told me.

I did, even though all I wanted to do was turn and see if Ryder was baring his neck to the blade in my sister's hand.

Yes, Crow said. *Go to Myra. Get the axe.*

It meant turning my back on Goap, Patrick, the king, and Mithra.

I hated to do it. Every inch of me was hot, screaming, but I stiffened my spine and strode toward Myra like nothing about the dead demons spread across the ground bothered me. As if the grisly dismembered body parts bobbing in the stream were no big deal.

As if the double-crossing prince, and asshole leprechaun weren't watching my every move.

As if the man I loved wasn't about to be killed.

Ryder had stopped in front of Myra and bent so that the angle of her downward swing would slice clean through his neck.

I was going to be sick.

It was everything I could do to not touch him and shove him out of the way.

Goap could snap time back into motion any second. Could have planned to wait until I stood here so that I would see Ryder's death close enough to feel the blood spray.

I reached for the axe handle and tugged. But Myra was fighting to hold on to it. I couldn't pry it out of her hands.

Steady, Crow said. *Try again.*

I tugged one more time, twisted harder, and the axe was mine.

Walk to Bathin. Hold the axe in your left hand.

I'm right handed, I said. *You are too.*

I'm ambidextrous and trying to save you. Left hand.

I switched the axe to my left hand. I was now carrying both demon weapons, the axe in my hand, the sword on my hip, and I had a strong need to do damage.

I stopped next to Bathin, feeling the gaze of Goap and Patrick following me.

The ground rumbled again. Stronger this time, harder. If Crow was right, Goap was losing hold on the time freeze. And when that happened, all hell would break loose.

The king moved one of his mouths, the god Mithra blinked.

Then the rumbling stopped, and they froze again.

"Losing your grip?" Crow told me to taunt Goap.

"Hesitating, Raven?" Goap jeered. "Or are you just waiting for your chance to betray me too? As if I'd allow that."

The quick draw of a breath—Patrick's—was the only warning I got.

Goap snapped his fingers.

The ground shook harder and harder, as if a thousand fists were pounding upward from below.

"I'm not losing control," Goap yelled over the buried thunder, "I am gaining it. Rise, my loyal dead!"

The world came undone.

The ground shook, a violent herky-jerky rumble that knocked me off my feet.

I landed with the axe still in my hand. The freeze was broken and everyone, everything, was chaos.

I rolled, twisted, tried to gain my feet. Flashes of battle came into view as the ground undulated.

Xtelle stabbed Mithra through the throat. Avnas pulverized the god's head with both mace and chains.

The demon king shoved Bathin away, like swatting a fly. Vychoro thrust his fists into the air and grew into a massive lizard creature with multiple mouths, all of which were roaring.

Bathin rolled to his feet, and attacked his lizard father, who lunged, mouths full of razor teeth, ready to rend, to tear.

Dead demons followed Goap's orders, and grew up out of the ground. They were putrid staggering lumps of flesh and bone with way too many sharp weapons.

There were hundreds of them. Thousands.

We were outnumbered.

Somehow, I caught Ryder's gaze through the hoard of dead demons between us. Ryder nodded. He knew we were not going to win.

I love you, he mouthed.

I love you, I mouthed.

And then the dead roared and attacked.

I pulled the sword, slashing with one hand, hacking

with the other. The demon weapons were light, responsive and hungry for blood.

I saw Bathin throw himself forward, chopping off one of his giant lizard father's giant lizard toes.

Then all I could see were too many disfigured heads, too many arms, some with grotesque bodies attached, all with weapons, stabbing, tearing, slashing.

I used the axe, the sword, smashing flesh and bone and fur, but I was tired. Several small cuts on my arms and legs stung, and a fleeting memory of demon scratches going toxic flashed through my mind.

A demon that looked like a cross between a crocodile and a worm dashed behind me and opened its huge mouth. It swallowed my backpack.

The backpack that was strapped on my back.

I yelled, and barely managed to slide my arms through the straps before being swallowed with it. I lost hold of the axe, and it disappeared into the dead demon mob.

Something grabbed my ankles, pulled. The sword was ripped from my hand.

I went down again, into soil that had gone rotten and soft as it disgorged more and more dead demons up through the dirt.

I pulled my knives and aimed for heads and throats.

Xtelle yelled: "Stab, stage right! Stab, stage left! Stab! Who's the livestock, no-lines now?" as she impaled Mithra over and over again, Avnas bashing him like a bloody drum at her side.

The last glimpse I had of Jean, was her sitting, back to a fountain, Hogan unconscious and bleeding in her lap as she shot monster after monster. Myra was wielding a short sword she'd pulled from one of the dead. She ran toward Jean, only to go down in the sea of hands.

Ryder stumbled toward me, bleeding and furious as he tried to fight his way free of the demons surrounding him, his only weapon a knife in his hand.

Then there was Rossi.

A sudden hit of cold air blasted the demons away from me and the vampire stood above me, magnificent in his vengeance, blood dripping from his saber and talons. "Up!" he yelled, lifting me off the ground away from the hands that clawed and tore. "Fly!"

He locked his arms under mine, and we were up, so high, so fast, I felt like I was falling instead of rising. He landed us on the roof of the temple under which the thrones lay broken and bloody.

"I have to get the others," Rossi said. "Stay here."

He was gone so fast, I braced my hands under me to keep from over balancing and falling off the roof.

From here I could see Goap and Patrick locked in battle, their weapons glowing with so much power I couldn't even make out the shape of them.

From here I could see Myra suddenly fly upward and disappear toward the jungle in an eye blink.

From here I could see Hogan, then Jean, then Ryder do the same.

From here I could see the king of hell, still a massive lizard, had pinned Bathin on his back, one giant claw planted in the middle of Bathin's chest. Bathin had a rock in his hand but that was all.

The Brute of All Evil's mouths merged into one maw that emitted a horrific roar.

I slapped my hands over my ears and screamed to try and break the pressure on my eardrums.

Then the demon that looked like a crocodile worm, the demon that had eaten my backpack, exploded.

In the scope of shit currently going wrong, it wasn't that big of a thing.

But Crow's laughter in my mind was triumphant. *This is gonna be so fucking good!*

Standing there, on the battlefield, in the middle of the recently exploded crocodile worm, covered in guts and gore, was a dragon-pig.

A very angry dragon-pig.

It snorted and shook off the remains of my backpack.

"No," I said. "It did not. It did not stow away in my backpack."

I wonder where it came up with that clever idea? Crow said.

"Run!" I yelled to it, as the demons, stunned by the explosion, recovered and surged toward it.

The dragon-pig tipped its darling little pink head and looked up at me. Its little curly tail wagged, and it *oink*ed, bouncing on all four feet, like it was excited to see me.

"Run, run, run!" I yelled. "Please, run!"

The dragon-pig followed where I was pointing. It saw Bathin on the ground, saw the demon king who had, for no reason I could understand, paused in the disemboweling of his son.

Then the king roared a single word with all three mouths: "No!"

The dragon-pig did not seem impressed.

One moment the dragon-pig was a cute pudgy little pink pig. The next moment it grew. Up and up, and out and out, until it was massive, bigger than the sky.

It was no longer a pig.

It had claimed its original form—black as midnight, scales shot through with burning red rivers of lava, wings of fire.

Dragon.

It swung its mighty tail and smashed the dead demons, smearing them across the battlefield like a layer of gory jam. It stepped on those who tried to run, pulverizing them into pulp.

The demon king roared and charged, growing tentacles, claws, and new heads with each step, every appendage more monstrous than the last.

The dragon spread its wings and lowered its head.

The demon king leaped—

—just as the dragon opened its jaws—

—and bit the king in half.

Both parts of the king slammed into the ground with a thunderous wet smack, and wriggled mindlessly across the battlefield, shrieking as they crushed the remaining dead demons.

The dragon extended its neck and chomped down on the front half of the demon king, chewed loudly, once, twice, three times, then it snapped up the second half and repeated the process.

The silence that followed was astounding. The dead demons were nothing but gory wet lumps of flesh. The battle was over. Goap and Patrick were nowhere to be seen.

"This is an outrage!" Xtelle yelled. "I will *not* be upstaged by a dragon in the climactic scene!"

A great gong rang out, drowning her voice. Once again, the ground trembled and shook.

Voices rose in wailing chorus, groaning and shrieking in pain. "The king is dead! The king is dead!"

Shit, Crow said in my mind. *Out of there. You all need to get out now, before every demon, every wanna-be demon, every asshole from here to the dick end of the universe shows up to claim rulership.*

I slipped on the temple's roof, trying to make my way down as the world did its best to rattle my brains. My hands skidded on the marble tiles, scraped and bleeding. I barely caught myself from going over the edge.

"Easy," Rossi said. He was there again, crouched beside me on the roof, the air cool around us.

His hair was a mess, and blood covered his face in a fierce battle mask. "Breaking your neck would be a terrible way to end all we've done here today."

"We have to go," I panted. "Crow says we have to go. Now."

"Everyone is in the jungle," Rossi said. "Bathin can take us to a stone from there. As soon as I find Bathin. Which I'll do as soon as you are safe."

He helped me stand, wrapped his arms around my waist. I smelled blood, sweat, and patchouli, then I was moving, fast. Too fast.

Then there was the green, green, green of the jungle. Then there were arms, familiar arms, that caught and held me.

"Ryder!"

"Laney, thank gods, Laney." He breathed into my hair as he gripped me tight, both of us clinging to the other.

A moment, two, and Rossi was back with Bathin.

"He's wounded," Rossi said, a bit unnecessarily since Bathin was holding his arm over a gut wound, and his eyes were unfocused. He slumped to the ground as soon as Rossi let go of him.

Myra strode over with her med kit.

"Where are Xtelle and Avnas?" I asked.

Bathin grimaced. "I told them to come. They didn't listen. Wanted…dramatic…exit."

He snapped his fingers. The jungle disappeared, replaced by red light.

We were inside a stone again, but Bathin was on the floor, unmoving.

"Passed out," Myra said, as she pulled his arm away so she could deal with his gut wound. After a pause, she pulled surgical gloves, goggles, forceps and sutures and a lighter out of her pack. "Rossi, I need you to kill these gut leeches when I pull them out."

Rossi stepped over, and there was the smell of butane. There was also the sound of Myra tugging wet things that screeched out of Bathin's belly, and dropping them to the floor.

I caught sight of one leech-like creature with visible fangs, before Rossi smashed it, and burned it with the lighter.

I shifted in Ryder's arms, not letting go of him. I didn't think I physically could let go of him.

Hogan and Jean were sitting, Hogan with his back against the stone. Jean sat in between his legs. They were passing a water bottle back and forth. Hogan looked more aware than I'd last seen him.

Jean offered us a full water bottle from her backpack.

"Thanks." I took it, swigged the liquid which I knew was only water, but that tasted amazingly sweet, then handed it to Ryder. He drank deeply until it was gone.

"Are you okay?" I asked both of them.

Hogan nodded. Jean rocked her hand back and forth in a fifty-fifty gesture.

"I think Hogan has a concussion," she said.

"Jean broke her ankle and won't wish me to heal it," Hogan said. "I'm not happy about that."

"Concussion," she said, like this had been an ongoing argument. "Heal thyself, genie. Then you can heal others."

"That makes sense," I said. "Why aren't you doing that?"

"He's exhausted," Jean said, when Hogan wouldn't answer. "Magic takes energy. Wishes take a *lot* of energy and focus. Why do you think all the legends say genies only grant three wishes?"

"Because the story wouldn't have any tension otherwise?"

She flashed me a grin. "Well, yeah. But also, there is a limit to wish giving. That's what the stories are rooted in."

"I can grant wishes," Hogan said, but I heard the exhaustion in his tone.

"Did you take pain-killers?" I asked Jean.

She nodded again. "Wrapped it in an ankle brace Myra had on her. It doesn't hurt if I don't move. You should sit down. We're safe here."

I wasn't sure safe was the right word, but as long as the stone wasn't found, we were probably okay.

"Let's sit," Ryder said. When I didn't move, when I took a step to go back to Myra and Rossi and make sure everything was okay with them and Bathin, he added, "I need to sit. I'm exhausted."

"Are you okay?" I asked, even though the words

sounded dumb as soon as they were out of my mouth. "Are you injured?" I corrected.

"I'm good for now," he said. "Nothing more serious than those cuts you have. We're okay. I'm okay."

I nodded. "But the cuts, are they poison?" I asked Rossi.

"No," he said, burning a leach the size of his arm. "I would know if they were. I think this stone has an anti-septic quality, or perhaps slight healing properties. It's very clever."

Ryder kissed the side of my temple and whispered: "Are you okay?"

"I think so," I said. "Yes. I think so."

"Good." He said. "Let's rest." Then he guided us over to sit next to Jean and Hogan.

CHAPTER NINETEEN

THE DRAGON-PIG POPPED into the stone about half an hour later. It spun in circles, *oink*ing and grunting and making happy little squeals.

"Someone's in a good mood," Jean noted.

The dragon-pig ran over to her on its stubby little legs, *oink*ed at her and growled, its eyes flashing before it *oink*ed again, tail wagging.

Jean laughed. "Yes, you were very fierce. I saw that. You ate the demon king."

The dragon-pig hopped, all four feet off the ground, and hopped and hopped, speeding around the edges of the stone.

Ryder, sitting with his arm over my shoulder chuckled. "Maybe we should have been adding demon to its diet."

I shook my head. "If it wants demon, it's gonna have to hunt its own. I'm never going back there again."

The dragon-pig was hopping our way, *oink*ing each time it touched down. It stopped next to us, long enough to put both front legs on my thigh, look me in the eye, and give a happy little *oink*.

It was so pleased with itself, I chuckled and rubbed behind its ears. "Good dragon. You saved us."

It made a satisfied growl, smoke rising from its nostrils, before nudging its head on Ryder's knee.

Ryder reached down and petted its head. "Very good dragon. So brave to save Delaney and all of us."

It kept its head down and made happy little mumbly sounds as Ryder scrubbed at the back of its neck.

"How's he doing?" I asked Myra.

She sat next to Bathin, her hand on his shoulder. "Still unconscious, but breathing easier. The wound is healing."

"Do you think he'll wake up soon?"

She frowned, looked down at him, then shook her head. "No. He's in a healing state, I think. There's more wrong with him than what shows on the outside."

"So," Jean said, "we're not getting out of this stone for a while."

Myra shook her head.

"Days? Weeks? Months?" I asked.

"I don't know," Myra said. "I don't know."

"We need another way out of the stone," I said.

"We need the stone to be in Ordinary," Rossi said. He was leaning against the wall. He'd used a pile of the wet wipes we'd packed to clean the blood and gore off his face and hands, but a thin coating of red clung to his lips and throat.

"Hogan can do it," Jean said.

"If someone makes a wish," Hogan said.

"We just need to wish ourselves to Ordinary?" Ryder asked.

"I'd be more specific than that," Hogan said. "The demon stone has some limits. It's made to respond to Bathin's magic more than any other."

"Can you tell us what we should wish?" Jean asked, tipping her head back to look at him.

"That's a little bit against the rules."

"Can you tell us if our wish will do what we want?" I asked.

"Yeah, I can," he said. "Pretty sure."

"Super idea," Jean said. "Let's rely on Sir Concussion here."

"I bumped my head," he said. "I didn't lose my hearing."

Bumped his head, Jean mouthed.

"We want to wish the stone to Ordinary," Myra said. "That should avoid messing with the boundaries and protections of Bathin's magic."

"We'll ask him to move the stone, with us in it," I added, "to Ordinary."

"But not in the ocean," Jean said. "Not in the sewer system. Not in the rock quarry, concrete trucks, bags of dog food."

"Let's be specific," Ryder suggested. "Say exactly where in Ordinary we want to be taken to."

"The station?" Jean asked.

"Too busy," Myra said. "Bertie's office?"

"I don't know what Bertie would do if a demon stone showed up on her desk," I said. "My house?"

"Or ours," Jean said. "The gnomes would probably guard it like treasure, and Hogan knows the interior of our house best."

"Does that matter?" Ryder asked.

She made a face. "I don't want to end up in a wall. Or a toilet."

"Yep, it matters," I decided. "Okay, Jean, make the wish."

"Me?" she asked.

"You know the rules of wishing better than all of us," I said.

Myra nodded, Rossi gave her a thumbs up, and Ryder grinned. "See what happens when you date a guy with powers?"

She bit her bottom lip. "Okay, hold on. I'm gonna take this slow, okay, babe?" She ran her hand down his thigh to his knee.

"Yep," Hogan said. "I'm not gonna grant some kind of last minute thrown-together trash wish. I have standards."

Jean grinned and relaxed. "Good. So here goes. I wish that you will grant the most positive outcome of my wish and move this stone, with all of us in it, safely and quickly to our living room, setting us down, carefully and gently onto our gaming table near the window without triggering any of Bathin's protections that may harm us or him, or trap us or him, or otherwise make me regret not spending this wish forcing you to heal your damn concussion."

Hogan smiled, and it was full of so much love, I leaned my head on Ryder's shoulder.

"Is that your wish?" he asked.

Jean closed her eyes for a moment, her lips moving as she replayed her words. "Yes. That is my wish. Please and thank you."

Hogan's eyes crinkled at the corners. "So polite.

How could I not grant such a polite wish? As you so wish, so shall it be."

The air became just a little warmer, and a light breeze brushed over me. It lasted for about five minutes, then the breeze stopped, and the warmth lowered to a more pleasant temperature.

"As you wish," Hogan whispered. Then he leaned his head back and closed his eyes.

"Hoges?" Jean said, twisting around, but trying not to move her ankle.

"Good," he said. "Tired. That was pretty damn boss."

Jean grinned. "Yeah, it was. Bad ass."

"How long do you think we'll be here?" Ryder asked.

I shrugged. "Until Bathin wakes up."

The dragon-pig, who had geared down to a stroll while nosing at the walls, waddled over to us. It plopped down next to my thigh. I dropped my hand on it.

I might have slept.

A WARM CIRCLE on my chest woke me. I blinked, trying to remember why I wasn't in my bed, why I was curled up against Ryder, and why his shirt was off. Then memories clicked into place like toggles being thrown, and I was awake.

I sat, lifting my head from Ryder's shoulder and looked around. Everyone else was sleeping except Rossi, who was sitting now. He raised his fingers in a silent greeting. I wondered if he had cast a sleep spell, or if we were all just that exhausted.

We'd fought demons and survived.

We'd fought a god and survived, though I didn't know if Mithra was still alive.

We'd killed the demon king.

I was sure there wouldn't be any terrible consequences for that.

But we were here, hopefully in Ordinary, alive, together.

The warmth flared on my chest. I reached down and pulled Crow's god stone away from my skin.

Crow?

Delaney, good. You're here. You're in Ordinary. I'll be there. Hold on.

We should be at Hogan's. We should be...

"...on the game table in a pretty little rock?" Crow stood in the center of the stone with us, a grin on his face. "Did I get that right?" He spread his arms wide.

I walked over to him, stepping into his hug and hugging him back. "You better really be you and not a leprechaun pulling a trick or a demon double-crossing us."

"I'm really me."

"How did you get here?" Myra asked.

"God stone. Delaney's wearing it."

"God stone?" she asked. "You stole it out of the library?"

"I did not. How could you accuse me of such a thing?"

"You never gave it to me, did you?" Myra narrowed her eyes. "You tricked me into thinking the stone you gave me was your god stone. That's dirty, Crow."

"Or a very clean trick that allowed me to help when you needed help?"

"No," Myra said. "It's the thing I said."

"Can you get us out of here?" Jean asked. "Out of the stone? Hogan needs a doctor and so does Bathin."

"And Jean," I said, stepping back from Crow. "She broke her ankle."

"Maybe just a fracture," she said.

"Still needs a doctor," I said.

Crow shook his head. "I can't release you. That's Bathin's power. But I did bring a hell of a healing spell. One I am assured will work on demons."

I smiled. "You're pretty good at this."

"Yes, I am."

He crouched next to Bathin and handed Myra the spell. The spell was carried by a crocheted yellow lace doily that looked like a sunflower blossom.

Myra nodded. "That's good. Really good, Crow. Okay."

Bathin's shirt was undone from when she had been digging things out of his gut. She placed the spell on his chest and spread it out so it draped his skin without any wrinkles.

Crow placed his palm over the spell. He whispered a word that sounded like Latin, and the doily glowed with buttery yellow light.

Nothing more happened for a minute. Then the doily dissolved into Bathin's skin and Bathin took a deeper breath, opening his eyes.

"Well, shit," he said, his gaze flicking from Crow to Myra. "That didn't go quite to plan." He grunted up into a sitting position, brushing off Myra's objections.

"Who moved my stone?" he demanded. "Hogan? How the—a wish. You wished my stone into Ordinary? I'm going to have to set new protections."

"Sure," Crow said. "But how about you snap

everyone out of here first? There are wounded who need doctors."

Bathin took in the rest of the space, all of us standing except for Hogan and Jean. Jean waved. "Ankle. No big deal." She jabbed her thumb over her shoulder. "Concussion."

"Bump," Hogan said, but he didn't open his eyes or move.

Ryder waved. "Cuts and bruises."

"And how did you get here?" Bathin asked Crow.

"Delaney has my god weapon, my power. Not even your travel stones could keep me away from it."

"Gods," Bathin said like they were the most annoying things in the universe. He took Myra's hand and stood next to her. "Easy then, everyone. Breathe. One, two, three."

I tried to follow his advice, but held my breath instead. Between one blink and the next, I was no longer in the stone, but standing in Hogan's living room, Ryder next to me.

The warm smell of cake and vanilla, and beyond that, the salty scent of marine air from a window left open a crack, filled the room.

"Wow," Jean said. "You're damn good." She and Hogan were on the couch, settled carefully so Jean's ankle was still outstretched, and Hogan's head was resting against the back cushions.

"I'll get the van ready," Myra said.

"You have a van?" Ryder asked.

"I rented one and left it here before we left," she said.

"Of course you did," Bathin said with a smile.

She touched Bathin's arm, and he turned and bent,

his gaze stopping her, holding her. Then he kissed her, gently, resting his forehead on hers for a moment and murmuring something so quiet I couldn't hear it.

Myra's eyes were closed and she nodded, then pulled away. She searched his face, looking for something, or maybe just making sure he was okay, then she headed to the door.

"Jean?" Rossi offered. "Might I offer myself as your crutch?"

That was enough to get us all moving. There were protests and negotiations, but finally, we got all of us, except Rossi, who said he could find his way home on his own, piled into the twelve-person van, buckled in, and headed to the hospital.

Good thing Myrrhis was on duty and more than happy to see all of us. I was too tired to come up with cover stories for demon wounds.

THE INJURIES WERE, thankfully, no worse than we'd thought. Jean's ankle was a bad sprain, but not broken. Hogan's concussion was minor. Ryder had torn his rotator cuff and was grumpy about having to wear his arm in a sling.

I had cuts and bruises everywhere, but hadn't even noticed most of them until the doctor got busy poking.

Myra had been hiding a cut on her thigh that needed stitches. Bathin's guts and knock on the head were on the mend, though he'd been instructed to stay off his feet, drink plenty of liquids, and get lots of sleep.

From the look Myra was giving him, she was going to make sure all of those things happened, repeatedly.

Bertie showed up, because of course she did.

"Delaney, I need a word with you." Bertie was in all gray, but her accessories sparkled in reds and hot pinks and oranges. She looked like a phoenix who'd just crawled out of the coal bin.

I followed her out of the waiting room, where we were all waiting for the last of the paperwork to be handled, and down a short hall to a small empty room that looked like someone's office we shouldn't be using.

"Do you know what day it is?"

"I've been told it's Tuesday. We left Sunday, before dawn. So we were gone for almost three days.

"Yes. Patrick hasn't been back."

"He was in hell. Sent by Goap, not the king."

"In league with the demons?" she asked.

I wanted to say yes. Patrick had kidnapped Ryder and let him be chained and injured. Anger flared in me, wide wings that wanted destruction, but I pushed that away and tried to look at the events through more neutral eyes.

Patrick's magic had been soured. We'd suspected the king, but Goap was a lot trickier than we'd given him credit for. Some of what Patrick had done might not have been in his control. He had said Goap had forced him to kidnap Ryder. Patrick may have only been a pawn in Goap's plans.

It was the kindest opinion I could dredge up for him.

"I think if he was on the side of demons, he didn't want to be," I said.

"His videos on Ordinary have been posting."

"And?"

"He's been…complimentary. But he has pointed out the drawbacks of coming to a small town like ours. Spotty wireless connections. No three, four, or five-star hotels. No twenty-four hour grocery stores or restaurants. Very small selection of bars. One theater. And only a couple coffee shops."

"Yeah, but they're really good coffee shops. What are you telling me, Bertie? I need you to be super clear with me. It's been a long day."

"We neither lost nor won the bet with Robyn. He didn't over-sell Ordinary, which means we should have an uptick in visitors who follow him, but I don't expect people from around the world to come knocking down our doors to book a room.

"He did a remarkably clever thing. He created attention that won't flood our resources and that is equal to that of Boring. I'm annoyed he was that capable."

"Well, luck falls on his side, as I understand it. Maybe he's shared a little of that with us."

She nodded. "There are other things you should know."

"Hit me, but not literally. I feel like a walking bruise."

"Most of the tourists have left, but we are still at capacity at all of our lodgings."

"Good."

"The murder mystery went so well, I am adding it to our annual events."

"Thanks for warning me."

She gave me a sour look. "Robyn and I are renegotiating our agreement, seeing as it was influenced by a leprechaun."

"Prudent."

"And I have taken over all matters of your wedding, which I will, of course, acquire Ryder's blessing for."

"What? No, I don't think that's a good idea. He's worked hard to put it all together."

"Yes, yes. And he has done a remarkable job," she said dismissively. "Except for the cheese."

"I'll tell him you said so."

"Tell him no such thing. But now, as a *gift*," she added, because she was a dirty rat and knew how to prey on my sense of fairness, "I will take the reins and steer the wedding to its glorious conclusion."

"I don't...I don't think he's going to want that."

"Ask him," she said briskly. "I am familiar with his plans and have done my homework. I know what he wants, who he's hired, and every detail he's dropped. I will carry the load, so that you and he can do nothing more than enjoy the event with those you love."

Like I said, a dirty rat. She knew how to use my heart against me too. "I'll talk to him."

"Of course."

"No guarantee he'll say yes."

"Of course."

"I'll let you know tomorrow."

"Yes. Of course you will."

She took my elbow and guided me out of the office, down to the waiting room where Ryder, in a hospital T-shirt he'd scored from someone, was slouched in a chair, half-asleep.

"Hey," he said. "Are you in trouble?"

I took his hand and tugged him up to his feet. "Not yet. Wanna go home? Maybe sleep for a century?"

He groaned softly. "Yes, please."

Myra came walking into the waiting area. "Okay, everyone's paperwork." She handed each of us a manila folder.

DEVON MONK

"Thanks," Jean said, her eyes a little shiny from the pain-killer they'd given her. "Can we go home now?"

"The van is waiting outside the door. I'll drive." She gave each of us a stern look.

None of us had the energy to argue with her.

SPUD, who had been spoiled by our neighbor, bounded through the front door, wriggling and beside himself with joy to see Ryder, me, and his favorite dragon-pig.

"Thanks for bringing him over," Ryder said. "And for watching him."

"Any time, you know that," Mr. Stein said. "He was a good boy, but he missed you." He nodded to the dog who cannon-balled into the pile of stuffies in front of the fireplace. He resurfaced with three toys shoved in his mouth.

I chuckled and started across the room to the stairs.

Ryder's voice faded as I made my way up to our room, and through that to the bathroom. I turned on the shower, peeled out of my clothes, kicked them into the corner, and stepped under the spray.

I shivered at the gentle warmth, then closed my eyes, letting soft heat flow across my skin, erasing the bone-deep chill I hadn't been able to shake.

A whoosh of cooler air stirred the steam in the room.

Over the sound of the spray, I heard Ryder. The click of his belt buckle, then, just like always, him realizing he'd have to take his boots off first, before he could take his pants off. He sat on the toilet lid, worked on his boots, heavy laces buzzing through metal grommets, then toed them off, shucking socks next.

I remembered he had one arm in a sling and slid the shower door to one side. "Need any help?" I asked.

He stared at me, his gaze warm and wanting. "You're beautiful."

I dragged my hand over my face to push away hair that was stuck in the side of my mouth. "Back atcha, gorgeous."

He huffed and held out his good arm. "The shirt's defeated me."

"I'll come to your rescue."

I stepped out of the shower, leaving it running and enjoyed the flash of lust that flickered in his gaze. "My hero," he breathed.

I unbuckled the sling and set it on the sink. Then I helped him get the T-shirt off his good arm and head and finally drew it carefully off his bad arm.

"Your bruises?" he asked.

"Better than your arm. Good," I said. "Need help with the boxers?" I waggled my eyebrows, and he smiled.

"I got it." He dug his thumb under his underwear waistband and pushed them down, working his good hand on either side until he could step out of them.

"I am absolutely filthy," he said, looking at the dirt and slime and other unknown smears covering his body.

"Yeah?" I said, catching his good hand and drawing him into the shower with me. "Prove it."

WHEN WE STUMBLED, weaving and exhausted into our bedroom, the fresh scent of the soap Ryder loved, and which I couldn't get enough of, having washed us stinging and clean, I almost didn't have enough left in me to pull back the covers.

"Shh," Ryder said. He tugged down our quilt and blankets, then guided me into our soft sheets, onto our soft mattress.

Heaven. Nirvana. Ecstasy.

I felt the bed dip as Ryder got in on the other side. He shifted, trying to get his arm comfortable. It wasn't in the sling, but I was too tired to fight him about it.

He made a final effort and turned on his side, facing me.

I inch-wormed over, tucking my knees against his thighs, and curling in closer, my head on the pillow he'd shoved his good arm under.

"I don't want to hurt your arm," I said.

"We're good," he mumbled.

"We lost the demon weapons."

"Mmmm."

"Xtelle might take a shot at the throne just to get out of paying her five-hundred dollar fine."

His only answer was a soft grunt. Then he was breathing deeply, his body heavy, muscles soft.

The door creaked, and Spud and the dragon-pig slunk into the room. Spud jumped on the bed first, carefully curling up behind Ryder's back. The dragon-pig was next, plodding up until it settled like a warm round heater at my back.

I opened my mouth to tell them not to bump Ryder's arm, but the dragon-pig nuzzled my neck, its breath warm and even.

Sleep came with soft clouds.

CHAPTER TWENTY

"ARE HATTER AND SHOE OUT THERE?" I stood up from the velvet loveseat, that looked like it'd been plucked off a museum shelf, and started to the door.

"Nope," Myra said, standing in front of Bertie's office door and catching my wrist. "No leaving this room. Not until it's time to walk down the aisle."

"But security. I need to check to make sure they're handling the crowd."

"Oh, my gods," Jean breathed. "This is amazing."

I turned and glared at the phone she was using to film me. "Put that down."

"Not on your life," she laughed. "These are precious, precious memories I am going to cackle over for years."

"Don't—" I moved to make a grab for the camera, but Myra held onto my wrist.

"Stop it," she said. "Both of you."

"Me?" Jean said.

"Stop antagonizing her."

I pointed at Jean. "Yeah. Stop antagonizing me."

"She's very delicate and dramatic right now," Myra added.

"Hey!" I said, betrayed.

But Myra was grinning, and the moment hit me. She was wearing a 1950s-style summer dress with a lace shrug, all of it in beautiful blues and purples. She had pearls at her ears and neck, and she'd tucked a tiny bright yellow rose in her hair.

She was beautiful.

"Oh no," she said, her gaze going everywhere on my face at once. "No crying. We just got your mascara right."

"What set you off this time?" Jean asked.

"You're just so beautiful," I told Myra.

Myra threw a panicked gaze over my shoulder.

"Hey," Jean said. "Hey, Delaney. Turn around, I need to tell you something."

I turned, the skirt of my very lacy, very formal, very white wedding gown—*wedding gown*—hushed around my feet like the softest ocean wave.

I sniffed.

"What about me?" Jean asked. "Am I pretty too?"

She had on a full-length dress with a pale orange under layer and a layer of yellow lace with butterflies stitched into it. Her hair was blonde and combed into soft waves. She'd tucked a trio of tiny, bright blue cornflowers behind her ear.

She was nodding. "I'm pretty too, right?"

I nodded and sniffed, trying to rein in the wild mix of emotion and fear—was it fear?—running through my veins.

"Good answer," she said, angling the phone. "Now look in the mirror."

I did. And my own image locked me in place.

My sisters both stepped up behind me, though Jean had to put her phone down to use her crutch. We'd been back in town for four days. All of us were still a little bruised up from the battle in hell.

I'd told Ryder we should postpone the wedding.

I'd told Bertie we should postpone the wedding.

They'd both told me firmly, that I was out of my mind.

Somehow, Bertie had pulled all the final details together. Ryder had told me, in near tears himself yesterday, that she'd gotten all the award-winning cheese he'd ever hoped for.

I was glad for the cheese, and happy she'd insisted we stay out of the rest of the preparation.

The station had mutinied and told me to take the week off. Ryder had already planned the week off from his business.

It had given us some time. Time to hold each other. Time to praise the dragon-pig and Spud. Time to walk the beach or stay at home in bed, binging shows. Some time for Ryder to get used to not being bound to a god, though I thought that change would take many more months.

It had been wonderful. A vacation I didn't know how much I needed.

Even the gods had given us a break, none of them dropping in to check on me, as none of them were worried about a demon attack since the demons were, according to Bathin, "launching all-out war to settle who gets the throne."

Xtelle and Avnas hadn't returned to Ordinary, so my bet was on them.

"See that terrified, ridiculous dark-haired woman in the mirror?" Jean asked.

I scowled at her. "I'm not terrified."

"Good. See her? That look on her face like she's going to feed someone to her pet dragon?"

I snorted. "That dragon doesn't need to eat for the next six months."

"Sure, but see her? That fierce sister of mine? She is not going to mess up her makeup is she?"

"No?"

"No. I've only ever seen her in a dress like twice in my life, and this pretty dress is made for dancing the night away. Right?"

"Right."

"And this walking down the aisle stuff?" She blew air through her lips. "Piece of easy peasy pie. You'll say your vows, he'll say his vows, you'll do the repeat after me thing and an I do. Then done. Over. You know what happens next?"

"I'm a married woman, and my whole world changes?"

"No. Hells, no. What happens next, is you eat a fancy dinner, drink champagne, and shove cake in Ryder's face."

She rested her head on my shoulder. "No crying, okay?"

"I'll try."

Myra nodded. "I brought you a blue handkerchief, that's your blue."

"My what?"

"Old, new, borrowed, blue. It's tradition," she said.

"The dress is new," Jean said. "You're old, so you don't have to worry about that one."

"Watch it," I warned her, but I was smiling, so it wasn't much of a deterrent. "I need a borrowed and an old. Come on, you two. You don't want to have me start my wedding on the wrong foot."

"Oh!" Jean said, "I brought a candy bar I found in the bottom of my purse. That's probably old."

"Myra?" I pleaded.

She walked over to a bag she'd left on Bertie's desk, rummaged around in it, and pulled out a small box.

"No tears," she warned.

"Promise."

She handed me the box. I opened the lid. There was a very small ruby heart on a thin gold chain.

"That was Mom's," Myra said. "It can be the old."

She didn't have to say any more. I nodded and took a couple breaths so I wouldn't tear up. "Thank you. Thank you for finding this. For bringing this."

"Wait," Jean said. "I have a borrowed thing for you! Here." She crutched over to where she'd left her purse on an empty chair and dug around. "I knew this was going to come in handy."

She thrust something out at me.

It was a gnome.

Or more to the point, it was a gnome head.

Headless Abner, who sometimes came alive and did a lot of talking.

"That's...um..."

"You don't want to start your marriage unlucky, do you Delaney?"

"No, but. Say, Myra, can I borrow—"

"Nope. I'm all out of stuff," she lied, like a Liar McLie Face. "You'll just have to take the head."

"Where am I even going to put it?"

"That's why your dress is so great," Jean said cheerily. "It's got pockets!"

She shoved the gnome head into my pocket. "Borrowed!" she crowed.

"Neat," I said.

Myra handed me the baby blue lace handkerchief. "Blue. There, now you're all set. All the luck."

"All the luck," Jean repeated.

I stared at the woman in the mirror who had two grinning sisters behind her. "All the luck."

I FLOATED.

There was a knock on the door. It was Bertie telling us it was time. That's when the floating started.

I walked down the hallway with Myra and Jean. The hall had always been empty and echoing, but now flowers flowed in green boughs from the ceiling, woven with fairy lights to the floor, where the light strands pooled, then spooled off, like burbling creeks, toward the big double doorway to the gymnasium.

I floated.

Following the rivers of twinkling lights, we stopped at one side of the door. Jean kissed me on the cheek. "No crying."

Myra kissed me on the other cheek. "Your vows are in your pocket."

Then Odin was there. "Blessings, child." He kissed my forehead before taking Jean's arm, wrapping his other around her so she didn't have to take her crutch.

Then Crow was there. "Blessings, Boo-boo." He kissed my temple and took Myra's arm.

There was music, I thought there had always been

music, but now I heard it, a sweet orchestral quartet that paused. Voices hushed.

New music began.

Jean and Odin stepped through the door.

Myra and Crow stepped through the door.

There was a hand at my elbow, encouraging me forward. I thought it was Bertie, but when I looked, she was gone. Only a twinkling of light and flowers surrounded me.

I floated.

The music changed, or maybe it just flowed, like a river of lights, note after note rising and tumbling, creating song out of joy.

Everyone stood, and it was endless, a sea of friends, an ocean of family spread out in a room that was twice as large as I remembered. Impossibly, three times. A room transformed.

It was no longer a gymnasium. In the back of my mind, where logic might still be working, I knew it was magic. A lot of magic.

The walls were gone, and instead, the shores of Ordinary spread out from sand to horizon. The sky was blue, soft, a few white clouds towering like castles in the sky. Sunlight glittered against waves, turning the curl and bow of rushing water into emerald, jade, turquoise, laced white with foam.

There were people on the beach I could see through the magic, which was probably explained as technology, some kind of new virtual reality thing, people of my town on the beach, all of them holding single flowers. They watched a big screen set in the sand showing a beautiful room, a beautiful wedding.

This room.

This wedding.

Everything else was swathed with green boughs and lights that flitted, as if butterflies or fairies were dancing in the green.

Flowers and ribbons wove up and up to the ceiling which was draped in huge gauzy canopies where the blue sky somehow flowed, shifting in the gentle sea breeze.

Magic. Some of the decorations were solid, real, but augmented with very subtle magic.

"Gnice gnuptials," a muffled little voice said from my pocket.

Part of me wondered if I should deal with that, but then there was a gentle pressure at my elbow again, bringing me back to the ground just long enough to know I had paused there in the doorway.

Everyone was watching me, they all held single flowers too. I recognized their faces, people I loved, but then the song lifted, and the light shifted, sunlight falling golden on one person. One man.

He wore a deep charcoal jacket and slacks, cut to fit his powerful body, his wide shoulders, his trim waist. Under the jacket was a white shirt, a jade vest the color of the curling waves, with what I thought was a golden pocket watch chain, and a dark bow tie.

His shoes were black and shiny.

I knew Crow stood, dressed in a lighter gray suit behind him. I knew Odin wore a lighter suit behind Crow. I knew Myra and Jean stood across from the men, both my sisters glowing like flowers.

With me in white, we looked like the ocean, like the water and waves and flowers and sand and sky that made this place what it was. I didn't know if Ryder had done that on purpose, didn't know if Bertie had somehow picked up on that lovely echo, but it was there.

Ordinary, the magic of it, the beauty of it, in all of us.

But that thought was only a second. Fleeting.

Because all I could see, the only reason my heart was beating, was the man who stood, with stars in his eyes, at the altar at the end of the room.

I wanted to run away with him.

I wanted to dance in his arms.

I wanted him to be mine forever.

I floated, this time with purpose. I wanted that man, and there was such a short distance I'd have to travel to have him.

With each step, I could better see his face. His love, fierce and bright, shone from him like a second light. His eyes glittered, tears unshed, and that, somehow, was all I needed in the world.

And then I was there, at the altar, in front of him, facing him. He winked, and I caught laughter in my mouth.

The music stopped. Everyone sat.

"Beloveds, welcome," a very deep and very familiar voice said.

It took me a second, maybe three, to fit that voice with what was happening.

In practice, Hera had been our officiant. I'd been honored to have the goddess of marriage marrying us. It made sense.

But this was Ordinary.

And Ordinary was anything but.

I turned to our officiant.

Than wore a very bespoke black suit with a bright

red Hawaiian shirt, black tie, and a black top hat. He looked like a tall, thin mortician on vacation, with a twinkle in his eyes.

Death. Death was going to marry us. When had that happened?

I glanced at Ryder to see if he was in on this. He gave me a smile.

I couldn't help it, I smiled back.

"Please, return to your repose," Than intoned.

Myra cleared her throat.

"Ah. Be seated," Than corrected. From the sounds behind me, everyone did as they were told.

"This, then, is a grand and rare event," Than began, "a moment when two hearts will be exchanged, and two lives will be joined. Those gathered are honored witnesses of this ending of one life and beginning of another.

"I am told this part of the ceremony is mine, to give wisdom or advice or guidance to all of us, and importantly to the two souls standing before me. I am also told to be brief."

There was a light flutter of laughter.

"Here then, is my wisdom: Savor.

"Savor the starlight, the moon, the rise of seasons, and fall of light. Savor the kindness of breath, the stretch of muscle, the spark of curiosity. Savor the laughter of friends, of songs sung off-key, the shout and giggle of children. Life is made of fleeting moments.

"Savor those moments. And in them, in the moments of life, every one, may you always find love."

He paused, and I blinked to keep the tears from falling.

"Good," he said, clapping his hands and rubbing

them together. "That went well. Now, it will be vows. I believe it is traditional for the groom to begin? Ryder. Do you have your vows?"

Ryder nodded and patted his pockets, sticking his fingers in at his hips and coming up empty.

Crow tapped his elbow and passed him a crumpled piece of graph paper.

"Thank you," Ryder said on a pent up breath. He uncrumpled the paper and tried to smooth it out. His hands trembled.

I couldn't read the words, but I could see some of them had been crossed out and scribbled over.

"Delaney, I wrote these vows a million times. In truth, I began writing them when I was too young to understand what love was. When I was too young to understand why the answer to my lonely heart was always you.

"But now, I know. You are the joy, the fire, the song in my heart. You always have been. I have loved you since the first day I saw you in kindergarten, punching that kid in the nose for stomping on all the crayons."

I laughed, but it came out hitched up, close to tears.

He dropped the paper. "I love you. I always have. I always will love you. Please let me share my life with you. Please share your life with me. I promise I will always stand by you, stand with you, my arms your safety, my soul your home."

I nodded and whispered, "Yes," which made the crowd chuckle.

"Sufficient," Than said. "Delaney, you will give Ryder your vows."

I reached into my pocket and heard a "Hey!" and

felt sharp little teeth nip my finger. I quickly pulled my hand out and checked my other pocket.

Empty.

A moment of panic washed over me.

My vows were stuck under a gnome head. A bitey gnome head.

"Delaney?" Than said.

"Yes. Um...I wrote my vows, too, but I don't have them right now, so this isn't going to be as pretty as what you said."

Ryder just shook his head, his eyes bright with tears, smiling as if I were the best thing he'd ever seen in his life.

I reached out for his hand, and he caught mine, holding, grounding me, giving me time.

"I love you," I said. "I knew that back in kindergarten too. I was too young to understand how love can grow and change, but I've known you all my life, Ryder Bailey. I want to know you for the rest of my life.

"More than that. I want to love you, hold you. I want to laugh with you, and argue with you, and sit around in my old jeans, barefoot, drinking beer on the beach with you. I want to watch the sun come up, and let you cook breakfast, because, fine, I'm a terrible cook.

"I want to watch the sunset in your arms. Please let me share my life with you. Please share your life with me. I promise I will love you. Always."

He squeezed my hand, and his eyes, filled and glossy, cleared as a single tear tracked his face. "Yes," he whispered, just as I had, and again, the crowd murmured.

"Adequate," Than said. "Now, are there rings to be exchanged?"

Ryder nodded and turned to Crow.

I looked back to Myra, whose cheeks were pink and eyelashes were wet. She took the bouquet from me and handed me a gold ring that was warm from being held safe in her palm.

I turned back to face Ryder.

"Well done," Than said. "All you need to do is repeat my words exactly. I am told there is no grade, and no consequences if you fail to follow my directions."

Crow make a sound that sounded like he was trying to hold back a laugh.

Than glared at him. Then turned his attention to us.

"Ryder Bailey, present the ring, but do not put it on her finger quite yet. First, repeat after me."

I lifted my left hand, and Ryder took it in his own, the ring ready in his other hand.

"Delaney Reed," Than said.

"Delaney Reed," Ryder said repeating Than's words. I knew Than was speaking, but all I could hear was Ryder.

"I, Ryder Bailey, take thee, Delaney Reed to be my lawfully wedded wife. To have and to hold, to love and to cherish, in sickness and health, for richer or poorer, until Death, who is a force to be feared, for his might and power are both unmatched, so too the swiftness of his scythe, the cold but not entirely cruel turn of his gaze…"

Bertie, and I knew it was Bertie, because I'd been on the receiving end of her displeasure for most of my life, cleared her throat loudly.

Than glared into the audience, then sighed.

"Where was I? Ah, yes. Ryder please continue to repeat after me."

"You are the love of my life, and you are my very

best friend. I give you this ring as a symbol of my love, my faith in our strength together, and a promise of my life united with yours. Forever."

"Place the ring on her finger," Than instructed.

Ryder the romantic fool, kissed the ring. Then he slid it onto my finger, fumbling a little with it on my knuckle, before settling it into place.

"Now Delaney," Than said. "You will repeat after me."

I did so, the words the same, including the overly-long death part, as I pledged myself to the man I had loved all my life. I kissed the ring the same as he had, and when I slid the ring on his finger, it settled there as if he had always worn it, as if he had always been mine.

"Now then. With the powers invested unto me by Get Ordained dot org, the State of Oregon, and the gods who bless this day, I pronounce you, married. You may kiss."

Ryder was smiling, though his cheeks were streaked. I was smiling too, tears pouring warm down my face.

"I love you," we whispered over each other's lips before we leaned in.

And kissed.

The cheer rose, loud and joyous, so loud I almost couldn't hear Than shout: "I now present to you, for the very first time, Delaney Bailey Reed and Ryder Bailey Reed, husband and wife!"

We ran down the aisle, hand in hand, amid cheers and flowers falling upon us.

· · ·

THE RECEPTION WAS A BLUR. We were kissed and hugged, blessed by gods, and given secret little magical boons and tokens.

I didn't think I could possibly hold still long enough to eat, but when the food arrived at our table, and Ryder breathed, "cheese," my stomach reminded me I hadn't eaten all day.

The banquet tables were laden with more food than I thought the whole town could put away in a week, flowers and lights scattered amongst it all.

There was cake, which we cut hand in hand.

Ryder fed me the first bite, and I fed him the first bite, and if we made a small mess of it, that just meant there was some kissing to clean things up.

The bridal bouquet toss didn't dissolve into a brawl, which I was pleased about, but even more pleased at the shocked look on Myra's face when she, standing at the back of the crowd, ended up with the flowers in her arms after said flowers had bounced off of the hands of half a dozen grasping people.

Jean howled when Myra said she hadn't seen that coming, and that it didn't mean anything.

Bathin just strode across the room and tugged Myra off to some side room where I hoped he kissed her silly.

There were toasts, and children running with balloons, and laughter, and dancing.

There were lights like stars, and sweet flowers, and ocean breezes.

And there was Ryder, the best, the only thing my heart could see.

We danced to a slow tune I wanted to hear every day of my life.

We laughed.

We snuck off to kiss, and were caught every time by someone who pulled us back out into the celebration.

Eventually, eventually, we finally did sneak away.

But not before Bertie handed us two duffle bags. "Myra said you'd want these," she said.

I opened my mouth to thank her, but she waved me away. "Go."

"Bert, my love," I heard a deep voice call. And Bertie, who I was pretty sure had been drinking, blushed and spun his way.

Tark was half troll and was short, wide, and strong. There was a gleam in his eye as he stood, his hand outstretched. "We dance!" he declared.

"We fly!" she responded, as she hurried to his side.

Ryder had unzipped one of the duffels. "How do you feel about getting into your favorite old jeans?"

"Are you kidding?"

He unzipped the other duffle and smiled. "It's almost sunset, isn't it?"

"I have no idea."

"That's okay," he said. "I'm pretty sure it is. Let's change. We have one more thing we need to do."

"I'm not doing it in high heels," I warned him.

"Nope," he said. "Bare feet all the way."

He took me by the hand to Bertie's office, where we took off our wedding finery and got into much more comfortable clothes.

And if our touches lingered, it wasn't for nearly enough time.

"Sunset," Ryder grumbled. "I am not going to blow this and have your sister mad at me for the rest of our lives."

"So romantic," I cooed.

He planted a hard kiss on my mouth, then pulled out of my reach. "Move it, Mrs. Bailey Reed. We have places to be."

I whined about it, but followed the man. Because how could I not?

"GOOD?" Ryder, sitting on the blanket beside me, asked.

"So good." I wriggled my toes in the sand at the edge of the blanket Myra had packed for us, enjoying the soft warmth of sun-heated sand becoming a soft coolness around my toes.

I was wearing jeans that had holes in them and a couple paint stains, and Dad's old Grateful Dead T-shirt that was faded, too big, and perfect.

Ryder had on jeans just as old and holey as mine, and a faded shirt that had Leonardo da Vinci's *Design for a Parabolic Compass* made to look like Pink Floyd's *Dark Side of The Moon* prism in the middle of it.

He had a beer in one hand and the wind in his hair.

He'd never been more beautiful to me.

"Think we'll be lucky and see the green flash when the sun sets behind the ocean?" he asked.

I must have taken too long to answer, because he looked over at me. "Hey, wife," he said with a smile.

"Hey, husband," I replied, the word new to me, filled with nuance I'd never understood before.

"You're looking at me," he said.

"Yeah."

"You're supposed to be looking at the sunset."

"Or I could just keep looking at you."

He smiled and moved closer so he could wrap his arm around my shoulder. Myra had packed beer and a

347

few snacks, two blankets—one for the sand, one to wrap around us—and a few sturdy pillows.

It was quiet here on this stretch of beach, only a few people out walking. They paid us no mind.

Ryder adjusted the blanket around us both, and I leaned my head on his shoulder.

"Watch the sun," Ryder said.

"Maybe I don't want today to end," I said.

He hummed and waited a moment. "Do you know the legend of the green flash of light when the sun slips into the sea?"

"It brings luck," I said.

"It brings luck in matters of the heart," he replied. "Let's watch for the flash of green."

It sounded important to him, like discovering the magical, mythical things in Ordinary were always important to him. I loved that, his curiosity, his delight in all things supernatural, his delight in the beauty of the world.

"I love you, Ryder Bailey Reed."

"I love you, Delaney Bailey Reed."

He caught my hand, the rings on our fingers clicking and slotting together. We held each other and watched the sun slip down and down, the ocean breathing and breathing.

Just as the sun winked green, just as Ryder's breath caught in wonder, I closed my eyes, and *savored* this feeling, this moment, knowing there would be so many more magical moments in our lives.

But I was in no rush to let this one end.

ACKNOWLEDGMENTS

Here we are! We've reached the ninth book in the Ordinary Magic series. I want to take a moment to thank the people who have helped bring this book together.

Thank you, Lou Harper, for the fabulous cover art. How exciting we finally get to see Delaney in something other than her leather jacket! You rock.

Thank you Sharon Elaine Thompson, for being so patient with me while I tried to get this book to you in time for copy edits before your big trip. Your sharp eyes and easy-going attitude always make copy edits a joy.

Big thanks to Dejsha Knight, for always jumping in at a moment's notice to point out not only the good stuff, but also the rough stuff. Your feedback and friendship is invaluable.

To my husband, Russ, and my sons, Kameron and Konner, thank you for sharing your lives with me. You are truly the best part of mine.

Last, but never least, thank you dear readers, for spending a little time in this magic town, with these magical people. I hope you've enjoyed your visits to Ordinary and that this trip is maybe just is a little extra-special in its own way. I hope you'll come back and visit again soon!

ABOUT THE AUTHOR

Devon Monk is a USA Today bestselling fantasy author. Her series include Ordinary Magic, Souls of the Road, West Hell Magic, House Immortal, Allie Beckstrom, Broken Magic, and the Age of Steam steampunk series. Her short fiction can be found in various anthologies and in her collection: A Cup of Normal.

Devon lives in lovely, rainy Oregon. When not writing, she is drinking too much coffee, watching hockey, or knitting ridiculous things.

Want to read more from Devon?

Follow her blog, sign up for her newsletter, or check out the social media below.

ALSO BY DEVON MONK

SOULS OF THE ROAD
Wayward Souls
Wayward Moon
Wayward Sky

ORDINARY MAGIC
Death and Relaxation
Devils and Details
Gods and Ends
Rock Paper Scissors
Dime a Demon
Hell's Spells
Sealed with a Tryst
At Death's Door
Nobody's Ghoul
Brute of All Evil

WEST HELL MAGIC
Hazard
Spark

HOUSE IMMORTAL
House Immortal

Infinity Bell

Crucible Zero

BROKEN MAGIC

Hell Bent

Stone Cold

Backlash

ALLIE BECKSTROM

Magic to the Bone

Magic in the Blood

Magic in the Shadows

Magic on the Storm

Magic at the Gate

Magic on the Hunt

Magic on the Line

Magic without Mercy

Magic for a Price

AGE OF STEAM

Dead Iron

Tin Swift

Cold Copper

Hang Fire (short story)

SHORT STORIES

A Cup of Normal (collection)

Yarrow, Sturdy and Bright (Once Upon a Curse anthology)

A Small Magic (Once Upon a Kiss anthology)

Little Flame (Once Upon a Ghost anthology)

Wish Upon a Straw (Once Upon a Wish anthology)